THE HOPE PEDDLER

BY BILL AND BRENDA ZAHN

Chapter 1:
"You're a stubborn S.O.B."

Middle America. A street like we all grew up on, or at least we all wish we'd grown up on. The kind that only gets better with memory.

The air's crisp, but the bright sun invites neighbors out of the house. Kids conquer new 10-speed bikes, dads perfect all-weather lawns. The dentist up the block hovers under the popped hood of his car like it's a patient in need of a root canal.

For the first time in months, everyone in the suburban neighborhood's active, if only for the mundane purpose of fixing a sprinkler head.

Bursting from one of the homes comes a middle-aged woman who's best known around the neighborhood as the piano lady, and not in a disparaging way. Every kid on the block learned how to tickle the ivories in her living room.

A full-figured gal in her 60s, she's wearing slippers and sweats, and beaming a wide, toothy smile at all the familiar faces. She's confident with every decision she's ever made, but that's all gonna change in about thirty seconds.

"Look at me!" says a redheaded six year old with pigtails and eyes ablaze with excitement.

The woman holds her breath as the girl's mouth springs open in a huge, toothless grin.

"Hot dog!" The woman claps. "Did you pull it yourself?"

"No. My daddy yanked it."

"Well, aren't you one of the bravest litt-"

"I ate a worm!"

The child bolts away as quickly as she arrived. The woman continues her mission, assured of another perfect, predictable day. She grabs the mailbox's contents, fixes the flag on the side and heads back up the driveway with the same pleasant trot.

Halfway up, she stops. Something's different. Something small, rectangular and bursting with color, beckoning from a faraway land.

Even for someone who's just recently given in to having a Facebook account, a postcard seems antiquated - someone putting pen to paper and sticking it in the mail. The man hours required to deliver it across an ocean.

The woman zones in on the white sand beach, the palm trees, the uncorrupted blue sky. Her instinct for celebrated foreign places was always defensive - "Nothing's better than home. Nothing." But this time, although she would never admit it, it's another story. It's enticing, exotic and just oozes relaxation.

She flips over the card to reveal an unfamiliar handwriting that's crafted in bold, confident strokes. A young woman's handwriting. But now there's a problem: This young woman has addressed the card to her husband.

The woman's casual stride turns into a march toward the front door. As she steps over the threshold going into the house, the welcome mat proclaims them as "The Wilsons."

"Henry, who the hell is 'April Showers'?" she demands.

Her husband sits lifelessly in his recliner holding a bag of potato chips, his face lit by the dim glow of midday cable news.

The woman waves the postcard in the air.

"She's got a lot to say to you." She's focused on the words in front of her. "'Henry,' it says, 'it's time to stop ignoring your doctor. He knows what he's talking about.'"

Husband and wife shoot each other a shocked look.

The husband shrugs it off. "Who'd you tell?! ... Ah, those quacks are just trying to sell drugs."

His exasperated wife shakes her head. "She's got one thing right. You are a stubborn S.O.B."

Inside another suburban home in Dallas, a frazzled soccer mom glares at a similar Hawaiian postcard as she takes a long, desperate drag of her cigarette. Children holler and play in front of the TV in the living room, piling like bean bags on top of each other with shrieks and screams.

Their mother turns abruptly to face them. "Dammit! Would ya shut up!"

The shouting quiets for two seconds, then kicks up even shriller than before, at ear-piercing pitches.

The woman's overly caffeinated friend grows impatient. "What else does she say?"

"I should be gentler with the people I love. I don't know how she knows me, but whoever this Amanda Hugginkiss is, she's got some nerve!"

The friend takes a long swig of her extra large energy drink. "She sounds like a real bitch."

Inside the mailroom of a swanky high-rise in the city, a well-tailored business man has finally come to the end of another grueling workday, just in time to go to bed and do it all over again in the morning.

Polished in his fitted suit, his shoulders droop as he opens his mailbox. When he was a slightly younger man, every woman would compliment him on his striking dimples. These days, they rarely make a showing at all.

Inside the mailbox, he discovers a similar postcard.

Reading the words at the bottom, for the first time in a long time, his eyes show signs of life:

"We both know there is change brewing in you, that spark of creativity ready to ignite.

Love, Sandy Beaches"

In government housing, a young mother reads to her kids from yet another postcard. She's animated as if she's telling a wonderful story. Wide-eyed, the kids circle their mother like bugs to a flame. On the front of the postcard is the image of a tropical beach with the words: "Having one shell of a time!"

In San Diego, a couple bickers in Spanish, both referencing the mysterious postcard.

In Utah, a man hangs a frame on the wall. He steps away to reveal that he's framed his postcard. It's crooked. He lovingly straightens it like someone would a diploma or award.

In Ohio, a high school guidance counselor sits across the desk from a scruffy 16 year old, who's decked out in a faded Rush t-shirt that must have belonged to his dad, and whose face, despite not seeing the business end of a razor for weeks, sprouts nothing more than pubescent peach fuzz.

"You know, it takes a lot to own a baseball team," the counselor's advising. His tired eyes have never left a postcard he's holding in his hand.

"No, I got this," says the student. "I figure I'll work a couple jobs - Shakey's Pizza's hiring - borrow some funds, I heard I got a rich aunt that lives in Delaware or Duluth or somethin' ..."

The counselor nods mechanically. He stares at the post-card, his face pained.

From Maine to Malibu, people across America find mysterious postcards mixed in with their usual electric bills and junk mail. Probing into their souls, their doubts, their problems with the kind of insight usually only reserved for trusted friends. Tucked into their daily spam like a whisper from somewhere far away. The messages seem tailored to their recipients, each one written in unique, hand-crafted prose that speaks directly to a specific person, but they all include a line that sparks imagination: "Next stop? New Orleans. I love Rusty Harpoon's, best bar in town."

Chapter 2:
"Some places don't wanna be found"

The thick, wooden door's so old and worn that it's almost indistinguishable from the brick wall where it's made its home since the 1930s, greeting every haggard face and forlorn spirit that's come its way. A deep mythology's woven into its fibers.

The porthole embedded just at eye level has a piece of plywood replacing the glass. It's the kind of door that says once you cross the threshold, you might not come out the same way you went in. Steeped in the history of the downtrodden who dwell inside, it's a door that would force any sane person into a moment of contemplation, because this door leads into Rusty Harpoon's.

At the end of a dark, narrow alley, Ryan stands frozen, unsure of what the next step will bring. He knows he's sometimes prone to overreact, and at this moment he's pretty sure that's exactly what's led him here. Now he's left the comforts of his steady, 9-to-5 job for what seems to be the beginning of a wild goose chase.

He wraps his fingers around the words on the postcard he's protected like a family heirloom for the past week and a half: "Next stop? Rusty Harpoon's," and the simple signature, "Wendy Breezes." From the moment he pulled it out of the mailbox mingled with spam, he's been consumed by it, hiding it under manila envelopes at work and behind reports he pretended to read at meetings.

At night, he barely slept at all. When he did, he was plagued by hazy dreams of Wendy Breezes. Nothing more than a dim figure with a face delegated to shadows, she spoke in faint whispers that were quickly drowned out by the commotion and noise of a raucous New Orleans. No matter how hard he tried to listen, he could never make out any discernible words. He got no answers, just the sense of her overwhelming presence.

He soon found himself staring down an airplane boarding ramp leading to a narrow metal tube - one that would fly him thousands of miles away from the cookie-cutter office building where his coworkers sat in neat little cubicle rows, the same coworkers who now fight the urge to glance over in dismay at his recently abandoned workspace.

His eyes again fell to the perfect picture of a white-sand beach lined with palm trees, the setting sun dropping behind the horizon just beyond the glistening waters.

He's now journeyed to this celebrated city only to end up facing a haggard door in a forgotten alleyway, with the shadows growing long as the sun descends in the sky.

"This as far as I go," says a raspy voice. "This place too rough fer me."

Ryan turns to face the man with the rumpled hair and unshaven face he met in the stoop of a building several blocks away. He reaches into his pocket and hands him a $10 bill.

"Thanks for the help," he says. "This place is hard to find, isn't it?"

The man looks down at what's probably more money than he's seen in a week, and what will most likely be wasted within the next hour on cheap booze. Shaking his head ominously, he says, "Some places don't wanna be found."

Ryan does a double take. Don't wanna be found? What does that mean?

His eyes strained from lack of sleep, he again focuses on the foreboding, battle-scarred wooden slab of a door. This is certainly more bleak and off-putting than the sophisticated jazz lounge his subconscious constructed, where a delicate Southern belle sipped mint juleps under the soft flicker of a candle as she lovingly crafted his postcard.

It's a far cry from the raging party that engulfed him when he arrived in New Orleans. He landed in a French Quarter buzzing with activity and noise, but within a few blocks, he found himself wandering increasingly decrepit streets where life seems to have ceased altogether.

But Ryan knows no one wins a race by stopping 10 feet before the finish line.

He wraps his fingers around the rusty, steel harpoon that serves as a door handle. He begins to pull, but finds that he needs to lean back and use a good deal of his weight to move the imposing door that almost seems to fight back - like it's trying to stop a young man from making a dumb mistake.

But Ryan's determined that this mistake is his to make.

The door finally relents to his forceful tugging. Inside, the dim lights and thick haze of cigarette smoke make it almost impossible to see, stinging his weary eyes. Stale, overplayed Southern rock lingers in the air, accompanied by the faint smell of greasy bar food.

Ryan pushes through the discomfort as he takes his first cautious step into the room. His eyes slowly adjust to the murky air. They begin to make out shapes and forms, illuminated by Christmas lights that seem to be strung along every wall, and small flames that emanate from the candles that mark every table.

Only a few slumped and haggard silhouettes adorn the saloon-style wooden bar. Ryan does everything in his power to cut through the fog of desolation and discern whether one of these candles illuminates a friendly face - the face of a lovely enchantress tucked away in some corner with an expression of measured patience as she awaits his arrival.

"I think you're lost," comes a deep voice from behind the bar. "The coed party you're probably looking for is up on Bourbon Street."

Ryan squints to make out the man's features. He clearly sports a full beard, and a t-shirt with bright letters that read, "The Buck Stops Here." At the bottom of the shirt, a picture of a shotgun makes it clear just how he's able to live up to the mantra. In his 50-something years, he's probably started more bar fights than he's ended.

Again, with his eyes adjusting, Ryan turns to scan the fairly limited room. He discovers a dingy, beat-up jukebox and a mess of mismatched yard-sale furniture. The walls are cluttered with scribbled graffiti and old license plates.

He takes a deep breath, as it finally dawns on him that he must stick out like a sore thumb in his loose tie and collared work shirt. He chuckles to himself at the thought of how ridiculous he must look.

Ryan's mother always claimed he had what she coined as an "accidental charm." Even in his most awkward moments, you couldn't help but love him. He was the type of kid who could win you over even when he was shoving Legos up his nose.

"Sorry," he tells the bartender, a bit embarrassed, "I was just under the impression I was gonna meet a friend here."

The man smirks. "This is a place you come to lose friends. Out the door and two blocks up on the left, there's 100,000 new friends to be made."

Ryan apologetically nods and begins to head for the old wooden door, but something makes him stop in his tracks.

"I came here to meet someone who, I know this sounds ridiculous, but I guess a fortune teller or something, a medium," he says.

"Someone who thinks they've tapped into the answers of the universe," Marcus says.

Ryan pauses. "Yeah, exactly."

"You sure this is a can you wanna open?"

Ryan's timid expression makes it clear he's a little hesitant.

"Too late to turn back now," Marcus announces before Ryan can even answer. He yells to the back of the room, "Hey swami! You got a lost soul up here!"

Ryan turns, and his eyes search the furthest regions of the bar, where two patio doors are swung wide open to frame an outdoor courtyard with sprawling trees that create a surprising garden atmosphere. More Christmas lights, these a brilliant white, illuminate simple tables shaded by umbrellas, making the patio glow through the grunge of the bar.

Ryan can feel a small jolt of electricity rush through him again.

In the doorway, backlit by the soft glow from outside, appears the outline of a figure with edges caressed by the light. Ryan desperately tries to glean even the smallest detail from the mysterious form.

"Woohoo!" the figure hollers in a deep, raspy voice that's clearly not female.

Ryan's increasingly concerned eyes shoot to the bartender, who gives him a wicked smile. "Buddy, you just let loose a wagon full of monkeys."

Into the low interior lighting steps a gangly man wearing weathered overalls and unkempt hair, whose eyes immediately lock squarely on Ryan. Ryan again looks to the bartender in a panic.

"I guarantee this is not the person I'm looking for," he says.

The bartender shakes his head. "I tried to give you an out." The gangly man's long, untamed arms dangle at his sides as he begins an awkward but confident stride across the room, only occasionally breaking eye contact with Ryan to greet a patron in his thick Cajun accent - "How ya doin', podna?" "Koman sa va?"

"Charlie, I like me some butterflies, yes I do," one barfly replies as he passes.

"Good fer you, buddy," Charlie says.

His stride leads him ever closer to Ryan, whose attempt to take a few steps backward is thwarted by the dilapidated jukebox.

Suddenly, Charlie's standing chest to chest with Ryan, gazing deeply into his eyes.

"Ya been travelin' many mile," he says, "an' yer wonderin' if ya made da right choice, ain't ya?"

Ryan's not sure whether to answer or try to make a quick break for the door. Sensing his bewilderment, Charlie gives him a reassuring pat on the shoulder.

"Look like ya need yerself a drink, son, before ya hear 'bout da awe-inspirin' wonders o' da universe."

Ryan glances back at the bartender, who only rolls his eyes.

Charlie takes a seat on the nearest bar stool and announces, "Two beer, Marcus."

The bartender pops the top on two ice cold beers and sets them on the bar.

Without looking back at Ryan, Charlie kicks out another bar stool and slaps the top as a kind of invitation. Ryan tells himself that this is the moment he should just accept his losses, swallow his pride and head home with his tail between his legs.

"If y'aimin' fer da door," Charlie tells him, "y'aimin' in da wrong direction."

He again slaps the top of the bar stool, and for some inexplicable reason, Ryan finds himself actually accepting the invitation of this unrefined stranger.

He reluctantly takes a seat.

"I gonna pass 'long a secret," Charlie says. "Dere eight diff'rent people in da world. Duplicated a few billion time, o'course. I tink you a numba six. Ya see, I a numba t'ree: Connect wit people, concerned wit dey well bein', but don't take care o' da ones truly close ta me, mainly myself."

"They're also late at paying their bar tabs," Marcus pipes in, handing him an overdue bill.

Ryan goes over it in his head. Maybe if he just keeps this quiet when he goes home, doesn't tell a soul, he can escape with a little pride. Either way, he's definitely earned himself another one of his dad's lectures.

He grabs the beer in front of him and takes a few quick swigs, hoping to wash away what he sees as impending regret.

Charlie begins to pull crumpled money out of his pocket and count it on the bar, his eyes narrowing as he clearly comes up short. "Jimmy Carta a numba t'ree," he says as he lays out the bills. "Ghandi a t'ree. Reagan, he a numba seven." He pauses as if what he has to say next deserves a little more attention. "Now numba eights, we all gotta look out fer dem numba eights, 'cause brotha ..."

"Sorry to cut you off," Ryan says, setting down his drink. "Thanks for the beer, but I think I better go."

He starts to get up.

"Ya don't realize it," Charlie says, "but ya come here lookin' fer me."

He meets Ryan's eyes, which betray defeat, and what almost looks like a bit of contempt. But Charlie's not giving up.

"Look me in da eye and tell me providence ain't brought us togetha."

Ryan begrudgingly accepts the eye contact. He suddenly shouts, "Oh my god!"

Charlie's excited by his reaction. "I knowed it!"

Ryan reaches into his pocket and, from a wad of travel brochures he pilfered from airport baggage claim, pulls one out.

"This is you!" He holds up the brochure with the unflattering picture of Charlie in mid-blink. It reads: "Charlie La Bouche's Swamp Tours: If you lose a leg to a gator, the tour is free!"

Charlie nods with pride as if recognized as a celebrity.

"Dat dere a joke. No one lost more'n a chunk o' dey ear, fuh shore," he says. "But hand down, best swamp tour in town. Ya get right in dere wit all da critter 'n creature o' da bayou. Good time guarantee. Only $29.95."

"What a weird coincidence," Ryan says, glancing again at Charlie's hastily snapped photo.

"No, brotha," Charlie says, "ain't no such ting as coincidence."

Ryan studies the man who's now gone back to unassumingly nursing his beer. Then, he scans the travel brochure that sings his praises.

"Best swamp tour ever!" - Sheryl, Phoenix, Az.; "This is the real deal. Best swamp tour around." - Scott, Cleveland, Ohio; "One afternoon with Charlie La Bouche and you'll be a changed person." - Owen, Trenton, New Jersey.

Ryan looks up to see Charlie searching for more change in his pockets. He abruptly pulls $5 out of his own wallet and slaps it on top of the bill.

His bewilderment turns to curiosity as he watches Charlie unload more items from his pockets - a Swiss Army knife, a rubber band, a pack of cigarettes and some gum.

"Tu veux? It got dat dere ginsing." Charlie offers the near-empty pack of gum to Ryan.

Ryan's got other things on his mind. He slowly reaches around to his back pocket, where he has his postcard tucked away.

"I want you to take a look at something," he says, "because it's just got me a little confused."

"Ev'ry last one confused," Charlie says, "but I believe we can betta ourself. Problem is, people more willin' ta listen ta advice from a stranga den dey own mama."

"Yeah," Ryan says, "but when you see this ... I'm telling you, there's something special here."

Before he can reveal the rectangular piece of cardstock, Ryan notices Charlie pulling a large wad of postcards from the front pocket of his overalls.

He freezes. "You write postcards?"

Charlie's mouth turns up in the grin of a cat who swallowed the canary. Ryan tries not to overreact.

"A whole bucket load," Charlie says. "Ta people all ova. Around da world. Make 'em feel good. Make 'em tink. I gettin' perty good at it, fuh shore." He gives Ryan a wink. "I use lots o' real flowery language."

Ryan can feel his gut twist into a knot.

Charlie leans in for the clincher. "I sign fake name, though. Joke name."

The only thing that pops into Ryan's mind is - Dammit! Larry was right! This was a total waste of time. They'll never let him live it down back home.

Resigned, he finally pulls the postcard out of his back pocket and hands it to Charlie. Charlie laughs as he grabs it.

"Dang," he says, "was ya surprised when ya got it?"

"You could say that," Ryan says.

"I jus' can't believe it. Did ya like it?"

"Well, I don't know if 'like it' is the way I would describe it."

Charlie squints to read the postcard, but has to pull out a thick pair of glasses. As soon as he reads the first few lines, his face becomes tinged with a bit of disappointment.

"Aw shoot," he says.

He looks up at Ryan and takes a deep breath.

"Dis ting woke ya up like ya been sleepin' yer whole life, didn't it?" he says. "Like a hammer knocked ya over da head. Made ya question everytin', even da cosmos, and what ya gonna do in yer short time on dis spinnin' hunk o' rock."

"Yeah, that's actually exactly how I would describe it," Ryan says. "I'm not sure whether to be amazed by you or really pissed off."

Charlie shakes his head. "Oh, dat ain't mine. Yer lucky. Ya got one o' da originals. Dey real good. Dey made wit magic, what we call juju."

"An original?" Ryan says with new life.

He knew Larry couldn't have been right. Larry's never right.

"With magic?" he says.

Charlie has a look of hidden knowledge on his face. A smirk reveals he's about to let Ryan in on it.

Two thousand miles away in a cookie-cutter office building, employees who sit in neat little cubicle rows fight the urge to look over at the nearby cube that was recently abruptly abandoned.

Larry has his cell phone pressed to his ear.

"Well, I refuse to believe I'm wrong about this," he says. "In that case, you can remove me from your mailing list, VIP group and monthly sticker club."

He hangs up.

"Stupid Ice Capades!"

Thirty-two and "big-boned," he sits nervously in his cramped, cluttered cubicle wearing short-sleeved attire and 30 extra pounds of stress.

It's a cube that's nestled dead center in a sea of cubicles that seems to stretch on forever, in an industrial building that's always either slightly over-air conditioned or slightly under-heated. In a place where all meals are microwaved in the crusty, radiation-emitting machine in the break room, and the sounds of muffled gossip and clicking keyboards create a constant background noise.

For the hundredth time since he got to work, Larry's eyes drift across the way into Ryan's abandoned cube.

The small workspace bears all the markings of a place that's been left in a hurry. A light jacket still hangs over the arm of the chair and a half-full coffee mug sits cold on the desk. The cubicle's sparsely decorated compared to most. It's the domain of someone who seems like they're waiting for something, who appears to be living in limbo.

Larry's leg bounces up and down with nervous energy and worry. To some degree, everyone in the office had noticed Ryan's weird behavior over the past couple of weeks, but most wouldn't have taken the time to think much about it.

Larry suddenly hears footsteps approaching down the hallway. He's filled with an inexplicable sense of foreboding. As usual, the last thing he wants to see are those three uniform male haircuts passing by the top of his cube.

The Red Tie Brigade, a group of nondescript middle managers whose power's limited to daily meetings with the big wigs and control over the dreaded "raise freezes," seem to stalk the hallways of Redding. No telling what would happen if they discovered that Ryan's M.I.A. No telling what kind of repercussions they would slowly inflict on him for this infraction.

Larry breathes a sigh of relief when he instead spots the curly blonde locks of one of the executive assistants. She stops in Ryan's cubicle and drops some kind of memo on his desk. Then, she spots Larry.

"Company meeting tomorrow," she says, handing him a memo.

"Ryan had to take a quick emergency leave," he blurts out.

The woman stares at him as if to say, "Why should I care?"

As she hurries off down the hallway, a head pops up over the wall of a nearby cube.

"Is that guy still sulking?" says a voice.

Larry turns to see Pokorski, an unapologetic geek who's lacking a couple of haircuts and has a mop of hair over his eyes.

"You know how he gets," Larry tells him.

"Come on, at least he *had* a girlfriend," Pokorski says. "I've never seen anyone take a breakup so badly."

"Well, it was eight months."

Pokorski gives a dismissive wave, but suddenly comes to a realization.

"Nah, he didn't go. He's fine. He's got that date tonight with that scary chick from accounting."

Outback Steakhouse bustles with the Friday night crowd. Monica, the "scary chick from accounting," glares at the door as she watches for the man she had to wait out an eight-month relationship before she could finally ask out.

In a back booth, she's dolled up to the nines, maybe to the tens. Her hair's teased high atop her head and she's wearing impressive stilettos. Like an eager child who made a card for their mother, she's gone way beyond simple effort into gaudy excess. Her chest sparkles with tiny flints of golden glitter. You can take the girl out of Long Island, but you can't take Long Island out of the girl.

With each ticking minute, her long, cherry-red fingernails tap harder on the table as she anxiously chews gum as if it contains an anti-aging antidote.

She stares across the now-stone-cold Bloomin' Onion to the glaringly empty seat across from her, her hand gripping an envelope that reads, "For Ryan," followed by a series of hearts and her signature.

Her eyes burning with humiliation, she pulls out the stack of crisp, new Hawaiian travel brochures she's organized by island, and abruptly rips them to shreds.

"I hope friggin' Wendy Breezes was worth losing this girl over," she mutters.

Although she keeps her secrets close to the chest, this enigmatic beauty's always ready for a party. She enjoys the fun of batting her eyes and flirting a little, but she's never willing to compromise her own eclectic personality. Truth is, she refuses to be tamed by anyone.

Then again, New Orleans has never disappointed her suitors.

Starting when French fur traders settled among the Native American villages, and the Spanish and French battled for years to claim her as their own, she's been the darling of many a race, religion and nationality.

She proudly wears the wardrobe of the Spanish, French and Haitians who've dressed her over the years. Though she lives to put on a good show, a sadness dwells beneath her extraverted nature. She's seen more than her fair share of floods, hurricanes, racial strife and bitter custody disputes.

They've all left their mark and created an underlying dark mysticism. But she'll always put on her best dress and offer tourists the time of their lives.

As night falls, people revel in the streets. A saxophone explodes in a dixie rhythm. The buzz of voices and music swells. Past the water front. Over the city. Into the French Quarter. Beads fly from balconies. Jazz bands play in small watering holes.

Lovers embrace in the landings of French-style door-ways, oblivious to the swell of humanity around them.

A stranger to this place might find themselves feeling like Dorothy as she took her first step down the Yellow Brick Road, immersed in a swirling party set among the architecture of a bygone era.

Ryan struggles to keep up with his enthusiastic tour guide. It seems as though Charlie knows every soul in the French Quarter. If someone walked up to him with a frown, they left with a smile.

Ryan squeezes in questions whenever he gets a chance, but it's not easy. People seem drawn to Charlie, as evidenced by the excess of beaded necklaces that now adorn his neck.

"Ya wouldn't know it from lookin' at me," Charlie says, raising his voice to be heard over the din of the crowd, "but t'ree week ago, I's just a good ol' boy makin' his livin' off da bayou. Not da enlightened man ya see here before ya. It like I wearin' blinders. Couldn't see ting da way dey really were."

He walks at his own relaxed pace, but Ryan feels as if he could easily fall behind the exuberant man in the hand-

26

me-down overalls who greets every passerby as if he's known them for years. Even Charlie's walk is happy. He's the type of person who seems like he's dancing, even when he's standing still.

"She got herself a gift," Charlie says. "I ain't smart 'nough ta know what t'is. ESP or sometin'. She can read souls, same as you can read a eye chart. She know what eatin' ya 'fore you even know."

"And she's always right?" Ryan says.

"She ain't like a news man reportin' fact. More like a weather man. She ain't necessarily sure where, when or how much, but she can tell when a storm comin'."

"When can I meet her? What's her name? It obviously can't be Wendy Breezes."

"Lily. She go ta Harpoon's every mornin'," Charlie says. "Dey open at eleven. She probably already know yer comin'."

Ryan struggles to keep his hopes in check, but he can't deny the surge of adrenaline rushing through his veins.

Charlie abruptly stops and turns his way.

"Prepare yerself," he says, "'cause once ya meet her, y'aint gonna be da same as ya was. It like da world take on a new color. Ya see ting with a diff'rent eye. An' whateva magic she got in store fer ya ..."

Ryan's glued to his every word. This is exactly what he wanted to hear, and he just prays that it's true.

"I tellin' ya, it powerful magic. It potent," Charlie says. "An' it gonna touch ev'ryting in yer life. Ev'ryone you know."

"Why do I get this weird feeling all of a sudden?" Larry says. "There's something in the air."

"Yeah, the smell of nervous sweating," Pokorski says.

"No, really. Something's going on. Something's happening."

With the early morning energy running high, and Larry going on no sleep thanks to anticipation about this meeting, the air's definitely charged with tension. Larry and Pokorski endure Redding's overly air conditioned auditorium as they watch Vice President of Operations Betty Parks dole out charts, graphs and profit margins to captive employees.

Larry glances again at the menacing company memo, then back up at the stage, where the well-toned, middle-aged woman clicks a button to advance the sterile, corporate presentation.

A large screen over the stage projects a Powerpoint image: "Redding: The future through teamwork."

"Which brings me to address some rumors that have been circulating," Betty says.

Larry and Pokorski simultaneously hold their breath.

"Relocation," Betty announces.

A stunned silence overtakes the auditorium, and Larry and Pokorski are almost unable to release the air they've sucked in.

A new slide pops up on the screen. A bad publicity image of: "Phoenix: Catch the heat!" Suddenly blasted a little too loudly comes "The Heat Is On" by Glenn Frey.

It takes several minutes before Pokorski's finally able to squeak out a few words.

"Ryan picked the worst possible time to go chase down Carmen Sandiego."

A woman with perfectly feathered hair lifts the lid off a pot brimming with bright red little creatures that resemble tiny lobsters, practically salivating as steam rises from it.

The home-grown instructional show was clearly filmed in an era when wide collars were still popular and a synthesized drum beat was the sign of a quality production.

"Okay, now ya'll are in for quite a treat." The woman snaps one of the crawfish in half.

"First, you suck the goodies out of this little critter's head."

Ryan quickly turns away from the TV in disgust.

It was around the age of 9 that he began obsessively calling in favors from countless friends going on trips, bugging family members who lived in different cities and writing formal requests to chambers of commerce around the world to gather hundreds of travel brochures that by now he's practically memorized. He's a virtual expert on Paris, Africa, New York, exotic Delaware, although he's never been to any of these places - or even outside his own state border, for that matter.

Something akin to a secret, underground currency has developed at Redding over the years. If you need anything, you slip Ryan a few travel brochures. If you're lucky enough that he doesn't already have them, he's yours for the day.

Ryan uses the ornate hotel bed as a staging area to sort his many glossy brochures, which until now have never made their way out of the safety of the shoebox at the back of his bedroom closet. After adding several crisp, new booklets to the New Orleans stack, including Charlie's, he carefully loads them all back into his backpack and tucks them away in the closet.

He checks the time - 11:03. Crap, this is it. He grabs his wallet and room key and quickly rushes for the door. As soon as he opens it, he comes face to face with a short woman who has her hand raised to knock.

Standing in front of a fully stocked cleaning cart, the woman's shocked to see him.

"Sorry." Ryan looks at her name tag. "Mila, do you think I could get a couple more mints?"

The woman glances around nervously.

"I tell you," she starts in her Eastern-European accent, "I not supposed ... one mint in room."

"One mint, right." Ryan nods and starts to head off.

Mila scans the hallway as if a SWAT team's about to bust through the window. Then, she discreetly grabs two mints and places them in Ryan's hand.

He nods his appreciation.

"Go, go," she says, as she hurriedly pushes her cart into the room.

The harpoon door handle that's been marred by years' worth of fingerprints looks like it very well could have been used to kill something at some point.

Ryan pops a mint in his mouth, hoping to calm his jitters.

For him, most events in life come and go with the significance of a trip to the grocery store, but this one's different. For some unexplained reason, this woman knows everything there is to know about his daily struggles and his unrelenting desire to run away from it all.

And if for some reason Charlie's right about her, could she also know about his gnawing regrets, his most private pain, the decisions he'd give anything to take back?

He's come here for one very important reason, and even though it'll take all he's got, he'll have to block out everything and everyone else.

With a deep breath and a mouth burning with the overpowering flavor of spearmint, he reaches for the door. His phone suddenly vibrates in his pocket. He groans, pulling it out to be confronted by an older picture of a wide-eyed and befuddled Larry in an outdated sweater.

Oh no, not now. He slides the phone back into his pocket, and decisively enters the bar.

There he finds Marcus diligently cleaning the counter in a t-shirt that reads, "Life Insurance By Smith & Wesson." The establishment's only customer's slumped lifelessly over his beer.

Ryan nods to Marcus, but gets no response.

His eyes drift to the back patio, which is still stuck in the peace and quiet of a pleasant New Orleans morning, with cherry blossoms fluttering down from a statuesque tree that splashes everything with pink accents.

One blossom dances on a gentle breeze with life and personality, twisting and careening through the air. Ryan follows it until it lands on the table of a woman who's shaded by a big, floppy hat.

She's poised in her white summer dress with her long, brown hair braided over one shoulder, a rim of sunlight around her.

Exactly what Ryan would have hoped to find here, this pretty woman whose sweeping pen strokes mark the back of a postcard. Not only one postcard, but she's got stacks and stacks of postcards piled up on her table.

There are two types of men in the world - those who ask women out for a cup of coffee, and those who ask them out for a drink. Ryan asks women out for an afternoon cup of frozen yogurt.

Approaching a stranger in a bar isn't his style, but nothing's ordinary anymore.

The stranger writes so diligently, and with the bright morning sun bathing her in translucent light, she's almost glowing. Ryan's transfixed by the image straight out of a black-and-white movie.

"That's called a woman," Marcus says. "They like flowers and ordering lots of crap from catalogs, and they tend to hate it when dudes gawk at them."

Ryan tries to snap out of his paralysis.

"How about a drink?" Marcus says.

"Yeah," Ryan says, "whatever she's having."

Rubbing his hands together, Marcus proclaims, "Hot damn! Another exotic Diet Coke with a slice of lemon."

"Um ... never mind."

Ryan instinctually heads in the direction of the woman who's scribbling so attentively, just the way she must have done when she reached out to a stranger in a neatly kept cubicle miles and zip codes away from here. Telling him there was more to see, probing his needs and frustrations.

He shields his eyes from the direct sunlight as he cautiously approaches the table. Even as he casts a shadow over the woman and her postcard, her focus remains unbroken.

From her point of view, the brim of her hat blocks the upper half of Ryan's body, reducing him to a pair of shaky legs with jeans and an untucked shirt.

Ryan's suddenly desperate to get a glimpse of her eyes under that obtrusive hat. He musters up the courage to break her state of concentration, but before he does ...

"Don't you think it's time to put those puppies to bed?" the woman interrupts.

Ryan checks out his overly worn, always-reliable sneakers.

Marcus' voice yells from the bar. "Is Little Johnny Stares-a-Lot bothering you?"

"I'm not a creep," Ryan tells him. "I'm just nervous."

"You have a really subtle way of approaching women," says the woman who, thanks to Charlie, Ryan knows to be Lily.

Terrified of blowing this all-important first impression, Ryan says, "Oh, I'm not trying to hit on you."

Lily finally looks straight at him with striking green eyes. She wears minimal makeup, just a hint of lip gloss, but her skin's even and smooth. She's dressed simply and without much jewelry.

Lily's a lot younger than Ryan expected. No older than 30.

She meets his eyes, which are wide with anticipation. Clearly, he's waiting for something.

"Well," she says, "you don't look like you need a hand out."

He takes a deep breath.

"I'm Ryan," he says, hoping for that look of immediate recognition, to be welcomed with open arms.

Instead, he's greeted with an indifferent stare.

"You sent me this," he says, carefully laying his cherished postcard in front of her.

It takes Lily a moment to study the delicate, looping letters.

"I did," she says.

Ryan finally begins to breathe again, the smallest sense of relief washing over him.

"Thank god. I'm not sure where to start. I've gotta be honest, it's amazing how well you know me."

Lily's aware that what she has to say next will probably come as a blow to this eager stranger. "I think you're reading a bit more into this than you should," she says as she starts to gather her postcards.

Ryan steps closer, not ready to let the moment slip away. "Charlie says you have special powers, a gift or something."

Lily carelessly shoves an old laptop and some pens into a large, pink bag that's stuffed to the brim. Ryan instinctually grabs for the postcard he's become so accustomed to protecting like a member of his family, in doing so knocking off the stack of cards that was already there.

"Oh geez, I'm sorry," he says, flustered.

He quickly kneels down to clean up the mess he's made.

Lily finishes scooping up her belongings, barely paying attention to the pile now scattered across the floor. As Ryan gathers up the cards, he begins to see names and cities - Minneapolis, Chicago, Detroit - all in the same handwriting as his own.

"Charlie's sweet," Lily says as she slings her bag over her shoulder, "but he gives in to superstition. It was nice meeting you, Ryan."

"Wait," he says. "This can't be it. I've travelled a thousand miles, risked my job and spent more money than I should to meet you."

"I've got a ton of errands. I'm sorry."

36

As Ryan collects all the postcards off the ground, Marcus gestures to Lily from inside: Want me to kick this guy out of here?

Lily looks down at the stranger who's working so hard to clean up his mess. He's in his late 20s and attractive. She gets a little grin on her face. Something about him tells her he was the kind of kid who was charming even when he was shoving Legos up his nose.

She waves Marcus off.

"All right," she tells Ryan, "but you gotta keep up. I move fast. Slow me down and I'll cut you loose."

Ryan nods as he hands her the newly stacked postcards.

They're out the door and down the dingy alley that leads from Rusty Harpoon's onto a street populated by battered buildings scarred with graffiti. In this section of town, the party died a long time ago, replaced by the pain of drudgery and daily struggle. With the quick turn of a corner, they're suddenly in a whole other world - the exuberant celebration that's always raging on Royal Street, where tourists and locals mingle under the gas lamps and on the ironwork balconies of vintage buildings.

Lily weaves her way through the crowd as Ryan races to keep up, and at the same time, to organize his jumbled thoughts.

"Why me ... why us?" he asks.

"I just pick names out of the phone book. I'm sorry if you thought it was something special. It was just meant to make you think about your life. Think about a change."

"What change?"

They make a sharp left down another street packed with tourists.

"People lead boring lives," she says. "They waste them away scrimping and saving for a day that may never come. I try to get them to live for today, not some idealized tomorrow."

"Oh, I get that. That's why I'm here. It just doesn't explain how you know all this stuff about me."

A quick right past the neon sign that marks the front door of Marie Laveau's House of Voodoo and Fortune, and they've entered a dark, cluttered den of voodoo magic. Posters of ghouls and spirits glare down from the walls. Shrunken heads hang low, almost scraping Ryan's hair, and the shelves contain skulls and magic card tricks, most of which say "Made in China" on the back.

Ryan's been transported into a narrow space that straddles between eery and touristy. Incense burns on a counter that's unmanned. There must be a smoke machine in the back, because the air's hazy and blurred.

Ryan and his mystery woman now dwell in the underworld come to life.

Lily barely glances around at the seedy shop. She heads confidently past the dried monkey paws and virility potions. Ryan obediently follows.

"Being vague goes a long way," she says.

Past the taro cards and dried mushrooms, she's shopping with purpose.

"Mine certainly wasn't vague," Ryan says.

"Or so you think. I guess that's my gift."

"So Charlie's right."

"Okay, gift is the wrong word." Lily turns to face Ryan. "Skill."

She grabs a box of exotic teas. "You're smart. Search your soul. Is it magic and I have an insight into your inner thoughts and feelings, or did I just paint a simple picture that allows you to fill in the gaps, and you read into it what you wanted to hear? Is it that I've harnessed some mystical power of the universe, or is it a simple formula of twenty percent horoscope, twenty percent fortune cookie and, if they're right in front of you, twenty percent facial expressions and body language? You should probably throw in ten percent instinct. If you don't have good instincts about people, they'll see right through it."

"Charlie says you're using magic," Ryan says, "so what do you mean by instinct?"

"Instinct. It's the same feeling you have when you're in a bar and you know some girl likes you from across the room. It's nothing."

"So what you're saying is my postcard is nothing more than a glorified fortune cookie?" Ryan says.

"Think of it this way," Lily says. "The road to wealth is not found by following the symbol of the dollar, but the shape of a heart, or ..."

She sets down her items and takes hold of Ryan's hands. Suddenly, an unexpected tingle shoots through his entire body. Her eyes lock into his, and it's like she's peering deep inside him.

"Ryan, following your current path to wealth is only getting you lost. Follow your heart, which is full of wonder and clearly has a lot of love to give."

Ryan succumbs to the intense connection of their stare.

Suddenly, Lily lets go of his hands and her eyes disengage. Just as quickly as the tingle overtook him, it's gone.

"See the difference?" she says. "It seems specific to you now. If everyone's name was suddenly printed on their fortune cookies, half the population would believe wholeheartedly."

Ryan knows what she's saying is absolutely true, but he can't get past the moment - that touch, the feeling, the depth of Lily's eyes.

Behind the counter appears a gaunt young man with dark, black lines around his eyes and a concert t-shirt, looking no more than 16 and oozing middle-class angst. He's still pouting from a highly emotional argument with his mother over the fact that if he's truly committed to this lifestyle, he needs to start buying his own eyeliner.

He picks up a skull and bones that not so subtly disguise a laser scanner.

Lily's not interested in conversation as she pays for her unique assortment of items. Pausing for a moment, something makes her turn back toward Ryan with a softer expression.

"Listen," she says, "leaving that cubicle of yours is the best thing you could have done. I think you made the right decision coming here. Clearly, this is what you need. The only problem is you're looking to me to show you some new direction. That's for you to figure out. You took the first step. I'm glad I wrote it. But remember, it is just a postcard."

She opens the box of tea and places a packet in Ryan's hand. "I helped you untie the ship. Now you decide where you're gonna sail."

Ryan tries to lock into her eyes again, hoping for the kind of moment he's only seen in others - the hint of clear recognition, the glimmer of complete connection between them - but now the only look she's giving him is a sympathetic one.

"Okay?" she says. "Are we good?"

"Yeah, we're good," Ryan lies.

"All right." Lily turns and leaves the shop with the shallow ring of the little bell over the exit.

Ryan watches the door slowly close.

"You're compassionate," a voice says, "yet can be stubborn and indifferent to others' feelings."

Ryan turns to see a couple of tourists behind him reading from a thick hardcover book titled *Dr. Wistorium's Book of Cosmic Alignment and Future Premonitional Insights.*

The other one rolls his eyes. "What idiot falls for this crap?"

In towns and cities across America, handwritten messages on the back of postcards seem to leap out and take hold of people as they muddle through their daily ruts. The anonymous words feel anything but vague, and almost eerily tap into their biggest worries and wildest daydreams. The confused recipients think they can shake the feeling when they leave for work or school, but they're surprised to find that a simple piece of mail has begun to permeate everything they say and do.

In a big city, the polished businessman tries to make it through his usual slew of meetings without overanalyzing the words he still can't figure out. His eyes drift out the window to the vast landscape of tall buildings, and even beyond that, to places he never gave much thought to before.

In between dragging her kids to various sports practices, the frazzled soccer mom steals every opportunity to read the words a stranger has addressed to her. At every red light, in the waiting room at the dentist office, at a game, she covertly sneaks a peek at the colorful Hawaiian postcard she has taped to the inside of a magazine.

In Ohio, the guidance counselor suffers through meetings with students whose big dreams contradict the list of real-life occupations he's printed out for them on a barely functioning printer - construction worker, plumber, accountant.

On his desk, always in his line of sight, rests a postcard that has him tortured as if he's trying to decode something written between the lines. He struggles to maintain eye contact as his thoughts drift back to the sweeping pen strokes that have him shaken to the core.

On Martin Street, the piano teacher listens to a young pupil plunk out notes on a baby grand. As she shoos away so many nagging thoughts, she's unaware that in the other room, her husband's gaze has again drifted from the uneventful ball game on TV to the simple words scribbled on a postcard that's propped against the lamp: "We all know there's magic out there to be found … Next stop? Exotic New Orleans."

Chapter 3:
"I'm not about to throw away four good years"

"Phoenix is probably the most exciting city on the planet. You've got desert views, restaurants, stores, museums." Larry turns a page in the packet he's scanning. "The thing is, with the cost of living out there, even in great school districts, we could actually think about retiring someday."

Pokorski shakes his head. "Janet's gonna be a tough sell."

Larry crinkles his brow in frustration. "The dry air's great for your skin."

"Not sure, but I think she might take that as an insult," Pokorski says. "Hey, isn't she always cold? She'll be dying to go."

"I don't have it all worked out yet. Janet's usually the one who would walk me through something like this."

Larry's always believed that if he ever had a heart attack, his wife, Janet, would save his life not with CPR, but with a simple look of "Knock it off!", and his heart would immediately return to its normal rhythm. She always seems to remain calm when everyone else panics.

"So, how did you tell …?" Larry stops cold.

"Who? Who'm I gonna tell?"

"I don't know … your parents?"

"They barely know where I live now," Pokorski says.

Suddenly, something crashes to the ground in the cubicle across from them. Larry feels an instinctual excitement at hearing signs of life in Ryan's workspace.

His excitement's short-lived. When there's another loud bang, he and Pokorski peek over the wall to see a dolled-up Monica ripping open an envelope and angrily dumping small pieces of glossy paper all over Ryan's desk - the remnants of his precious brochures.

"Think you're hot stuff?" Monica mumbles in her thick Long Island accent. "Grow up ... frickin' Bloomin' Onion."

Larry and Pokorski exchange a look of horror. It's intensified when Larry's phone rings.

"It's Ryan," he whispers.

He answers it like a teenager trying to hide their bad boyfriend from their parents, but gets right to the point.

"So, are you ready to come back?" he asks.

"What?" Ryan says.

There's more banging as Monica continues her rampage. She lifts a framed photo off Ryan's desk and holds it dramatically over the ground, braced to destroy it.

Pokorski cowers in Larry's cubicle. "I'm so scared." He peeks over the wall again. "Those accounting types are sure strict about their expense reports."

"Uh, I might have to call you back," Larry tells Ryan, "but I can pick you up at the airport anytime. Just let me know."

Monica's struggling to carry out the destruction. She finally lets out an exasperated growl and slams the picture back down on the desk.

As she stands there, her anger turns inward. She knows she continues to sabotage her own goals. Done with bad boys, exhausted of wild romps with men of no substance, she's finally ready for something other than the rough and tough Long Island kid. Trouble is, she has no idea how to reel in the marrying kind.

It took forever to get Ryan to agree to go on a date with her, and just like that, some woman 1,000 miles away stole him from her.

How's she supposed to find a solid relationship when the good ones up and vanish? How can she compete with a woman Ryan's never even seen before who scribbles a message on a postcard and turns his whole world upside down?

Having found herself woefully unable to inflict damage in Ryan's cube, Monica storms out into the hallway. With no outlet for her anger, she turns to the belabored office copy machine that churns out faded duplicates with a loud hum.

Her foot delivers a vigorous kick that reverberates throughout the cubicle maze. Her eyes light up, and she brutally unleashes every ounce of her fury in solid, repetitive kicks that would make David Beckham proud.

"I don't know if you've talked to Monica," Larry says into the phone, "but you might want to invest in a really nice Hallmark card when you get back."

Ryan's not listening. Through the endless stream of tourists, he's spotted a battered pick-up truck driving down Bourbon Street. He waves to Charlie, who despite having his windows rolled down, doesn't seem to notice.

More banging and cursing through the phone draws Ryan's attention.

"And possibly a restraining order," Larry says.

"Right," Ryan says with a tinge of fear, "that's probably a good idea."

He looks up again and sees that the truck has moved on down the road. He begins walking faster to follow it.

"By the way," Larry says. "I couldn't cancel the tickets, so you're stuck. And the kids will be mad if you're not here for the Ice Capades."

"Okay, Larry," Ryan says as he tries to weave his way through the crowd.

"Listen, you gotta get back here. You just taking off like this does not look good," Larry says, "People have noticed."

"Got it."

"I know it's been a tough month. Break ups are hard."

"I gotta go."

Ryan looks up to see Charlie's truck stopped at a light not too far away.

"Hey, I'm interested in a swamp tour!" Ryan yells from the sidewalk.

Charlie glances over in disbelief. "Mais, ain't you a sight! Dere da lady killa."

He motions for Ryan to hop in the truck.

"Honestly, right now it just feels like all the ladies want to kill me," Ryan says as he takes a seat.

As Charlie drives, the ornate beauty of the French Quarter slowly dissipates and the road winds into rural country lined with striking Louisiana greenery.

"Well, ya best take dat swamp tour good 'n quick," Charlie says. "I tinkin' 'bout sellin' my business, startin' dat new chapta."

"Oh wow," Ryan says, "that's a big step."

"Sure is," Charlie says. "Dere lots o' folk just itchin' ta buy it off my hands. I get me dat money, go see me da big ol' world out dere."

"Now see, that takes guts," Ryan says. "I wish I could do that. Screw what everyone else thinks, do what you wanna do."

"Darn straight. Matta fact, ya willin' ta help me lay down a fresh coat o' paint and shore up a coupla 2x4's, get everytin' in order, I give ya yer tour on da house."

"I'm in," Ryan says.

Charlie gives him a little nudge. "Dis stay betwixt us fer now, k podna?"

Ryan nods that the information's safe with him.

Charlie finally pulls into a dirt lot that's almost completely empty except for a couple of old junk cars.

The ramshackle building's marked with a rusty sign that reads "Bobby Jack's Bait & Tackle Supplies." It's probably been there for 100 years, and seen every shade of business take place under its roof. It's the kind of shop where the locals have caught on to the fact that everything is perpetually "on sale."

Ryan doesn't get much of a chance to absorb the unique establishment. For Charlie and the folks around here, this is just everyday, and everyday stuff needs to get done.

It's hard to keep up with Charlie as he slides open the glass door to the shop and enters a room that's poorly lit by long, fluorescent tubes, with Merle Haggard serenading from a scratchy old speaker on the ceiling. Ryan's struck by the pungent, nasty aroma of fish. He tries his best not to breathe in, as he surveys the rustic decor.

Metal replicas of sea creatures snagged with hooks hang everywhere, and the walls are strung with large nets, and fishing poles that could catch anything from a minnow to a shark.

Charlie grabs a white, five-gallon bucket and begins filling it with plastic worms, jigs and spinners.

"So ..." Ryan says as he hurries to catch up.

"Not what you's expectin', huh?" Charlie says. "I shoulda give ya some warnin'. She can be entêté ... pig-headed."

"Well, she drew some definite lines in the sand," Ryan says as he follows behind.

Charlie sorts through items on the cluttered shelves. "Now dis li'l sucka here gonna catch ya some prime bluegill. Dem's some stubborn sons o' guns."

He moves on to another aisle filled with miscellaneous fishing paraphernalia, with Ryan close behind.

"Hey, Junior, how much fer dis?" he shouts to the gawky teenager behind the counter.

"Marked down from 10," Junior returns. "It seven dollar."

"It always seven dollar," Charlie mutters under his breath.

He throws the gadget into his bucket anyway and continues on down the aisle.

"Don't take it pers'nal, podna," he tells Ryan. "She ain't took kindly ta me da first time, neitha. She quite da looka, fuh shore."

"Hard not to notice," Ryan says. "I'm sure someone like her gets lots of interest. What else do you know about her?"

"Uh, not much. Everytin' she own perty much in dat bag o' hers. She move 'round a fair bit."

Charlie suddenly gets a huge smile on his face and throws a ridiculously oversized fake worm in with the rest of his bounty.

Ryan pulls his well-worn postcard out of his back pocket. "Sadly, she made it very clear we're definitely on different wavelengths, and I hate to tell you, but she was adamant that this thing has nothing to do with magic."

Charlie stops cold and sets down his bucket. Ryan's surprised to get his full attention for the first time.

"Dat 'bout as true as dese here fer sale signs," he says.

Junior grumbles in protest from across the room.

"She tell a good tale," Charlie says. "Lemme ask ya, how'd she know dat despite how much I love readin' 'bout ancient Rome and da Pyramids and such, I quit school in da eight grade. I want ya ta tink real hard. Whatever she told ya today, ya know she said sometin' ya just can't explain."

Ryan dismisses the idea, but Charlie's unwavering, his eyes locked on his skeptical friend.

"I show ya sometin' gonna change yer mind fer good," he says. "I gonna open dem eyes o' yers, an' once dey open, ya gonna see dat she don't just got magic ..." he pauses, excitement in his voice, "... she downright glowin' wit' it."

Inside the modest suburban tract home, the wooden spice rack hangs a little crooked on the wall, but it's packed to the brim with family essentials like oregano and basil. The white tile countertop's clean, although the grout's stained from daily use. But all that's more than made up for by the well-watered potted plants in the windowsill and the children's artwork that decorates the refrigerator.

Penne's reaching a boiling point on the stove as the kids mope around cleaning up their toys, and Janet's juggling a phone call with her sister in Albuquerque about their parents' upcoming anniversary. As she stirs the sauce, she compiles the next day's to-do list. And somehow, through it all, she's perfectly orchestrating everything.

Larry stares at the front door knowing for sure this is the scene he's about to interrupt with the lame speech he's been practicing all day. He grips a manila envelope that contains an HR packet - "What The Relocation Means To You."

Relocation! It's the kind of earth-shattering news that usually has him completely flipping out, but he knows he's only feet away from Janet, and she'll have a clear plan to maneuver through the turmoil.

He takes a moment to shore up his reserves. When he opens the door, he's immediately deflated by the lack of even the hint of an aroma of peppers and onions drifting in from the kitchen. There are no pots clanking, no TVs blaring.

His gut sinks when he trips over a child's toy truck left lying in the entryway.

That's when a father's worry really kicks into high gear. Has Janet rushed one of the kids to the emergency room? Did someone hurt them?

Larry rushes into the house, to find Janet sitting in the family room.

"Oh my god," he says, "you had me so worried."

She's sunken into the couch, her eyes distant. Making his way toward her, Larry tucks the packet behind his back. Any stressful news will have to wait.

"Larry," Janet says, "I've cleaned this house 2,752 times."

"Today?" Larry says.

"No, I cleaned it for the 2,752nd time."

"Are you mad at me?" he says as he takes a seat and places the envelope behind him.

"No."

"Are you mad at the kids?"

Janet's eyes are puffy and her hair's pulled back in an untidy ponytail. She's wearing her old, ratty sweatpants that usually never leave the back of the closet.

She shakes her head.

"I'm not mad at the kids. Well, I took it out on the kids. I yelled at them pretty good earlier. They're in their room now eating 'Mommy feels guilty' ice cream and watching that stupid kitten movie they've practically memorized. Look around, I've cleaned this house 2,752 times, and does it look any better than it did the first day we moved in?"

"Yes," Larry says cautiously.

"Honestly."

"No. I'm sorry."

Janet's eyes have the hollow stare of exhaustion.

"For 2,752 days, I have cleaned this house everyday, and the next day it's dirty again, and so I clean it again, and the next day it's dirty again. Everyday this remote control will be sticky. I know it will be sticky. So I get out a wipe and clean it off. But it gets sticky again. This is my life, Larry. This is what I do."

Larry's staring at her, at a complete loss for words.

"You read Ryan's postcard," Janet says. "I read the postcard, and the moment I read it, it was like something came over me. I turned it over and saw the picture of that white sandy beach, and all I could think about was putting my toes in that sand. I'm bored of this house. I'm bored of the TV. I'm bored of the view."

"Are you bored of me?" Larry asks.

Janet turns toward him and finally makes eye contact.

"No, but we're boring. Is this what we wanted, Larry? I keep secretly hoping you'll come home with some unexpected surprise, that when I say, 'How was work?', you'll tell me there's some exciting change, or a new direction I never saw coming."

She points to the envelope that Larry's discreetly placed behind him. "Like, I know that stupid thing you brought home is probably just a stack of 401K documents and crap you're gonna ask me to file, somewhere, but wouldn't it be nice if it contained a winning lottery ticket, or the details of a trip to Hawaii?"

Larry can't believe what he's hearing. He takes a deep breath. "You know how they say, 'Be careful what you wish for'?"

"Dem people tought she was one o' dem socialites. All prim an' propa. Let 'er into balls and such like she a princess. No one knowed." Charlie's stopped to look up at a desolate, three-story house whose windows are dark - 1140 Royal Street. It has the ghostly calm of a dwelling that was deserted by the living long ago.

"Goes ta show ya no one know nuttin'."

Ryan shakes his head. "Guess not."

A crooked smile crosses Charlie's lips. He's having a lot of fun trying to put a scare into this fish out of water.

"Dey found dem slaves all gnarled up, bound by dey feet and hands, in a world o' hurt. She peeled off one o' dey skin, and twisted one's bones 'til he look like a crab ..."

"Okay," Ryan stops him.

It's one thing to hear the stories on a Travel Channel documentary, but here in person, it's literally too close to home. More than a harmless ghost story, it's flesh and blood. Everyone knows this place is haunted by the tormented, angry souls of the slaves tortured by Madame LaLaurie.

What seemed like an innocent fire led to officials discovering mangled and battered slaves tied up in the kitchen by an evil, cruel woman who came off as a mannered pillar of the community.

"'Cause o' dat fire, dey find all dem people. And here da ting, no one know how dat fire got goin'. Da police ain't figure it out. Da firemen don't even know. Folk say some otha force at work. A force dat wanna free dem poor soul."

"New Orleans ain't all jazz and beignets, is it?" Ryan says.

As creepy as it all sounds, this house is probably just a wood-and-nails structure with creaky floorboards and a draft upstairs. Nothing a contractor couldn't fix. Maybe it's haunted by a few rats and dust mites. But because of superstition and ghost stories, no one dares even cross the threshold anymore. Because of superstition, this majestic, old house with all its history is just a rotting structure dying of neglect and decay.

"But Charlie," Ryan says, "anything could have started that fire."

Charlie sizes up his skeptical friend. "So ya don't believe dere nuttin' else out dere? Spirits? Dark magic? Dat juju we ain't understand? Even good magic? Kind make tings happen? Kind help ya out in a pinch? Without magic, yer tellin' me dat li'l ol' postcard found it way ta you just when ya needed it most?"

"This morning I might have agreed with you, but after what she said ..."

"She know more'n ya tink," Charlie says. "She keep her cards close ta da chest. Lemme show ya sometin'. Do as I do."

They stand side by side, and Charlie closes his eyes tight.

"Go on," he prompts. "Close 'em up real good."

Ryan shrugs, then follows directions and shuts his eyes, too, not exactly sure where this is all heading, but fully in the moment.

Something about having his eyes closed immediately renders the world so silent and still, but every small sound becomes amplified like it's booming. Each footstep becomes distinguishable from the next - the sober tourist's steady stroll compared to the off-kilter clomping of a drunk. Voices of strangers take on vivid nuances that allow Ryan to picture people's faces.

Ryan loses himself in the darkness for a moment, then something strikes him.

"Uh, why are you staring at me?" he asks Charlie.

"How'd ya know I's starin' at ya?"

"I don't know." Ryan opens his eyes.

Sure enough, Charlie's watching him.

Ryan could feel Charlie's eyes on his face like it was an actual physical sensation. It's the same way he'd know if someone was standing next to his bed in the dark of night.

"And ya know it ain't da first time ya know'd dat feelin'," Charlie says. "Someone standin' behind ya. Ya tink 'bout a good ol' boy y'ain't seen in years and dey call up da very next day? Or maybe a song pop in yer head, den ya turn on da radio and boom, dere t'is."

Charlie smiles.

"Ya can't explain it, but ya knew I's lookin' atcha. Ya could feel it. Almost see me, right? Gotta be da juju ..."

Ryan sees a new spark in Charlie's eyes. The look of genuine belief. He's not selling a thing - no malice, no gimmicks or agenda. The last few weeks, thanks to Lily, have nearly been a religious experience for Charlie, and he wants nothing more than for Ryan to experience the same thing.

"Or maybe dat just happ'n when two folk share a true spiritual connection," Charlie says. "Shoot, I dunno. But ya know it sometin' special. And don't ya be a fool tinkin' she ain't got buckets of it."

At a far back table on Rusty Harpoon's quiet patio, Ryan's mystery woman's bathed in early morning sunlight.

With her trademark hat shading her expressive eyes and soft features, she looks like an old-time movie actress who's trying to create privacy in a public forum. She's not a part of this place, doesn't look like the others, but she's comfortable enough not to feign interest in anyone.

A cherry blossom drifts on a soft breeze until it lands directly on top of the postcard that's commanding her focus. She cooly wipes it away.

In front of her sits a large stack of postcards. Some are already marked to Minneapolis or Seattle. Some still lack any address. Those are the ones with the most promise, because they could go to absolutely anyone.

Out the corner of her eye, she catches movement from inside the bar. The heavy front door slowly begins to open, then quickly shuts. There it goes again. And again. Each time, a little outside light sneaks into the room just enough to illuminate a few of the tables.

Lily notices that Marcus has also become focused on the door. He seems a little annoyed as he wipes down tables in a t-shirt that reads, "Tougher'n a Two Dollar Steak."

"I'm too old to deal with this crap," he grumbles. "If even half these drunks would pay their tabs, I could actually hire someone, instead of breaking my own back day after day."

Lily barely looks up from her postcard.

"There are only two professions - doctor and bartender - that require bedside manner," she says. "These people just want someone to listen to their problems. They want a therapist. Turn on your bedside manner, pretend you care, and not only might they pay their bills, they might actually leave you a tip."

For the first time in a long time, Marcus isn't completely writing off what someone's said to him.

Outside the weathered door, his hand gripping the harpoon handle, Ryan holds his phone to his ear.

"For the last time," he says, "I really have to go."

"You need to get on the next plane back here," Larry tells him.

"When I'm ready."

"Listen, relationships can be hard," Larry says, as his eyes fall to the crumpled relocation packet that's been ripped in half. "Sometimes I envy you being single again."

Ryan can hear the crack in his voice. After all these years, he knows what that means. He lets go of the door handle and takes a deep breath.

"Where are you right now?" he asks.

There's a pause. "The War Room."

"Let's be honest, Larry, you're sitting in a closet."

Off one of Redding's back hallways, Larry's alone at an old fold-up table surrounded by four folding chairs with paint stains. The forgotten storage room's only lit by a bulb overhead that flickers like it's on its deathbed. Along the wall sit fax machines and old printers left in the dust of the technology age. It's a museum that includes a bulky calculator circa 1985.

Ryan and Larry haven't been in the closet, which they've affectionately labeled "the War Room," since someone's last relatively insignificant crisis. It's served as the headquarters for rumors, gossip, speculation and, on lighter days, conversations about shocking events on their favorite TV shows.

The small, isolated man cave is discreetly located down the hall, around the corner and next to the gunky drinking fountain no one will go near because rumor has it Dennis Hickman used it as a urinal several Christmas parties ago.

"We've been sitting in a closet pretending the little stuff matters," Ryan says as he begins to open the door again.

Larry's silent, struggling to realign the pieces of the ripped packet.

"This isn't little stuff," he says.

That gives Ryan a moment of pause. "Larry, you know things work out."

"The company's relocating to Phoenix, and if you don't get back here right away, they're gonna fire you."

Larry hears silence on the other end of the phone, and immediately regrets his words.

"I'm sorry, buddy. I'm sorry to tell you like that. I don't mean to add more stress to your life. It's just, you need to get back here immediately, right now."

"Okay," Ryan says, "thanks for the heads up. I've really got to go. I'll call you later."

"Buddy, I know you're going through a lot. I shouldn't have just blurted it out like that. Promise you'll call me later."

"Yeah, yeah. I'll give you a call."

"No," Larry says, "if I don't hear from you, I'm calling in the cavalry."

"I promise, okay? Now can I please go?"

From her table on the back patio, Lily finally sees light flood into the bar as the door opens all the way.

"You have a really hard time making decisions," she says when Ryan approaches. "I didn't think you'd ever make it over here."

"How did you even know I was coming?" he says.
Lily's amused.

"Oh, come on. Obviously you were gonna talk to Charlie last night, and I'm sure he has you convinced I can cast spells and turn people into frogs."

"Sure, I guess," Ryan says. "Maybe Charlie's wrong, but how about this, I never told you I worked in a cubicle."

Lily lays down her pen and grants him eye contact.

"Your hands are too soft to have done any manual labor," she says. "And, no offense, but your clothes aren't nice enough to imply any serious income. I took a guess. If I was wrong, it would seem like a metaphor. If I was right, I seem like a genius."

"You knew Charlie didn't finish the eighth grade," Ryan says.

"People give off more information than they realize," she explains. "He didn't know about the Boston Tea Party. You learn that in ninth grade, and it's a pretty simple concept. He thought it was just a bunch of old ladies harping over tea, so he clearly didn't learn it."

Even though he's sensing a defensive wall, Ryan summons his courage and takes a seat.

"Yesterday you said that when you write these postcards, you used twenty percent horoscope, twenty percent fortune cookie and twenty percent facial expressions. Even if we dismiss the idea that there's some special quality to what you call 'intuition,' which you said is 10 percent, you're still missing 30 percent."

Over Ryan's shoulder, Lily can see Marcus listening to their whole conversation. His frustrated expression says, "You're really gonna engage this guy?"

Her attention's back to Ryan. Something's going on inside her head, like she's deciding whether to give him what he's asking for, whether she wants to open this considerable can of worms.

He's aiming his big, blue, puppy-dog eyes at her and she's struck by his genuine eagerness. He could be handsome if he tried. Nice features, probably attracts some attention he might not even notice.

"I'll assume the other 30 percent involves the Vulcan mind meld," he says.

Lily quickly glances back at Marcus, who just rolls his eyes at her willingness to bring what he considers another idiot into her life.

A grin sneaks across her face.

"All right, smart ass," she tells Ryan, her decision made. "The fact that people simply want to believe. You can't sell anything unless some part of that person wants to buy. I'm peddling hope. Everybody's in the market for that."

Ryan grabs a blank postcard from one of the stacks. "You already got Charlie writing them. Show me how to write one."

Lily gently takes it from him.

"First off, Charlie picked that up on his own," she says. "I take no responsibility there. And second, you need to stop encouraging him. The more you listen to his superstitious nonsense, the more you embolden him."

"Okay, I promise. So, what do I need to learn? Where do I start?"

A smirk crosses Lily's lips as she studies his face - the unassuming spark in his eyes, the corner of his mouth curled up in just the slightest of grins, his brow always slightly furrowed, almost sad, even when he's smiling. Although she knows better, she's being won over by his accidental charm.

"Lunch," she says.

She quickly gathers her postcards and drops them into her overstuffed bag. She's off and running at a record pace again, but Ryan's more prepared for her spontaneity this time. He manages to keep up.

As Marcus wipes down the counter, his eyes follow the pair through the empty bar.

"Hey, you gonna order and run?" He holds out a Diet Coke with lemon.

Lily barely glances in his direction. "You drink it."

"It's still gotta go on your tab," he says. "I'm trying to run a business here."

Lily gives him an almost reprimanding look. "Remember what I told you?"

Her comment seems to strike a chord, and the obvious attitude on Marcus' face subsides. He pours the soda down the sink. Through clenched teeth, he manages to mutter, "Have a good afternoon."

The streets of New Orleans teem with activity. At barely noon, tourists have tired eyes, overextended from not wanting to miss a second of their adventure.

Lily goes from 0 to 90 in the blink of an eye. When you live life out of a suitcase, you have nothing to check or consider before you make whatever last-second decision strikes you.

She walks quickly ahead of Ryan, but her mouth turns up into a smile as she glances over her shoulder from time to time to see that he's behind her.

"So," Ryan says, "have you always traveled alone?"

"You in the mood for a hamburger?" Lily throws out.

"Hamburger? You're not a vegetarian? Not some New Age vegan or something?"

"Are you just a wise guy or are you really this clueless?" Lily says. "Where have I been every morning?"

"A bar ..."

"Do they have any vegetarian food on the menu?"

"No."

"I enjoy dead animal flesh," Lily says. "I've worn fur and I say kill all the whales - save the plankton. No one gives a shit about plankton."

"Not to mention brine shrimp. Imagine being labeled a 'sea monkey'."

Lily looks coyly at Ryan. "Yeah, the monkey of the sea is clearly the octopus."

Ryan's invigorated by her understanding of his oddball humor.

"You know," he says, "I've always read that you shouldn't travel without a companion."

Lily glances back at him with a wicked smile. "Why? Because I might meet some strange creep in a bar in New Orleans?"

Out of nowhere, her attention's drawn by a heavy-set woman looking lost and confused on the street corner. The disoriented tourist meticulously studies a fold-out map, then the street signs, then back to the map, which doesn't seem to offer her the comfort she's desperately seeking.

Lily changes direction to head toward her. At her side, she leans in to help.

"Oh my god, it's like these maps were designed with an Etch A Sketch."

"Yeah," the woman says, "it's ridiculous."

"And it doesn't help that this place is like a maze."

"Tell me about it. I think I've been in this exact spot three times already. I just keep going around the block."

Back home, Ryan's seen coworkers who've shared a lunch table and even met each other's children barely make eye contact in the hallways, but Lily feels an uncommon sense of comfort with this anonymous person who just happened to enter her line of sight.

As if struck by a sudden thought, Lily lowers the unruly map.

"You know what?" she says. "You came here to get away, to lose yourself in the atmosphere. But you're not doing that, are you? Come on, you and I both know you're thinking about what's going on at home."

The stranger nods.

"We get caught up in all this stupid crap, and the moment we try to get away, it seems to sprout legs and follow us," Lily says. "Am I right?"

The woman's tapped into her every word, her eyes engaged.

"Trust me, I've been there." Lily pauses to make eye contact before discreetly lowering her voice. "Why am I getting this overwhelming feeling that there was an older man in your life? Someone who meant a lot to you."

"My grandpa."

"Yeah, grandpa. And why am I hearing this phrase, something he would say to you?"

Right there on the street, the tourist delves back into her deepest memories at the prompting of a total stranger. "Life's but what we make it, and why not make it a jelly donut?" Her face lightens at the thought.

Lily shrugs her shoulders, her expression saying, "And …?"

The woman's locked into her like she's found a dear friend in a sea of strangers.

"And I'm not doing that right now, am I?" she says.

Lily reaches into her oversized purse and pulls out a delicate, lacy pouch containing a single bag of tea. She ceremoniously places it in the woman's hand.

"Do me and Grandpa a favor," she says. "Forget about what's going on at home. Take five minutes to unwind. Drink some tea. It'll all work out."

With her un-styled hair tucked behind her ear, the tourist zones in on the ornate gift that very well could have been part of a royal tea service in some exotic land.

"You have the number for your hotel?" Lily asks.

A nod yes.

From down the street, Ryan watches the whole exchange unfold in wonderment.

"Allow yourself to get lost," Lily says. "Enjoy everything you see. Taste some new food. Buy something strange. Then, call the hotel. They'll send a cab to pick you up."

The relieved tourist stares into Lily's eyes. "Thank you, I will."

"No," Lily says, "thank Grandpa."

She smiles at the woman, who chokes back a bit of emotion as she says, "He was the best."

The stranger struggles to make sense of this unbelievable chance meeting, but as she watches Lily walk away, a smile creeps across her face. She folds up the map and looks again to the fancy packet of tea in her hand. Then, she contentedly wanders off into the vast crowd.

Lily's on the move again, jetting around oncoming tourists on the sidewalk. Ryan runs up alongside her.

"Okay, I don't know what you just did there," he says, "but you're telling me there's nothing to this? I saw what happened. How did you know about her grandfather?"

"People give off more information than you think," she says. "Let me guess, you're wearing crew socks with three stripes around the top."

Ryan looks down at his feet, confused.

"Both times I've seen you you've been wearing the same worn-out sneakers," Lily explains. "Since you haven't bothered to get new shoes, I'm guessing you've also hung onto the gym socks you wore in college."

"There are four stripes," Ryan says.

"It also tells me you probably paid your own way through college. You're clearly not willing to replace things until they're falling apart at the seams, which means you understand the value of a buck. If you got a free ride, I doubt you'd be so frugal."

"Where did you go to school?" Ryan asks.

Lily ignores the question. "Up to 30 seconds ago, that woman wasn't having fun. She wasn't giving in to the experience. Look around. There is so much to absorb here. She shouldn't be spending her whole day with her face in a map. If you're going to travel and see the world, then see it! Don't have your nose in some travel book."

Ryan's now self conscious and shoves his new wad of travel brochures deeper into his pocket.

Lily stops in front of a brightly lit building with large front windows in the retro style of a 1950s diner. A pink neon sign reads, "Sticky Buns."

"You have a prophesy for someone in here?" Ryan says.

"No, but you might."

They open the door to an old-time diner with red stools lining a black-and-white bar. An upbeat tune blasts through the room. The floor's checkered and the walls are decorated with posters of music divas who have illuminated the world with their grand personalities and larger-than-life talents, and wardrobes.

Bland by comparison, Ryan and Lily take their seats at the counter. They've entered a time warp. Within seconds, an effeminate waiter has dropped off menus that match the decor.

"So, Charlie says you travel a lot," Ryan says, not even looking at the menu. "Sounds great. I'm really a traveler at heart."

Lily gives him a sideways glance. "I don't see a lot of adventurer in you."

"I'm all about adventure. In fact, this afternoon I'm going with Charlie to help fix up his swamp tour business."

This catches Lily's attention. "Now, what did I warn you about that?"

"I know, I know. I'll be on good behavior. But I am getting a free swamp tour out of it. You interested in joining us?"

"We'll see."

Something else has drawn Lily's attention. She nudges Ryan and motions for him to watch the waiter, who's meandering in their direction.

For the first time, Ryan takes notice of the man who gracefully sways to the music from the jukebox, performing his duties while perfectly in sync with the rhythm.

When he reaches their table, he speaks melodically in a feminine, Southern drawl.

"Coffee, tea or somethin' fizzy?" he says.

"Something fizzy, please," Lily says.

Ryan raises his eyebrows.

"Something carbonated," she explains.

"Something fizzy it is. Actually ..." Ryan looks at Lily with a bit of excitement, "diet fizzy, please ... with a slice of lemon!"

Lily's glance says, "Okay, good for you," a little confused by his enthusiasm.

The waiter's elegant in his movements as he glides away, inspired by the song.

"He's wasting his time here," Ryan says. "He should be in New York or something."

"You should tell him that."

Ryan shakes his head no. He peruses the large, plastic menu and finds that every dish is named after a famous diva. The Streisand sausage sandwich. The Liza Minnelli mozzarella sticks.

"And you think you're gonna be able to write post-cards?" Lily scolds.

"Listen, that's anonymous. Telling someone to their face, that's a whole different ball game."

The waiter's coming and Ryan silently pleads for Lily not to say anything. Meanwhile, her eyes are fixed on the man whose every movement is compelled by the song. It's obvious to Ryan that she enjoys people-watching, that she's completely immersed in studying this intriguing stranger.

The waiter places their drinks on coasters that bare Elvis' face.

"Fizzy for you, and a diet fizzy for you, with lemon!"

Lily's eyes are focused. Ryan feels an almost obsessive need to know what's going on inside that mind of hers.

The waiter's voice startles him out of his trance.

"What can I get for you, sweetie?"

"I'd like ..." Lily starts.

"I was talkin' to him." The waiter points at Ryan, who's suddenly flustered. "I'm teasin'! Look at his face. That's precious. What is it, dear?"

"The Hamburger Pattie Labelle," Lily says.

The waiter jots it down.

When it's Ryan's turn, Lily shows him an item on the menu.

"You should really try this one," she says. "I've had it. It's good."

"Really?" Ryan reads the description. "Okay. I'll have the beefy Madonna."

The waiter grins and gives Lily a wink. He races to a large bell over the chef as customers stop talking to watch him. The room's abuzz.

Ryan glares at Lily. "What did you do?"

"What?" she says. "You had the whole menu to choose from."

Ding. Ding. Ding.

"We have a wiener, folks!" the waiter yells.

The full-figured male cook cheers as he wipes beads of sweat from his forehead. Everyone watches the waiter strut to the jukebox to drop in a few coins. With the push of a button, Madonna's singing and the rhythm's thumping like a heartbeat in the small diner. The patrons clap along in unison as the waiter glides across the floor, belting out the words to "Material Girl." The cook and dishwasher dance out of the kitchen to join him. The room's erupted in excitement.

Lily throws her hands in the air. She takes off her hat to expose her flowing, brown hair.

Ryan's looking at her accusingly.

"Oh, I'm sorry," she says with a bit of sass. "I thought you wanted the full experience."

Ryan shakes his head. Lily's definitely not gonna make this easy.

He adjusts on his metal stool. With the shedding of inhibitions all around him, he's even more self-conscious of his own stiff demeanor. He finally notices that everyone in the place, with the exception of Lily, is male. Men with mustaches, business men, weightlifters, single male tourists. Every single one of them enthralled with the music. Everyone having fun.

Before Ryan can flinch, the waiter grabs his hands and gently coaxes them into flamboyant dance moves, pulling him out of his complacency. Ryan gives a forced smile, trying to hide his clear discomfort with the situation.

Lily pats him on the back, at the same time pushing him to get out of his chair. He shakes his head defiantly.

With every flip of the burgers, the cook strikes poses straight out of a fashion shoot. The burly man flips, then freezes, then flips again. Vogue all the way.

The waiter struts around like he's channeling the spirits of a hundred full-figured, big-haired divas from eras gone by. The music swells as Madonna aims for that last, leave-'em-wanting-more note. Just as she's about to let it fly, the waiter jumps up on the counter, almost stepping on several fingers, and nails the high note as if he's on stage at Carnegie Hall.

He skillfully holds it right along with the Material Girl.

Then, the music abruptly stops. Patrons let out a unanimous "aahhhh" as the restaurant returns to business as usual as if nothing happened. As if it hadn't just experienced a spontaneous dance party. The waiter gracefully descends from the counter.

"Now, what did you order again?" he asks Ryan.

"Oh, a beefy Madon-" Ryan stops himself. "Okay. You almost got me."

The waiter gives him a wink. Ryan takes a deep breath and musters up some courage, looking to Lily. Her challenging stare says, "Okay, what are you gonna do now?"

"You should really be in New York, you know - dancing," Ryan says. "You're really talented. I - I mean, don't let your talent go to waste."

He can't even look the man in the eye.

"What a sweetheart," the waiter says, "but not for me."

"Really?" Lily says. "You've got the moves. You're young. You can make it."

The waiter shakes his head. "My partner would never go, and I ain't about to throw away four good years." He gives Ryan a nudge. "That's what love does to ya!"

Ryan nods that he understands, and looks to Lily. Her stoic face reveals that she's not impressed with the answer.

The waiter rips off their order ticket and places it on the hook. He looks to the robust cook in the kitchen and yells, "One Kabbala special and a huge Fro!"

Chapter 4:

"They'll see you coming a mile - make that a kilometer - away"

"Listen, I know it's a lot and the timing's bad, but I think this is a good chance to have that new beginning you've been talking about," Larry says at the prompting of Janet's voicemail. Although he's maintaining a calm voice, he's staring at the ripped HR packet that's been taped back together.

His eyes drift again over the wall of his cubicle.

"Pokorski should be out of his meeting any minute now, and then I'll probably have some great news for you," he says. "I bet they're offering him all kinds of amazing stuff. Maybe if you'd just taken a second to read the packet, you'd know about the relocation bonus. We could put that toward something exciting out there, like a great backyard with a pool. Everyone in Phoenix has a pool. You can swim all year there."

He's distracted by Pokorski's socially awkward haircut passing by the wall.

"Love you. I'll see you tonight. Gotta go."

When Pokorski doesn't pop in to see him, Larry covertly maneuvers his body so he's half standing and half crouched behind the short cubicle barrier.

From his awkward position, he can peek into the technology central that is Pokorski's workspace. Where most people have photos of their significant others or their kids, Pokorski displays framed pictures of Steve Jobs and Bill Gates - the two self-made brainiacs who used to serve as inspiration for his dreams of being a computer god in his own business, and who now only serve as sad reminders of a dream that he feels has passed him by. He's got more geeky electronic gadgets than personal chotskies and knickknacks.

Pokorski's sitting there slumped in his office chair with his back to Larry. Larry's concerned, and even more so when he sees that resting on the desk on top of a manila envelope is some kind of formal document that begins with the ominous words, "We regret to inform you …"

Lily places an ornate tea packet in the man's hand, and Ryan can see the amazing transformation, even from across the street. Where the frumpy tourist in the fanny pack had dragged his feet as if trying to disappear into the crowd, he now stands up straight with his head held high.

He grasps Lily's hand with a shake of gratitude as if she's just performed the Heimlich on him.

She casually crosses back over to Ryan.

"Well, whatever extra brain cells you were born with that allow you to just go up and talk to a stranger like that, I was not gifted with that kind of courage," Ryan says as they resume their walk past souvenir shops and bars.

"What are you talking about?" Lily says. "You had the courage to get on a plane and come to this crazy place looking for a person you never met before. Give yourself a little credit."

Ryan laughs to himself. "Listen, I sat in that airport for two and a half hours because I kept giving up my ticket, convincing myself I actually wanted the complimentary flight voucher they threw at me. I was practically sweating I was so scared. I couldn't stop hearing my father's 'words of wisdom' in my head."

Lily rolls her eyes.

"Parents have a lot to say, but then again, so do Hallmark cards. Like my mom …" She puts on her best imitation of a maternal sage. "'Buildings may crumble, rivers may dry up, but when it comes to matters of the human heart, all things can be mended.' For some reason, advice always sounds better coming from a stranger. Maybe your words sent that waiter running off to New York."

"Oh my god." Ryan's flooded with embarrassing memories. "That was terrible."

"Why? Because they're gay?"

"Are you kidding? That was the least of my worries."

Lily suppresses a laugh. "Your dancing wasn't that bad."

They stroll down Canal Street to the sound of a spirited jazz band fronted by a curvaceous ragtime singer.

"I just don't like being the odd man out," Ryan says. "I felt like everyone was watching me."

"Don't beat yourself up about it." Lily stops at a large shop window. "Everyone feels that way. If anyone was the 'odd man out,' it was me. That's what really living life is about. If you're not feeling out of place or uncomfortable once in a while, you're not doing something new or exciting. You think the first time someone decided to get on a plane and fly to Mongolia, they weren't scared? They didn't feel out of place, with their strange clothes and weird way of talking? Sometimes it can be the same just going to a different part of your own town."

Ryan laughs. "Well, in the future I'm only gonna travel to European countries."

"That's not the point," Lily says. "The point is about doing something you're not comfortable doing."

Ryan nods. "Well, I did just give a gay dancing waiter career advice."

They stop at the alley leading to Rusty Harpoon's.

"But seriously," he says, "it's just nice that guy has somebody. He's not alone."

Lily shakes her head. "Actually, that's his biggest problem."

"You think love is his biggest problem?"

"Sure. He let himself get tied down. One day, he'll be an old man saying, 'I could have been a dancer on Broadway, or worked in Hollywood.' He'll resent his partner for holding him back. It's sad, really."

"I never thought about it that way."

"That relationship'll probably last a couple more years," Lily says. "The odds are against them. It'll end, he'll be late thirties, out of shape. Then he'll suddenly say to himself, 'It's not too late. I can still make it,' knowing very well he won't. But he goes anyway, fails miserably, 'cause his fat ass can't move like it used to. All because of some clingy person who kept him around for their own selfish needs."

Ryan bristles. "Wow, optimistic."

"Realistic," Lily says. "The best thing that could happen to that guy is that he gets dumped, wakes up and finds himself on a new path that finally leads him where he really needs to be."

She notices that Ryan's been immediately affected by what she said. The gears seem to be in motion in his head. Maybe she went a little too far.

"Then again …" she starts.

She's interrupted by a loud honking. She and Ryan turn to see Charlie's old pick-up truck with rust spots on the hood, and Charlie leaning out the window.

"Come on, you two! Time ta do us some celebratin'! Who up fer oystas 'n moondogs?"

Ryan and Lily just look at each other, as the horn blows several more times.

With the main copy machine still bruised and beaten, the throwback model tucked away down one of Redding's back hallways remains Monica's only option.

It sputters and hums as she feeds in expense reports, at the same time holding a phone to her ear.

"No, I don't friggin' know. It's just not working, taking up space on my living room floor," she says a little too loudly, as usual. "Three hundred bucks? I can't afford that!"

Monica pauses when she sees a strange movement down the hall - a door opens, then closes, then partially opens again. She quickly hangs up the phone.

A little spooked, she forgets her work and slowly, cautiously heads down the narrow corridor, grimacing as she passes the old drinking fountain forever sullied by Dennis Hickman.

The door to a small storage closet starts to open, then abruptly closes. Monica tentatively steps closer.

She feels like one of those idiots in a horror movie who just has to go check out the scary sound coming from the dark room, when what they should do is run as fast as they can.

As Monica approaches, she can hear the clear sound of stressed voices inside. Stressed, nerdy voices.

She throws open the door. There stand Larry and Pokorski with wide, fearful eyes.

"Oh … my …. god!" Monica says.

"No, no, no!" Larry shouts.

"It's not what it looks like," Pokorski insists.

"What in the …?" Monica scans past the frazzled men to see a ratty old card table full of pretzels, chips and sodas, and a couple of travel books with pictures of the desert Southwest.

"You guys talking about Phoenix?" she says, suddenly interested. "Oh my god, rumor is they're already cutting people."

Pokorski's face turns a little red. He looks to Larry, then abruptly heads for the door. As he brushes past Monica, Larry yells after him, "Pokorski, come on!"

That gets Monica's attention. "Oh my god. Is that Michael Pokorski?"

She forgets Larry, and follows Pokorski out into the hallway.

Left all alone under the dim light of the overhead bulb, Larry's thoughts turn immediately to fear and worry. If they're willing to lay off the best computer guy at the company, why would they even hesitate to get rid of the guy who freaked out about a break up and went AWOL at the worst possible moment in the company's history?

Ryan's got everything to lose - stock options, a pension, seniority. While he's off sulking about the past, he's playing with his future.

"You're like that big-brain computer guy!" Monica squeals in the hallway.

Only feet from the gunky drinking fountain, no one else in sight, a worried Pokorski wipes beads of sweat from his forehead.

"I may have exaggerated a little on those expense reports," he says. "I'm so sorry …"

"Are you kidding? Everybody lies on those things. No, what I'm talking about is you earning a home-cooked meal fit for a king, Mr. Superstar Computer Man."

In front of Ryan sits a plate of oysters on the half shell on a bed of ice.

He hasn't touched one of them, even though Charlie and Lily, squeezed in next to him at a cramped booth in the back of Salty Jim's Sea Shack, have devoured a dozen each.

Although Ryan's trying not to be obvious, he's having a hard time taking his gaze off Lily - her eyes sparkling with fun and joy, her laugh completely effortless, her natural charm.

She doesn't seem to notice, too caught up in dressing oysters and joking around with Charlie.

The pretty young waitress with the styled blonde hair returns to their table. As is typical with Ryan, he's almost oblivious to her hints of interest in him. It's not that he's indifferent to the charms of young, attractive women. It's just that it goes right over his head.

It barely registers when the waitress flashes him a sideways glance and a not-so-subtle Southern smile.

"Can I get you a refill?" she says, touching his arm.

"Uh, I think Diet Coke will be coming out of my eyeballs if I say yes to that," Ryan says.

"Don't worry, sweetie. I got towels in the back, so whatever you want."

Suddenly, an oyster's shoved in Ryan's face. He looks over to see Lily holding it.

When he glances back at the waitress, her annoyed face says, "Boy, she's pushy." The woman's expression isn't lost on Lily, but she keeps her attention on Ryan.

"You'll never know if you don't try it," she says. "Come on, who's the odd man out now?"

She places the oyster in his hand. He stares at it for a moment. As soon as Lily moves to finish off the last of her wine, he covertly uses his napkin to swipe the slimy creature from its shell.

"Good boy!" Lily says. "Not bad, huh?"

"You were right," Ryan proclaims.

Lily gets a little grin on her face - I told you so.

Even though Ryan knows he's lying through his teeth, he basks in the temporary thrill of her approval.

"See here," Charlie says, "try da touloulou." He makes a hand gesture where his fingers look like they're running.

"He means crab," Lily says.

She's already polished off a few drinks at Charlie's encouragement, and both have shed at least one layer of inhibition thanks to the fermenting of grapes.

All around them, tourists enjoy the new, eclectic environment, alcohol coursing like electricity through their veins. The artificial freedom of vacation has shattered their chains. They'll go back to hotels tonight, instead of all the silly worries waiting for them back home - the things that won't even matter in a month or a year. You can be anyone you want on vacation. Talk more, drink more, sleep more, make stupid mistakes you can leave behind on the night table, along with a tip for the housekeepers who'll never spill your secrets.

You can pass a Creole evenin' eatin' oysters under the watchful eye of the local catch, which is proudly displayed on the wall alongside a few alligator skulls.

The alcohol's really settled in by the time the live music erupts from the stage at the back of the room. Lily immediately heads toward the tiny dance floor.

Charlie leans in toward Ryan.

"Dat girl itchin' ta dance," Charlie says. He gives Ryan an encouraging nudge. "Only a fool let 'er dance alone."

Ryan tenses a little. If eating oysters was stepping outside his comfort zone, actually going out on that floor and dancing would be several plane rides away from it.

The 1970s cover band performing on stage is fully made up in tight, faded bell bottoms, shirts unbuttoned to show their '70s smooth chests and long hair they enjoy flipping obsessively. They're rocking the classics with power, fueled by a few too many Hurricanes. A cheap banner proclaims them the "Psychedelic Moondogs."

They're fronted by a thin man with wild hair and pronounced bags under his eyes. He goes by the rock moniker Randy Sparkles, but his drivers license would claim his name is Darrell Zumbrowski.

Right away, Charlie dominates the room with his gangly moves, always the life of the party. His tattered blue jeans sag to reveal his underwear. He truly embodies the saying, "Dance like there's no one watching."

Lily cheers on the band, clapping along to the rocking drum beat. Her sun dress flows with her every movement, and Ryan could watch her dance all night. Face flushed with exhilaration, she feels the music from somewhere deep inside.

Ryan doesn't care what she says, Charlie's right, she does have a glow about her, something she's not revealing. Is it magic, or just a spark of some kind that he can't quite put his finger on?

Lily slowly turns in his direction and gives him a smile. Then, her attention's back to the dance floor.

Charlie's words echo in Ryan's head: Only a fool would let her dance alone. He holds his breath, and takes that first big step out of his safety zone and into the thick crowd of partiers.

Just as he does, the band shifts gears to a romantic power ballad. With a scarf tied around his head, Randy Sparkles embraces the microphone as if he's about to make hot, sweaty love to it.

Like a hidden force has parted the Red Sea, people begin to clear the dance floor, almost creating a direct path between Ryan and Lily.

Ryan can feel the butterflies fluttering in his stomach. That instinct that tells us all to run away is now screaming warnings in his ear. But suddenly, Lily turns and looks his way.

Maybe Charlie knows what he's talking about. Just when you need to hear a song, it comes on the radio. Just when you think about an old friend, they show up.

Just when you enter a crowded dance floor, the crowd parts for you to reveal the girl you didn't know you were looking for waiting on the other side.

Ryan continues his slow march, passing by Charlie, who now has a girl on each arm. Not a pretty girl, but a girl nonetheless.

When he finally reaches Lily, he gently holds out his hand to her. She looks down at it, then back up at his face. He can sense that she's conflicted, but she must be feeling this energy, too.

Finally, Lily takes his hand and leans in toward his ear so close that he can feel her warm breath against his cheek.

"You know what," she says, "we'd just step on each other's toes."

Ryan looks down to see Lily's bare feet right next to his big, thick sneakers. She's left her flip-flops back at the bar stool. They both let out a nervous chuckle as Lily's eyes implore, "Let's not make this more awkward than it needs to be."

Just as quickly as the magic engulfed Ryan, it now fades.

Lily turns him around, gives him a pat on the back and guides him in the direction of the bar, promising, "Next round's on me."

Boogying with his companions, Charlie becomes concerned as he watches Ryan and Lily exit the dance floor. He bids his dance partners farewell with a chivalrous kiss on each of their hands, but can't walk away without dispensing two travel brochures for the best darn swamp tour in town.

"Only a few day left, mes cheris," he says.

The girls gaze in wonder at the awe-inspiring photo of Charlie in mid-blink.

Once Charlie gets back to the bar, he's anxious to make things happen. "Why ain't we movin' our feet?"

"'Cause we're drinking," Lily tells him, glancing over at Ryan and noticing his dejected demeanor.

"Don'tcha know dancin' da spice o' life?" Charlie says.

He motions toward the dance floor that's slowly filling up with people again.

Ignoring his prompts, Lily hands him a shot glass, and also puts one in front of Ryan. She holds up her own glass in a direct challenge to her friends. Ryan gently declines.

"Okay," Charlie says, "but den we goin' back out dere, us t'ree. Ya don't know true joy 'til ya feel da rhythm wit' anotha person at yer side."

He gives Ryan a little nod, and out the corner of his mouth whispers, "I tryin', buddy."

A little uncomfortable with Charlie's prodding, Ryan glances down at the bar. His eyes land on a cardboard coaster. It portrays beautiful people celebrating something really great on a perfect white-sand beach, smiles all around. Large, bold letters proclaim, "You're not the life of the party ... until you are." There in the center of the bikini-clad women stands a man of average attractiveness holding up a frothy beer and looking like the coolest dude on Earth.

Ryan shakes his head at the idea.

Just as he's ready to completely pack it in for the day, he looks up again to find Lily's eyes meeting his. She offers him a little grin that says, "Are we still friends?" He musters a smile to let her off the hook, but it's clear from her behavior that she sees him as just a bumbling little puppy dog, when what she's looking for is a German Shepherd.

"Ready ta hit da floor?" Charlie's not giving up.

Lily holds up a finger. "One more round, then we'll really embarrass ourselves."

Charlie hurriedly summons the bartender. "We need us anotha round quick. Music callin'."

Suddenly, through the din of the crowd and the pounding beat, Ryan makes out the sound of angry voices coming from across the room. He looks to see their pretty, blonde waitress in a heated argument with an angry, red-faced man who must be her boss. He's straight out of the '70s in his horribly outdated plaid tie, but even more impressive is his beautifully coiffed toupee that doesn't match the gray underneath. He's dishing out quite the verbal thrashing.

After bringing the waitress to the verge of tears, the manager storms off in frustration.

Ryan just sits there for a moment. He watches the poor woman return to her thankless work. Then, a moment of self loathing overtakes him.

If this was Lily, that waitress would already have a packet of tea in her hand and they'd be bonding over dead grandparents and cheap pastries.

The bartender sets another round of shots in front of them. Charlie glances in Ryan's direction to assure him there's still hope for that magical moment on the dance floor, but Ryan's not even paying attention. His eyes are locked on the frustrated waitress.

"Let's do this!" Lily announces as she holds up her glass. "One, two ..."

To both Lily and Charlie's surprise, on three, Ryan grabs the shot glass that's been sitting neglected in front of him, and tosses back the small amount of alcohol. It stings all the way down his throat. He wipes his mouth like a cowboy at a saloon, then quickly stands up and abruptly marches off.

"Where's he going?" Lily asks.

"I tink he goin' ta get him dat girl," Charlie says.

That catches Lily's attention. Her head turns toward Ryan, who's approaching the dejected waitress.

"He can do better than her," she mutters under her breath.

Charlie raises an eyebrow at her remark, and gives her a little smile.

She flashes him a look that leaves no room for interpretation. "Oh, come on."

As Ryan heads toward the waitress, he sees her picking up grimy ashtrays and wiping up the spilt beer and food crumbs underneath. Some of the ashes fall onto her shirt as she dumps them in a trashcan. If that's not humiliating enough, she has to reach into a full glass of water to fish out the 73-cent tip some jerk dropped in.

When she looks up to see Ryan standing in front of her, her spirits seem to lift a little.

"Oh, hey," she says.

"I came over here because I could hear you all the way from the bar ..." Ryan says.

"I know. He's crazy, but I need this job."

She eyes the manager, who's just stepped out of his office.

Back at the bar, Charlie gives Lily a little nudge with his elbow. "Look like our boy gonna get hisself a date."

Even without the nudge, Lily was already locked into the waitress' friendly exchange with Ryan.

"I wonder what line he usin'," Charlie says. Regardless of her reaction, he's smart enough to know when he's pushing someone's buttons.

They both watch on. If they only knew.

Ryan struggles to keep his voice low in the noisy atmosphere.

"No, you don't," he tells the woman. "That guy's doing nothing but holding you back."

Her expression sours a little. "Yeah, well this job does pay my bills."

She's not getting it. Ryan knows he has to muster the right words to change this woman's life. "You know, you don't have to stay in this dump."

A bit of anger flashes across the waitress' face. What was once a cute guy with big, puppy-dog eyes has quickly transformed into just another drunk moron.

"Uh, you know what, why don't you head back to your seat and I'll take your order in a minute."

Ryan looks back to see that Charlie's giving him a huge grin, but Lily's more focused on finally downing her shot of tequila. He has to get her attention.

"I mean, you don't have to stay here," he says. "You're in New Orleans, for god's sake. Look around you! You've got a vacation paradise right outside your door. Quit, leave. You're wasting your life here being a waitress."

Now, he's clearly struck a nerve. "What do you mean 'being a waitress'? What's wrong with waitressing? Puts a roof over my head."

"Nothing, but I bet you had dreams and goals. You could be a model or something."

"Oh, and I'm nothin' but a failure? Just servin' jerks like you?"

She quickly stops herself. This happens all the time - idiots with too much to say who think her name is "sweet-heart," make a pass or just outright grab her ass. She's not going to defend her entire life to some guy wearing Dock-ers.

When she turns to walk away, Ryan grabs her arm.

That doesn't sit well with a woman who, as the sole girl in a family of five brothers, wrestled down and gutted her own fish before she owned her first Barbie.

"Please listen," Ryan says. "You should go out and see the world. You can do better than this place."

The waitress yanks her arm free. Ryan quickly releases. He's clearly violated this woman's personal space, but he musters his courage. The message is too important. Before he can get out another word, she steps closer.

"Okay, so you're gonna pay my bills, huh? I'm three days away from having my water shut off. You gonna cover that for me? You gonna pay my overdue phone bill?"

Ryan glances toward the bar and sees that Lily has her back to him. What he can't see is that out of his earshot, Charlie's whispering, "Would ita killed ya ta give dat boy a dance?"

Lily doesn't acknowledge him, and just orders another drink.

Ryan faces the waitress with all sincerity, knowing this might be his last chance. He reaches into his back pocket to pull something out.

"I know it's not a bag of tea," he says, holding up the inspirational cardboard coaster, "but the quote really applies to both of us."

He sighs and looks back with sadness at Lily, who's still turned the other way facing the bar.

"People like us sit on the sidelines. We never do anything of significance. Trust me, I know what it's like to live a sad, wasted, nothing kind of life."

He turns back around to see that the coaster is now lying on the floor. The waitress' punch suddenly lands like a crack across his face, bending and bruising every bone in his nose as he slams to the ground. Then comes the first sensation of trickling blood.

Defeated and exhausted, Ryan lets his head smack hard against the wooden dance floor, and goes limp.

Suddenly, a couple of hands reach out to lift him off the ground. He's looking straight into the eyes of a clearly concerned Charlie.

At the bar, Lily notices that her companion has rushed off. She turns around to see Charlie standing with his arm around Ryan. Even from so far away, she can make out a trickle of blood dripping from Ryan's nose.

She quickly rushes in their direction.

When she arrives, Charlie hands Ryan over to her, whispering, "Dat girl got herself a nice left hook."

Lily carefully leads Ryan toward the bar.

"I guess that's what happens when you flirt with temperamental bar maids," she says, trying to suppress a smile.

She plops him onto a barstool, and Ryan looks back through blurry eyes to see the waitress in a full-on shouting match with her manager. Charlie's given up his attempt to smooth things over and is backing away.

"I wasn't flirting with her," Ryan says. "I was trying to change her life. I was trying to be you."

The smile Lily fought to suppress now disappears.

Ryan's still obsessed with watching the waitress and her manager make angry hand gestures at each other. The manager motions toward Ryan, whose bloody nose doesn't exactly say, "Come eat at Salty Jim's." The waitress flings an inspirational coaster at her boss, then sends pure hatred Ryan's way.

"I should go fix this," Ryan says.

Lily places her hand on his chest to stop him from moving.

With one more burst of anger, the waitress and her boss really have it out. She throws down her apron and follows his pointed finger toward the front door, bursting into tears as she loses her only source of income.

Ryan closes his eyes in overwhelming guilt.

They open when he feels Lily place her hands on either side of his face and, like a worried mother, try to examine his nose. He keeps turning regretfully toward the door, but Lily grabs his face.

"Look at me," she says. "That's the best thing that could have happened to her."

Ryan stares into her eyes, which are open and inviting as she checks out his injury from several angles. A little blood trickles down from his throbbing, red nose, but all he can feel now are Lily's warm, soft hands pressed into his skin.

He succumbs to her rotating his head so she can get a better view.

He's a little startled when Charlie, a would-be Marcus Welby, shoves the twisted-up corner of a napkin up his nose and steps back to assess his handiwork.

"What did I do to that poor woman?" Ryan says.

Lily shakes her head.

"Places like this are traps. Sometimes people have to be forced into their new decisions, because they'll never make the choice themselves. But next time, just remember ...," she squares up his face so she can look him directly in the eye, "... you train a mouse by tempting him with the hunk of cheese, not by telling him he's stuck in a maze."

Larry removes his work badge and places a stack of Phoenix travel brochures on the kitchen table, which he notices looks strangely naked without all the junk that's usually accumulated there. He glances around to see that every surface of the kitchen has a fresh sheen, and the lemony aroma of disinfectant scents the air.

There's also no trace of the unruly stack of bills and refinance offers that's always been a permanent fixture on the counter.

His eyes drift to the arcadia door, and outside to where Janet's on the back patio talking to a strange man.

"Yeah," he hears her say, "if you could create a little shade here, that would be great, and tear out these ..."

"What's going on here?" Larry steps outside to get a closer look at the man in the utility belt who's chalking up measurements on the concrete.

"This is Warren, our new contractor," Janet says. "We're gonna put in the deck and the awning, and guess what, you're getting that built-in barbecue with the fridge and rotisserie."

Warren just nods his confirmation with a little wave.

Larry looks to the small but well-maintained backyard that's lined with lawn chairs and tiki torches, and which now bears countless chalk markings.

"Janet, we can't pretend this isn't happening," he says. "I'm sorry, Warren, but we won't be needing your services."

The contractor pauses, then starts to get up.

"Keep measuring, Warren," Janet says. She gives Larry a defiant glare. "This is where our children were born, where we made our plans, where we were gonna take on the world."

Larry shakes his head. "Yesterday, this was a prison from which there was no escape."

Janet's unfazed. "Larry, if you're going to Phoenix, you're going alone."

"You actually handed her a coaster?" Lily doubles over laughing.

Ryan accepts her teasing. "Yes, but you should have seen the quote. It was great."

Lily and Charlie stumble down a street that's mostly emptied of tourists at this late hour, accompanied by a perfectly sober Ryan. Even when she's tipsy, Lily exudes an irresistible light and energy.

Ryan tries not to be obvious about the fact that he's noticed a change in Charlie's demeanor. Charlie's more withdrawn, as if something's brewing inside him. Many times, he's drifting off into his own thoughts.

"Come on," Lily chides, "how great could a quote on a bar coaster really be?"

She comfortably meanders closer into Ryan's personal space, just as they reach Charlie's truck.

"I know it's stupid," Ryan says, "but you give everyone tea, so this was my thing. It was a really great quote."

"Listen, if you think you get a great quote off a coaster, we're gonna have to rethink this whole postcard thing."

They're interrupted by the sound of coughing and hacking.

"Lord, dem oystas swimmin' in my gut." Charlie's face has drained of all color as he bends over in the street.

Lily leans in toward Ryan. "Any idea what we were really celebrating tonight?"

"Not really," Ryan says.

Lily loses her balance and casually lets herself rest against his shoulder.

She grasps his arm for support. He's well aware that the alcohol's numbing her inhibitions, and what feels like bonding or affection may actually be a woman with no sense of equilibrium, a woman who won't remember any of this in the morning.

Charlie finally lets loose and begins vomiting in a way that sounds like he's purging major organs.

Ryan grabs Lily by both arms and leans her against Charlie's truck.

"You gonna be all right here for a minute?" he asks.

He looks straight at Lily, and finds that she's staring at him with a warm smile. She places her hands on both his arms and focuses in on him, connecting with his gaze.

"You have nice eyes," she says.

"Well, that's the only good thing my mother gave me," Ryan jokes, again having to restrain his emotions and re-mind himself that Lily's compromised right now. "I'm gonna go check on Charlie. You wait right here."

"Okay," Lily says, "don't be long."

Ryan rushes toward Charlie, who's buckled over in pain.

"What exactly were we celebrating tonight, buddy?" he gently asks.

"Shh." Charlie puts his finger to his lips and glances in Lily's direction. "Ya do believe in magic, right? Ya believe in it?"

Ryan hesitates. He looks back toward Lily. Even in her weakened state, leaning against the truck, she has a certain innate beauty.

"I do, Charlie," he says.

"I knew it, podna."

"All right, let's get you in the truck. Let's get you home."

Ryan helps Charlie maneuver toward the cab, where Lily's leaning against the passenger door. Gently moving her out of the way, Ryan guides Charlie to climb in.

A fleeting look of worry says Lily's finally noticed the pain on the face of the usually exuberant man.

She stands there watching Ryan carefully pull the seatbelt over Charlie's lap, moving out of the way just as Charlie does a dramatic dry heave. Ryan doesn't even flinch from the horrible smell, or from Charlie's dirty clothes, even though he didn't even know Charlie a week ago.

Lily's eyes are fixed on him as he talks his friend through the pain.

"Can you get the bucket out of the back?" Ryan asks her.

She nods, and heads to the cluttered truck bed to sift through old crab traps and junk metal. She finds the fresh, white, five-gallon bucket and delivers it to Ryan.

He nudges his slumped friend. "Here you go, Charlie."

He pulls him up to a sitting position and places the bucket between his knees.

"Oh yeah. Tanks, podna," Charlie mutters. "You all right, brotha."

"You're good," Lily says.

"Not my first rodeo," Ryan tells her.

When Ryan takes his place in the driver's seat, Lily finally climbs into the truck. She glances over to see Charlie's ghost-pale face and bloodshot eyes.

As Ryan slowly maneuvers the sputtering vehicle, Charlie again lunges forward with a horrible sound.

Ryan and Lily scoot away from Charlie and brace for what seems to be an inevitable gross-out moment. All they need is one of those chain reactions where none of them can keep their food down.

Suddenly, Lily points to a building on the left.

"Up here," she says.

More and more comfortable with the geriatric movements of the truck, Ryan pulls over to the curb.

Lily gets out, but then turns around and leans into the cab.

"Now don't get lost out there. Make sure you come back."

"I will," Ryan says.

Lily covers her mouth with her hand so Charlie can't see. "What's the story?"

Something in Ryan's gut tells him Charlie's mood has something to do with his business, but he made a promise. He shrugs and plays naive.

"I'll see you tomorrow?" Lily says.

Ryan sits up straighter in his seat. "Nothing could keep me away."

"Promise?"

"I promise."

Lily looks at him with a smile, her eyes bright and genuine. Maybe it's the alcohol, or maybe it's the moment.

She steps up onto the curb. As the truck pulls away, Ryan looks back to watch her as long as he can before he has to focus on the road. Suddenly, Charlie lets out another noisy dry heave.

Despite jittery hands, Pokorski performs his task with careful precision, hiding a gnawing fear and doubt as he squats over Monica's relic of a computer like a dedicated surgeon. His high waters ride up and a small light adorns his headband.

Even though the skilled computer technician knows exactly what's wrong with the machine, for the past 10 minutes he's kept his head inside it pretending to do a detailed diagnosis.

He jumps a little when Monica announces, "Linguini with clams! You can finish that after you have some food in your belly."

Even though the air hangs heavy with the luscious aroma of garlic, oregano and onion, Pokorski's dragging as he glances over and sees Monica pouring two glasses of wine. He's never been much of a conversationalist, let alone with an attractive but domineering woman who seems to have no qualms about squashing men the moment they get on her bad side.

"Come on, no one eats cold pasta in my house!" Monica says. "I was gonna literally jump off a freakin' bridge. Thank god you're here to work your miracles."

Pokorski turns off his headlamp and finally boots up the computer that's required so much tinkering. A series of unpleasant sounds erupt from the machine, and the error messages on the screen confirm his worst fears.

"Why's the screen still blue?" Monica asks.

Pokorski approaches the table with his head down. "I'm sorry ... I .. I can't eat your food. I've wasted your time. I can't fix your computer. I tried a few workarounds, but your motherboard's completely shot."

Monica stops what she's doing. Pokorski braces himself. He doesn't want to end up like the now-leaky copier that's clinging to life outside Ryan's office.

As if she didn't hear a word he said, Monica continues to ladle out pasta onto two plates, and returns the pot to the stove. Before she turns back, she seems to be dabbing her eyes with a napkin.

Instead of him getting a barrage of insults, Pokorski finds himself in the awkward position of not knowing how to respond. Is he supposed to go over there and comfort her?

Before he can even make a move ...

"Well, shoo," she says. She tries to put a slight playful tone to her voice, but she's clearly struggling with a bit of emotion. "Go wash up. We're gonna eat."

Pokorski finally lets out the breath he's been holding, and makes his way toward the bathroom. Before he gets around the corner, Monica says, "There's a bunch of pictures on there. Do you think we can save them or ...?"

From the tone of her voice, she seems to already know the answer.

"Yes! I think the drive is fine," Pokorski says. "I think I can salvage everything. I'll make it my sole mission to get every scrap of data off that thing."

Monica breathes easier.

"Well, scoot then," she says. "I won't tolerate filthy hands eating my food."

She gives him a smile. Relieved, Pokorski returns it with a thankful grin before hurrying off to clean up.

Monica steadies herself with a deep breath. Dishing out the pasta, she notices the banged-up corner of her kitchen table, and self-consciously covers it with the tablecloth.

The tasteful curtains and lacy rugs make her studio apartment much more homey than most people would expect from her. It still reflects her eclectic New York tastes, but at a more tolerable level.

But a few doilies can't hide the chipped paint and dripping sink of a living space in need of serious repair.

Pokorski returns, and finds the tiny kitchen table set in style with wine glasses, flowers and two plates spilling over with the most beautiful, clam-topped pasta.

He takes his place at the table as Monica lays her napkin across her lap.

He's been so nervous all evening, this is the first chance he's had to really notice this new side of Monica. It's one of the rare times she's not glamorized to the hilt. Her make up is faded from the day, and she's slipped into worn jeans and a tank top. And rarest of all, she's barefoot, not a stiletto in sight.

By not even trying, this woman has managed to achieve an even higher level of beauty. And for the first time, at least in Pokorski's eyes, she's almost approachable.

But he knows that tomorrow the heels will be back on, the smoky eye shadow heavy as ever, and she'll have to duck under doorways to keep from denting her big, teased hair.

"Sorry, before we start, I hope you don't mind. I'm still a good girl at heart."

Monica holds out her hands across the table. Pokorski timidly takes them, and finds that they're warm to the touch.

"God, we thank you for the food you provide, the family we love and the beautiful world we live in," she says. "We also thank you for the kindness of strangers."

Pokorski looks up. When he does, he sees a small smile on Monica's face.

"Amen," she says.

And though not particularly religious, Pokorski follows her lead. "Amen."

Ryan maneuvers Charlie's pick-up truck, which has been on life support for years, down swampy backroads that have been washed out by too many violent rainstorms. Charlie slouches low in the passenger seat.

"So," Ryan says, "what were we celebrating tonight?"

"Can ya keep a secret?"

Ryan nods. "It feels like half my life is keeping secrets."

"Okay," Charlie says, "we celebratin' my independence. I had ta cut loose dem ties."

As the truck bounces, his face grows more and more pale.

"What do you mean?" Ryan says. "What ties?"

"I told my gaienne - my lady friend - I sellin' my business. Dat part weren't so good. She heard betta news. But den I told her we's goin' ta see da world." A sadness crosses Charlie's face. "She don't wanna go. Dat when tings got a li'l heated. I had ta draw some line in da sand. She said if I goin', I goin' alone …" He pauses. "So I mighta told her I's goin' alone."

Ryan navigates what's now a narrow dirt path. The truck's dim headlights barely illuminate patches of dense shrubbery. He used to think the wooded area near his grandparents' house was overgrown, but here, the trees and brush swallow up everything except the road, and it feels like they're ready to overtake that, too, with spines that can crawl and spread.

"Wow," Ryan says, "that's a really big step."

"I can't waste my life away in some swampy corna o' da world. Lily right. Dere places ta explore, places I ain't never see before. Tings dat change me forever once I lay eyes on 'em. Real perty places wit' tall buildings an' people I ain't never talk to. Food I ain't never ate." He looks up at the road. "Make a left just 'round da bend. Promise me one ting. I pass out, ya take out my gold teeth so's I don't choke on 'em."

Ryan reluctantly nods.

"You a good friend," Charlie says. "Y'ain't even mentioned I made water when I passed out fer a spell."

Ryan tries to look stoic despite this new information.

As the truck approaches a large clearing, the thick brush slowly thins out to frame a vast, dark sky filled with millions of stars.

The blue tones of night are interrupted by the dim, warm glow of the windows of a little trailer perched in the clearing. From what Ryan can see, its all-weather white paint has chipped and frayed, and it tilts a little.

Ryan parks Charlie's truck in the muddy lot out front and slowly approaches the rundown trailer, on alert for what he might be confronted with behind that faded door at the top of the steps.

When he musters the nerve to knock, the door slowly opens to reveal a blonde woman with puffy eyes, although one of them is obscured by an eye patch. She's attractive, but the swamp has definitely taken its toll. Half of her is hidden behind the door, and it's clear she has something large and heavy in her hand, something that gives her the confidence to handle whoever's shown up at her door this late at night.

"Sorry for waking you," Ryan says. "Is this the home of Charlie La Bouche?"

The woman looks at him suspiciously. "Used ta be."

Ryan notices that this woman shares Charlie's thick Cajun accent. Although he was always taught never to stare, he studies her face in an attempt to decide how old she is.

"Thank god," he says. "This is the fourth trailer I've been to. He passed out at the last exit. Oh, here."

He pulls Charlie's gold teeth from his pocket and hands them to the woman, who's looking at him coldly.

"Ya can't drop him here," she says. "He ain't my mess no more."

"By the way, I'm Ryan." Ryan offers his hand, but tries to brush it off when she refuses.

"Listen," he says, "it was my idea to bring him here. I don't know what happened, but Charlie comes across as the impulsive type to me. If he has a chance to sleep it off, I have a feeling things might look different in the morning."

The woman mulls it over. She glances at the truck, where Charlie's a sack of potatoes in the front seat. Her eyes soften.

"Dat him?" she says.

"It is."

She reluctantly motions for Ryan to bring Charlie in.

With his hands wrapped around Charlie's torso, Ryan drags him out of the truck and across the grass like a crash test dummy that's drooling, snoring and slowly losing his trousers.

He enters a trailer that's small and cluttered, with several alligator skulls mounted on the wall, and a picture of a gold-toothed Charlie proudly displaying a huge fish he must have caught.

Ryan pauses, still holding Charlie with all his strength. The woman gives him a sympathetic nod. She looks at Charlie, who along the way has lost both shoes and whose pants are barely hanging on around his knees, exposing his colorful boxer shorts. Ryan's clearly struggling to support Charlie's weight.

"I know. He heavy dat way," the woman says. "By da by, I Crystal."

Ryan stands there with his back strained. He's not even trying to keep Charlie's pants up anymore.

Crystal notices his discomfort.

"Bedroom dataway," she says.

Ryan flops Charlie onto a bed that's covered with a hand-sewn country quilt, and decides it's best to just leave his pants right where they are. The bedroom's a surprising tribute to a life Charlie claims he's about to abandon - comfortable and cozy without any pretense.

Charlie and Crystal have lived there a long time together. Their hobbies and interests have merged to form a homey sweetness that puts Ryan at ease as soon as he walks in. Even their clothes effortlessly coexist in the cluttered closet.

Framed pictures on the night stand tell a deep story - Crystal wearing oversized hip waders; Crystal on the ground in hand-to-hand combat with an alligator; Crystal holding a trophy, her foot on top of the defeated alligator, with Charlie gazing on in earnest admiration.

The couple must have even shared a loyal hound dog, because they're posing in bed with him like a happy family. The old photo shows a dog who's so floppy, exhausted and comfortable that he was obviously the most well-loved pooch that ever lived. When that dog died, it must have hit Charlie as hard as if he'd lost a brother.

As Charlie snores like a chain saw, Ryan makes his way back into a living room that's more of a tackle box than a home, with fishing poles propped against the walls and all kinds of hanging lures and nets. Aquatic conquests are mounted like trophies of work well done. Even the patchwork of furniture reclaimed from third-tier yard sales - a plastic end table, a TV with rabbit ears on a crate - marks some sort of achievement.

It's a place where you can kick up your dirty mud boots while you throw back a beer at the end of a hot, humid day on the swamp.

The kitchen's practically in the living room, but it has a purpose all its own. Its shelves are fully stocked with bags of French rolls, huge jars of pickles and bargain-sized bags of potatoes. Despite the clutter of the rest of the living area, the kitchen appears to be a well-oiled machine set up for one task and one task alone - to cap off each swamp tour with a meal fit for a cajun king: po' boy, genuine dill pickle and homemade cajun chips.

Crystal's sitting in a ripped, faux-leather armchair in the living room with a tear running from her one eye.

"So, I'm just gonna go," Ryan says. "Again, I'm sure first thing in the morning, he'll come around."

"Tanks fer bringin' him home," Crystal says.

Ryan's headed for the door, when he stops. "Uh, actually, I drove here in Charlie's truck." He's thinking. "I'll sleep in the truck."

"You can grab some shuteye on dat dere divan." Crystal points to the sofa that's covered in newspapers and clothing. Ryan smiles to hide the fact that he'd pretty much choose any other option over this awkward, uncomfortable arrangement.

This couch that's seen its share of muddy boots and messy supper stains is about the furthest thing from the fresh, white sheets waiting for him back at his hotel.

"Mind if I ..." he motions to clean up.

"Knock yerself out."

Ryan gathers up the old newspapers and notices a strong fishy smell. He looks at Crystal.

"Charlie land hisself a big ol' catch a while back," she explains. "I bein' rude. Yer hungry. I can fry some up quick as a lick."

Ryan puts up his hands in polite decline. He grabs an armful of dirty laundry and the Sunday edition, and makes a pile on the floor.

As he's hunched over, he's suddenly staring into the huge, brown eyes of a droopy hound dog who's slumped at the end of the couch. The dog makes a lazy attempt to sniff the newspaper, then gives up. He's almost a piece of furniture, eyelids heavy and a chunk of one ear missing. In the picture in the bedroom, he looks like a puppy compared to his current condition.

"Now Rufus, you be a good host," Crystal says.

Ryan's eyes again fall to the couch, which is cleared enough that he can see the torn, 1970s fabric.

Crystal's studying him from the armchair. "So, what he tell ya?"

"Not much," Ryan says, "but I get the feeling he's torn up about whatever happened."

"He been actin' so funny past couple week. Like da Charlie I love left t'ree week ago. Ya know, I only got one eye, but I see a good soul better'n anybody. Dat ol' boy got one o' da best I ever see."

Crystal's defeated and broken, almost sinking into the Lazy Boy that makes her look so small.

"Who gonna love a girl wit one eye? Who gonna love somebody wit no periph'ral vision?"

Ryan shrugs.

Crystal shakes her head. "Don't make no sense. Did he tell ya he sellin' his tour business? He sellin' it! Dat man love him da swamp. He love showin' people da beauty of it. Now he gonna 'go see da world'? Dat boy baptized in swamp water, from his Daddy ta his Daddy's Daddy ta his Great-Grandpop before dat. He da last one on dis whole bayou still givin' real swamp tours, not some fancy boat tour wit da big fan on da back and some company name on da side. Charlie givin' up his tour business like a mama givin' up her baby."

Ryan tries to sound reassuring. "Like I said, you might find things changed in the morning."

"Dis just don't make no sense. It dat bitch he met. He been goin' ta da Quarter a whole hell of a lot lately. Comin' back talkin' all philosophical like. She been fillin' his head wit nonsense. He got a good life right here. He always was a sucka fer someone talkin' hocus pocus."

Ryan squirms in his seat, searching for anything to focus on besides the pain on Crystal's face.

"I guess we've all been doing a little soul searching lately," he says.

"I see she sunk dem claws in you, too," Crystal says, shooting daggers at him. "Ya'll both coo-yon, like a couple love struck teenagers. Dat woman put 'er spell on you two fools. Ya'll hexed, fuh shore. Charlie say she ain't been home in a year. A year! Ya gotta ask yerself what she runnin' from. What she hidin'? And where she get money ta just wander 'round carefree?"

"I don't know," Ryan says. "I'm not sure."

"If I's you I'd sew yer wallet ta yer ass 'fore she get hold o' it," Crystal says. She looks him up and down. "By da way you dressed, y'ain't from 'round dese part. Ya got yourself a lady at home?"

The question catches Ryan off guard. It takes him a moment to answer ... "No."

"Eitha way, best if ya just go home and make right wit' yer kin."

"Of course," Ryan says.

Crystal's not entirely buying his answer. She quickly stands up.

"Well, I tell ya what. Dis here ship sailed. Dis girl not waitin' 'round for some ol' boy who can't make up his mind. An' whoeva you got back home ain't gonna wait 'round fer whateva shenanigan you got planned, neitha."

"I'm not somebody who normally plans 'shenanigans,'" Ryan says.

Crystal starts to head toward the bedroom. Ryan wishes he could say something comforting.

"I'm sure things will be better in the …"

"In yer heart, ya know whateva you boys chasin' ain't right," Crystal says.

She gives him a weighty look, and walks off into the other room.

Ryan watches her disappear from sight, before slowly leaning back on the couch and starting to take off his shoes. With his nose beginning to throb again and his feet tired and sore, he's reminded that the long, turbulent night has taken so much out of him … and that's nothing compared to what it's done to Charlie.

Through the open bedroom door, he can see Crystal bending down to wipe Charlie's face with a washcloth. Her eyes filled with anger and pain, she cleans off the wear and tear of a difficult night that's left Charlie limp and lifeless. She pulls his pants from around his ankles and lays them over the back of the rocking chair. As she pulls the blanket up to his neck, she mutters, "Ya know sometin'? You nuttin' but a ol' fool."

The shaking of the couch startles Ryan. He looks over to see Rufus' plump body spread out across the entire spot he so carefully cleared. The dog's wet tongue hangs all the way out of his mouth.

"So that's how you're gonna play it, huh?" Ryan whispers.

His only option is to squeeze in next to the bulky, mouth-breathing canine.

"Scootch over."

The plump hound dog doesn't respond to his gentle nudging. After some jockeying for position, Ryan finally secures about a quarter of the couch's narrow length for himself, but try as he might, he can't keep his eyes closed.

They keep drifting upward toward the ceiling, to an outdated glass light fixture that's still dimly lit and giving off a soft glow. Despite its flickering, faltering bulb, it's attracting every bug who managed to sneak into the trailer when the front door was open.

Dozens of small, flying insects obsessively hover around the light as if it's some kind of mecca, instead of just a bulb that needs to be changed.

Ryan locks into one little bug who's not flying anywhere. The poor guy's hurrying around the outer edge of the light fixture, in a real tizzy, covering the same ground over and over. He's circling the very edge of the glass with dogged determination, clearly convinced this is the path to something and he's almost there. That it's just a little further.

With increasing discomfort, Ryan watches him go around and around without getting anywhere, in a circular trap he doesn't even realize he's in. And all he finds himself thinking is: Why doesn't that idiot just fly away?

Larry wrestles with the throw pillow and thrashes about until he finds an acceptable position on the small living room couch. He pulls up the thin blanket he found in the closet.

Down the hallway, he can see light peeking out from under his bedroom door, where Janet's alone in their comfortable king-sized bed.

He holds his cell phone right up to his face in the dark room. All he sees is the time: 12:14 a.m. Hope fades with each passing second, and all he can do is mutter under his breath: "Dammit, you promised you'd call."

Chapter 5:

"Best get all yer ducks in a row quick as ya can"

Ryan stretches his legs on the lumpy couch, yawning as the first rays of sun sneak through the holes in the curtains. His back aches and his stomach feels ... damp.

He looks down to see that Rufus has snuggled up against him on the couch with his head resting on his stomach, his drool forming a nice puddle on his shirt.

Suddenly, the sound of Cajun French bursts from the bedroom. Still groggy, Ryan sits up. The sleeping pooch grunts his disapproval.

"Sorry," Ryan says, "our one-night stand is over, buddy."

Charlie erupts from the bedroom with only his shirt, a worn baseball cap and boxer shorts, and a defiant look on his face that doesn't match his disheveled appearance.

"We best be goin'," he says as he pulls on his mud boots and busts out the front door.

Rufus waddles after Charlie with the lopsided limp of a not-particularly-healthy octogenarian.

Ryan hurries to throw on his shoes, afraid he'll be left behind in Charlie's trailer/tackle box. Just as he's about to reach the door ... "Don't you move," Crystal commands.

With a sagging expression emphasized by his limp ears, Rufus watches on as a couple of plastic bags full of clothing and what appears to be a mounted animal head are hurriedly loaded into the back of Charlie's truck.

Charlie throws in some more odds and ends, and walks over to where several small boats are lined up under a wooden sign engraved with the words "Charlie's Swamp Tours." Each boat has been lovingly christened with a name hand-painted by Charlie himself: Swamp Princess, Reed Warrior, Country Queen. Charlie searches each one with purpose.

Back inside the humble trailer, Ryan waits as Crystal leans over a stove that's seen its share of down-and-dirty home cooking. She's skillfully frying up fish in an old aluminum pan that's scratched and discolored.

"See how he get? He act crazy. Can't hardly see straight," she says. "Ever since he find out yer li'l know-it-all girlfriend 'bout ta spread her wings an' fly away on anotha fool's adventure, he straight outta his head."

Ryan snaps to attention. "What? When? Where's she going?"

"Don't know," Crystal says. "Weren't invited."

Charlie turns the key in the ignition and revs the noisy engine as a clear message to Ryan that it's time to go.

Ryan comes rushing out of the trailer.

As he approaches the truck, the trailer's beat-up screen door bursts open, and he and Charlie watch items being hurled out one by one - a full tackle box, a pair of pants, a few shirts.

Ryan starts to climb in the cab, but he's rudely cut off by a determined but shaky intruder.

"Not you, Rufus," Charlie says as his elderly dog does everything in his power to maneuver his chubby body so he can jump in on the passenger side.

Frustrated with waiting, Ryan gives the dog the final shove he needs and climbs in after him. Charlie looks at his pathetic lump of a pooch and decides to let him be.

Before Ryan can buckle, Charlie peels out with his hands clenching the steering wheel, headed down a dirt road marred by holes and trenches.

Charlie studies the newspaper rolled up in Ryan's lap.

"Fish," Ryan explains.

Charlie nods. "She don't let nobody go without feedin' em."

"Why didn't you tell me Lily's leaving?" Ryan says.

Charlie's stoic, but his eyes reflect a bit of guilt.

"'Cause I ain't even s'pposed ta know. I was hopin' last night you's gonna close da deal an' get yerself invited along."

Ryan's clearly got something on his mind. "Charlie, I'm starting to think you selling your business is a big deal. You might want to take some more time to think about it."

Charlie shakes his head. "We gotta grab life 'n take it while we got da chance. Can't neitha one o' us jus' sit around waitin'."

"I just got here," Ryan says. "She can't leave yet. I can't go back empty handed. I still have too many questions."

"Best get all yer ducks in a row quick as ya can, and cut yerself loose from whateva ties holdin' ya back, 'cause she like a whirlwind o' energy. Whereva she goin', dat da place ta be. An' I tellin' ya right now, dat place ain't home." He pauses. "Dat go fer both o' us."

He can see that Ryan's eyes are focused, filled with concern.

"It time fer us ta stop bein' li'l boys, scared o' what might be 'round ev'ry corna," Charlie says. "It time ta take da bull by da horn."

He gets a little worried when he realizes he hasn't seen Ryan blink in the past few minutes.

He tries to reassure his friend. "Ya just need ta take a deep breath, clear yer mind an' ask yerself dis simple question - what worth more, da librarian or da books?"

Ryan's circuits are still on overload. He struggles to even understand Charlie's words.

"If da library caught fire and ya had ta pick betwixt savin' da librarian or da books, what would ya choose?"

Ryan shrugs his shoulders. He spits out, "The librarian?"

Charlie's eyes fall to the rearview mirror, where his small trailer at the edge of the swamp slowly shrinks into the distance.

"I tink I just chose da books," he says.

Sometimes life slaps you across the face and leaves you standing there wide-eyed, unable to move, peering out into the fog and haze of an unclear future. Knowing your next step will somehow be different than every one that's come before it. But unable to convince yourself to take it.

In a high-rise office building, the polished businessman stares numbly at a phone that's incessantly ringing. He endures the sound until it finally goes to voicemail.

In the silence that follows, he turns his eyes to the wide office windows that showcase a view of the horizon which, until recently, always seemed so distant and out of reach.

In Ohio, the guidance counselor's vacant eyes watch students pass his car in the parking lot of Hillside High School, heavy backpacks weighing them down.

He's not sure why he's still sitting there, but as he pulled into work for the day, he had the distinct feeling of having nowhere to go - nowhere that mattered anyway.

Suddenly, he puts the car in reverse. His eyes are intense and focused as he drives across the parking lot toward the open road.

The Midwestern piano teacher managed to smile her way through an early-morning lesson, but it's getting harder to take the clanking of off-key notes. She waves as her student skips off down the driveway toward school.

Once the girl's out of sight, she closes the front door and right away notices the absence of the ever-present blaring of the TV. She hurries into the kitchen, only to find her husband sitting at the table looking unusually serious.

"Have a seat," he says, holding up the well-worn postcard. "We can't keep ignoring the elephant in the room."

"Wait, wait. What do you mean a secret meeting?" Larry says.

"I don't know," Pokorski says. "That's what Monica said. Ryan had some kind of secret meeting with Betty Parks last week."

"And?" Larry prompts.

"That was it. Then we just moved on to other conversation."

"So you had the queen of gossip cornered, and it turns out you're the only person in the world who can get her to completely shut up."

"Actually, she's really interesting," Pokorski says.

Larry looks at him like he's insane.

Pokorski's obviously a little embarrassed by his admission, and changes the subject. "Maybe Ryan got notice. That would definitely explain why he ran off. First you get dumped, then you get canned. I'd be surprised if he ever comes back."

"You're jumping the gun," Larry says.

Suddenly, someone clears their throat. The guys glance over to see the Red Tie Brigade standing in the doorway.

The men are dressed in long-sleeved shirts, suspenders and, as the name implies, red power ties. These middle managers laugh in controlled bursts, have personalized mugs and take the houseboat out to the lake on the weekends.

"Pokorski," one of them says in that tone that makes everyone feel three inches tall. "We've got something for you."

He holds in his hands a pink, rectangular cake box.

These days, the company's abuzz with strange cake-eating rituals designed to remind people that they're valuable and irreplaceable as they're being booted out the door.

Head down, Pokorski gives Larry a defeated wave, and obediently allows himself to be escorted away by the Red Tie Brigade.

Larry watches as they lead him down the hallway to one of Redding's long, narrow conference rooms. As the door slowly closes, Larry can see a handful of managers and assistants trying to put on a happy face for the condemned man.

At Redding, your fate's delivered to you in the form of a bright pink box.

"Okay, we need to talk," Ryan announces as he makes a hasty entrance into Rusty Harpoon's.

He's surprised to find his words falling on deaf ears, or no ears at all, thanks to a big empty room and an unoccupied back patio.

"All right," Marcus says. "Politics, religion or your favorite boy band? You pick."

Ryan ignores him.

Marcus suddenly remembers Lily's advice, and tries to correct his bad attitude. He swallows his pride, ready to put on his best "bedside manner."

It's too late. Ryan's already heading through the wooden doors that lead outside. He's surprised to find a quiet, empty space where Lily's cluttered bag and oversized hat occupy her favorite table. There's no Lily in sight, but she's left her trademark stack of postcards.

For the first time, Ryan's completely unchaperoned with Lily's mysterious pink bag full of everything, the portal into her life that she never lets out of her sight. Not only that, it hangs invitingly open.

Ryan's overcome by an unbearable curiosity. What's in there? A plane ticket with information about Lily's plans? A legal document? Something with her hometown on it?

Marcus' voice interrupts his thoughts.

"How 'bout a couple drinks?" he says, actually trying to use his nice, big-boy voice as he sets two Diet Cokes with lemon slices on the table. "This is your usual, right? Probably watching your sugar?"

Ryan spins around to look him in the eye. "I get it, you're mocking me. You think I'm a wimp because I'm not a slobbering drunk like everyone else in here. I go to a regular job every day and I do what I'm supposed to do. I'm a good son who actually listens to my father's advice."

Marcus knew he could never pull it off. He drops the facade, and his old self quickly emerges.

"No," he says, "I think you're a wimp for entirely different reasons."

Ryan closes the gap between them.

No stranger to a good old-fashioned bar confrontation, Marcus raises an eyebrow - you wanna go? The idea of a brawl isn't exactly intimidating to this seasoned tough guy whose shirt proclaims, "My Cow Died Last Night So I Don't Need Your Bull."

Suddenly, Lily appears in the doorway.

"All right," she says. "Stop before you two embarrass yourselves."

Marcus disengages and walks away muttering, "You know where to find me if you wanna dance, hotshot."

Ryan sees that Lily's eyes are tired and puffy. It's hard to tell whether she's showing the signs of a night of fun and heavy drinking, or a night filled with heavy emotion.

She walks around the table, and as she does, her eyes fall to her conspicuously open bag, which she quickly and decisively cinches shut. Ryan's jaw clenches as he watches his one opportunity slip away.

Lily's suddenly grabbing his hand and pulling him down into the seat next to her. She carefully places her hands on either side of his face to take inventory of the damage to his slightly less swollen, busted-up nose. It must be bad, based on her concerned eyes. Ryan lets her move his head from side to side, her hands warm and gentle.

"Well," Lily says, "it looks like it's healing."

Ryan knows he has to broach the subject.

"I promise I didn't indulge him," he says, "but ... Charlie's selling his swamp tour business. He thinks he's gonna follow in your footsteps."

"What?" Lily immediately grabs her bag and stands up. "Looks like my plans for the day have changed."

"Where are you going?"

"To talk him out of it," Lily says. "You realize this is the last swamp tour where you're actually in a wooden boat right on the water with a man who knows every plant and animal in the bayou, just like his father, and his grandfather, and his ..."

"Yeah, I got the whole lecture from Crystal last night," Ryan says. "I get it, it's important."

"Well, let's go then." Lily's on her feet and heading inside.

"Wait, I can't. I promised I wouldn't tell you. He'd never trust me again, and I get the sense he has a real stubborn streak."

Lily stops in her tracks. "You think? Okay, so what's your big solution, 'cause I'm not about to have this on my shoulders."

"Listen," Ryan says, "I'm meeting up with him tonight. I'll talk him out of it then. I'll get a couple drinks in him, get him laughing and talk some sense into him."

He motions for Lily to return to the table.

She gives him a skeptical look. "Why do I get the feeling you're just gonna end up talking him into it?"

"What's that supposed to mean?"

"Same reason you shouldn't be writing postcards. And the same reason you got a bloody nose last night. There's an art to these things. Most of the time, trying to talk someone out of something just solidifies their ideas."

"Then show me," Ryan says. "No more riddles, no more mysteries. Show me what to do."

Lily gives him an impatient sideways glance.

Ryan takes a deep breath, with the look of a guy who's about to take out his dignity and lay it on the table.

"Seriously," he says, "I'm tired of being the guy who's always wrong about these things. I want to be able to look at someone and know how to say the right thing, for once."

Lily's expression softens a bit. She meets Ryan's eyes, and she can see just a touch of redness - the symptom of a lack of sleep, maybe the stress of the situation. But the one thing she can't deny is the hint of sadness behind them.

"Okay," she concedes.

Before Ryan can even breathe a sigh of relief, she says, "But you're talking Charlie out of this. I'm dead serious. This is all on you."

"Of course," Ryan says, "absolutely, absolutely. We've got seven hours before I meet up with him."

He's surprised to see the serious expression on Lily's face - more serious than he's ever seen before.

"But here's the bad news," she tells him. "Before you can even remotely know what to say, before you have any chance, you have to see what a person feels … and once you see it, once you know, there's no turning back. Everybody's hiding something. Everyone has something tucked away, and once you get a peek inside, you may not like what you see. Most of us don't."

Through some cleverness and jimmy-rigging, Pokorski's wired up Monica's hard drive to his laptop. Not surprisingly, he watches pictures transfer that are exactly what he would expect of the native New Yorker who knows she's attractive and enjoys showing it off. Monica on the town with her friends, Monica in a bikini at the beach - Pokorski stops to take that one in for a second.

He clicks from one picture to another, making sure the party-girl images transfer properly and he can save them as promised.

Just as his disgust with her image is about to peak, he's caught off guard by a new batch of photos that pop up. There's a pretty, 13-year-old Monica wearing a long, winter coat and standing in front of a dingy, working-class home. Her face is solemn, almost sad.

Pokorski lingers for a moment, then clicks on more images: Monica in an apron at the stove; Monica walking with an older woman in a neighborhood that's anything but glamorous; Monica wearing a simple dress, ready for some kind of dance.

With each click of the mouse, Pokorski scans through the silent story of a latchkey kid who was raised by her grandmother, an old-world Italian woman who provided an expressive, abiding love in the most difficult of circumstances, and through the simplest of gestures.

It all plays out through the eyes of a young girl who stands with her back to the camera, glancing over her shoulder with the weight of life and circumstance written all over her face.

Weary travelers jockey for position at the luggage claim area for Louis Armstrong New Orleans International Airport. With sharp eyes and hair triggers, they shimmy for the few coveted spaces closest to the conveyor belt.

Ryan's eager to get started. "Okay, who are we giving advice to here? I don't have any tea bags. Did you bring some?"

"That's not how it works," Lily says.

The luggage spills out a shoot and onto a belt that's slowly rotating around the hub. Each bag has its own personality. The big ones seem arduous and bloated, barely able to stand upright. They slump on the belt like overweight hound dogs waiting for their owners to rescue them.

Other bags are light and efficient, svelte accessories whose owners have treated them with lots of care.

"What about that lady over there?" Ryan says. "She looks really stressed."

"Everybody here is stressed," Lily says. "Are you serious or not?"

"Yes, I'm dead serious."

Lily shakes her head. "It's like you're trying to ride a motorcycle when you haven't even taken the training wheels off your bike yet. Slow down."

She settles in and scans the large, open room. Her eyes fall to a colorful wall mural depicting the jazz stylings of Louis Armstrong.

"See, this is why I love New Orleans," she says. "This place used to be named after this daredevil aviator named John Moisant, who died in a fiery plane wreck here a hundred years ago. Logical, right? But this is the home of po' boys and river boats, and everything's a party, so they re-named it after a trumpeter. They don't need to explain it. Disorder like that makes sense here."

Lily and Ryan have perched themselves in a perfect spot to blend in with the crowd, who all wear the classic airport mask - expressionless, tired, on the edge of a break-down or a nap. Completely done with human interaction.

Lily examines everyone with a detached amusement, while Ryan tries to fight off the panic caused by her slow, go-nowhere pace. His impatience overwhelms him.

"They think a little vacation will make everything bet-ter," Lily says. "Every year, they accumulate a half dozen lumps to the head from the general hard knocks of life."

Her eyes land on a woman who's almost visibly trying to will her bags to appear on the belt as her children grab for luggage that isn't theirs.

"They go away for a week, come back and comb over the five remaining lumps as if those never existed."

Ryan nods, trying to imprint her every word on his brain.

Lily looks over at him. "Relax, we're gonna start sim-ple, okay? What do you notice about all these people?"

Ryan swallows hard and scans the large crowd that's perpetually on the move. Hundreds of people with distinc-tive hairstyles, clothing, facial features. Hundreds, even thousands, of tiny bits of data to collect. He can feel his breathing grow more shallow and his heartbeat accelerate.

Could a simple bottle of water be the clue he's looking for? Or the way someone holds their cell phone? A few words spoken in passing? Is he focusing on the wrong things while something obvious goes right over his head?

These are the kind of lessons he should be learning over the course of years, not in a single day.

Impatient with his lack of response, Lily says, "They're all waiting for their bags. Where are their eyes?"

"On the luggage carousel."

"Why are they looking there?"

Ryan scrambles for an answer. "Because they all want to get their bags."

Lily rolls her eyes. "Come on, these are your subjects. What they do in certain situations has to do with genetics, inbred personality, their background, their parents and everything that's happened to them since before the day they popped out into the world. Now, is *everyone* looking at the carousel?"

Ryan tries his best to make the world melt away so he can achieve a focused, zen-like state.

He examines countless faces. But then, there it is. Something finally catches his eye. A man standing nearby turns his head in a conspicuous way. Ryan zones in on the 30-something businessman who's polished beyond the norm, with shoes that probably cost more than Ryan's entire wardrobe.

The stranger's head makes another jerky turn to skim the crowd.

"There you go." Lily gives Ryan an almost condescending pat on the back.

Ryan brushes off her tone, relieved to have passed the test.

But then Lily says, "All right. Think you can do it again? I wouldn't want you to break a sweat or anything."

Flustered, Ryan tries to clear his head and focus on people's movements. Most of the time, they're only scratching their noses or taking a drink of water. It's almost impossible to distinguish anything significant in this sea of strangers.

Then, a middle-aged woman catches his attention, and he realizes it's not because she's moving, but because she's actually moving less than everyone else. All the motion's in her eyes.

"Yeah," Ryan says, "that lady over there. It looks like she's staring at the airport employees, then back to the carousel, then maybe over to security."

Lily nods. "What you're seeing is fear. These are both people in moments of fear. This is how you looked when you first walked into Harpoon's."

Ryan bristles. "That's not how I looked."

"Okay, sure it isn't ..." Lily says. "All right, tell me what their fear is."

"Uh …" He weighs his answer. "I assume they're scared they're gonna lose their bags."

Lily sighs, but quickly suppresses her impatience. "Okay."

"I don't know, maybe they're paranoid."

Lily points discreetly at the businessman. "Him. He's staring at everyone else, afraid that someone will steal his bag, so he must have something important in there. He's scoping everyone out to find the thieves, 'cause they're out there.

"It has to do with how people perceive their lives. Are they past, present or future oriented? People's lives are ruled by their deep-set beliefs about time. You take that guy's bag, and you've stolen more than a monogrammed leather attache case that cost as much as my refrigerator. You've stolen his time. Time is his life blood, because he's always on his way to the future. That's where he makes deals. That's where the action happens. That's where he has more status, greater success. Today is just a vehicle for reaching tomorrow."

The businessman's in his own head, studying everyone who walks by. Ryan now sees his tailored suit and watch that looks like it's clearly real gold, and the condescension in his eyes when he looks at his fellow passengers.

"But the thing is, he's clearly not in the first-class section," Lily says. "He's flying coach, which means he's in debt up to his eyeballs. That means he's all flash with no substance. He's presenting an image, hoping someone will buy it."

She looks to see if Ryan's paying attention. Seeing that he's listening, she continues.

"The woman, she's staring at the employees, not the other travelers. She's thinking, who can I turn to when my bag doesn't show up? Who's gonna help me? She hasn't even lost her bag yet, and she's already looking for someone to help her out of her predicament."

The middle-aged woman keeps a close eye on the security guard.

"The future's a lurking worry for her," Lily says. "That's where the next shoe's about to drop. She's past oriented. That's where she remembers all the good times. When things were better, and memories play like a sappy movie."

In teacher mode, Lily's eyes meet Ryan's.

"In moments of fear, if you look close enough, people are more than happy to tell you who they really are."

A smile crosses her lips.

"Here's a hard one," she says. "Where's the security guard looking?"

Ryan glances over at the serious man wearing an airport security uniform.

"Oh god," he says, "I think he's looking at us."

"Exactly."

Lily abruptly grabs Ryan's hand and pulls him across the crowded airport terminal and quickly out onto the busy sidewalk.

"What was that for?" he says.

Once they're outside and out of sight, Lily peeks in through the glass doors. She nods to Ryan that he should look, too.

The security guard is glancing around as if he's looking for them, and saying something into his walkie talkie. Ryan's shocked. They weren't doing anything wrong, but Lily's sudden actions made it look like they were.

The activity hasn't been lost on the people gathered around baggage claim. Travelers are now getting their bags with a bit more caution, eyes on their surroundings.

"You wanna see people being themselves," Lily says, "give them a simple dose of fear."

Alone in a vinyl booth, Janet stares blankly out onto an empty downtown street that serves as the hub of the bed-room community she's called home for seven years. Ask anyone and they'll tell you - it's a nice place to live, and Redding's the only game in town.

Her fingernails are getting a workout as she keeps chewing on them.

With whipped cream and milkshake smeared across their faces, her kids have forgotten both their manners and their much-lauded "inside voices" as they play in the next booth. Luckily, the small diner has almost no customers at this time of day.

Janet barely blinks when her phone signals yet another message. No way she's ready to hear Larry's stressed-out voice again.

She's slightly startled when a man appears at her table.

"You asked for the manager?"

He's dressed in a short-sleeved shirt and name badge. His eyes turn to Janet's unruly kids, then back to her. She tries to hide her embarrassment as her children jump and make ruckus in the next booth.

"Sorry about the kids," she says. "I guess I was spacing out. That's happening a lot lately. They're a little ..."

She quickly hands him the application for the waitressing job.

"Sorry if it's messy. I haven't filled one of these out in a long time. I hope I did it right. Sorry."

The manager studies her face, and sees the desperation in her eyes. From experience, he knows that when you see a woman of her age with two kids filling out an application like this, something's gone very wrong.

"I'm sure it's fine," he says. "We are a little shorthanded."

He watches her trying to appear nonchalant while her fingernails return to her mouth.

"I'll look it over," he says.

The hostess leads Monica and Pokorski through the pizza joint filled with noisy customers. This is the kind of place that defines hole in the wall. It's small and in a terrible location, and it's not the kind of structure where you'd expect people to be preparing food, but it's a place that, on the weekends, has a line stretching out the door and down the street.

Pokorski's fixed on Monica as he follows her through the considerable crowd. Her hair's big, as usual, but its full, dark layers cascade down her back as she walks with a natural confidence. It's the same easy manner she had when she looked at him, free of makeup and jewelry, across a plate of beautiful, homemade pasta.

But a brash voice interrupts his thoughts.

"Are you kidding me? It has to be by the window."

Pokorski looks up to see Monica directing the busy waitress with clear attitude on her face.

His eyes fall to the floor as the waitress leads them across the crowded restaurant toward a table by the window, which has to be quickly cleaned as they approach.

146

In her no-nonsense way, Monica proceeds to order a pizza to exact, complicated specifications. Although what she orders sounds amazing, Pokorski's a little taken aback that she didn't even ask for his input.

But when the authentic New York "pie" finally arrives, the light, perfectly crisped dough's piled high with prosciutto, sausage and a colorful assortment of toppings that make it look almost like a piece of art.

Pokorski's overactive nerves have left him ravenous, and he dives right into the heavenly creation. One bite and the look on his face makes it clear that the taste has surpassed all his expectations.

Monica watches as he thoroughly enjoys the meal.

He has a gentle, unassuming demeanor, really doesn't want to be noticed at all. He's kind of cute with his boyishly un-styled hair and clothes chosen without the slightest hint of vanity.

She really hopes he doesn't notice the little smile she's having trouble hiding.

"They make that dough by hand from their own family recipe," she says, "and I see these guys at the Farmer's Market every week picking out the best vegetables. So many places are just going through the motions, but when there's real passion in the cooking, there's nothing like it. Best pie I've had since back home."

She takes a bite, and holds up a finger to make a point.

"I'm telling you, the whole world's problems could be solved if everyone just baked each other one dish from their childhood. I mean, I don't care if it's bologna on white bread. If it comes from your heart, and if you love it, I'll love it, too."

Pokorski glances up at her. For a moment, there's no glitz and glamour, no pretense. She's real and open.

And that makes him remember … he reaches into his pocket and pulls out a flash drive.

"Uh, I was able to get all your pictures on here," he says.

Monica squeals with joy as he hands it to her. Suddenly, though, her demeanor changes and her face becomes a little pained. She wraps her hand around the small object and gazes upon it like it's something precious she had braced herself to never see again. Behind the heavy mascara and dark eye liner, Pokorski gets a quick glimpse of that young Italian girl looking back over her shoulder at the world as if pleading for something undefinable. Of a woman longing to connect with something that's passed, to a time that although rough and challenging, held the key to her most cherished memories.

The late-90s rust bucket of a car is adorned only with a simple cross that hangs from the rearview mirror. Monica's parked outside Redding, but neither she nor Pokorski have made any move to get out.

When Pokorski finally goes to open the door, it suddenly locks. His eyes shoot to Monica.

"How about if we don't go back inside?" she says.

Pokorski's nerves are kicking in again. "What do you mean?"

"Listen, if they're gonna fire me, they're gonna fire me, and there's no way they're gonna fire you," she says. "I miss this thing every year, all because of this stupid place, and … I'm gonna go. I'm going."

Pokorski feels the car begin to move.

"Wait …" he says in a panic.

"You taught me something today," Monica says.

"No, no, I don't think I did."

"Yes, you did. Precious moments and memories can slip away if we don't take care of them, and I'm about to take care of some today. And I want you to go with me."

Pokorski wants so bad to tell her to stop the car and let him out immediately, but he instead sits motionless as they drive toward Redding's large main exit.

Charlie has his eyes locked on the stack of official-looking paperwork that must be a half-inch thick.

"You just need to sign on the dotted line, buddy, and we'll get you out of here right away," says a voice behind him.

Charlie's eyes drift to the professionally designed logo on the door: "Southern Tours and Adventures Inc." The stark, white corporate office is sparsely decorated with a few high-end chairs and a coffee station in the corner.

"Just wherever you see one of those little yellow tabs," says Jim, the man Charlie introduced himself to with a handshake just an hour ago. "We need your John Hancock. We're excited to get out there and get to work."

Charlie's hesitant.

"It a real quiet piece o' land out dere," he says. "Folk like ta keep ta demself. Dem big ol' fans on da boats tend ta block out da natural beauty o' da swampland."

"I hate to break it to you, Charlie, but people don't care about that stuff. They just want an exciting ride through the glades. But come on, you know that. You're the one going off on a big adventure yourself, right?"

Charlie nods. He leans in to sign his "John Hancock" on the top document, but Jim stops him at the last second.

"You got a trailer there on the land?" he says. "A girl-friend?"

"Yes, sir. She gonna come 'round," Charlie says, "once she see dat money. Who gonna turn down gettin' a chance ta see Cleopatra an' such?"

Jim can sense Charlie's lack of confidence.

"Just so we're clear," he says, "I can only give her two weeks if she doesn't see it that way. Then, we gotta tear it all down. We're gonna need all that space for the hot dog stand, and we're putting in one of those big bouncy houses for the kids, and a souvenir shop. It'll be great, gators and crap everywhere. You know, swamp stuff."

Charlie can barely stomach the comment, but he nods and says, "Yeah, okay."

At the bustling counter of a retro-50s hotspot, Ryan can't hold back his wide grin as he watches an old acquaintance happily shimmy across the room to the pop stylings of the Material Girl. Perched next to Lily on a barstool, he's so excited to relive the experience that his body sways to the music with almost no discernible embarrassment, immersed in the crowd that's cheering and applauding.

The moment someone uttered the ominous phrase, "Uh, I'll have the Beefy Madonna," Lily playfully nudged Ryan to enjoy the show.

The lights dimmed, the jukebox sprang to life and a spontaneous dance party erupted. Ryan immediately spotted a young girl covering her face with her hands and shrinking down in her chair in an effort to disappear altogether. Right away, he recognized her discomfort. It's the way he must have looked when Lily first sprung this place on him not so long ago.

It's so different from the way he feels now.

But as the music blares, his mind begins to spin with the harsh realization that time's quickly slipping away. Lily could be gone tomorrow, and he's still so unprepared.

Since this morning, no matter where they went in the city, Lily had some insight or another for every person they saw, whether it be a guy in a t-shirt holding an energy drink or an elderly woman with hearing aids. She zeroed in on the smallest clues that revealed their entire worlds. Meanwhile, Ryan felt like he missed every clue.

Lily could spot a single guy from blocks away just because of the wrinkles in his shirt, or a new mother because of the bags under her eyes. For some reason, Ryan's brain couldn't click into the same insights. As Lily fired lesson after lesson at him, it was like he was trying to sip from a firehose.

But he never let on to Lily that he was struggling. He kept up a good front.

Sitting at this retro bar, awash in the fun and energy of a captivating city, it's easy to forget the struggles he's had throughout the day.

As the waiter gracefully dances past them, Ryan looks to Lily. He's surprised to find that she's giving him a subtle, unexpected smile. There's something there - a twinkle in her eye.

She's having a good time.

Suddenly, she grabs his hand and says, "Come on."

They charge out of the restaurant. Ryan has no idea where they're going, but with that smile of Lily's and her mischievous energy, it could be just about anywhere.

"Are you waiting for an invitation?" Lily says.

Ryan looks over to see that she's placed her foot on one of the rusty rungs of the precarious-looking ladder that climbs up the back of the old Maramount Hotel.

"Are you sure we're supposed to be here?" he says.

"I said no dumb questions," Lily reprimands.

"I've been listening. You never said that."

Lily points to the large "No Trespassing" sign tacked to the wall. "Of course we're not supposed to be here," she says. "That's exactly why we're here."

As a matter of fact, several signs declare the ladder off limits. Truth is, even if the police would allow it, only a fool would take the ill-advised climb that leads straight up toward a sky ablaze with the most beautiful orange sunset.

Ryan moves to speak, but realizes that Lily's already climbed half a dozen rungs in her quest to reach the rooftop. He sets off after her, willing to face arrest and possible bodily injury to follow her lead.

As he climbs higher and higher, he feels the rusty steps creak and bend under his feet, but he continues upward toward the almost blindingly vibrant sky.

Suddenly, the whole ladder vibrates and shakes like it's lost its anchor to the wall. Ryan's eyes shoot to Lily, who's barely hanging on several steps above him. His whole body tenses for action. As bone-breaking as it sounds, it wouldn't be so bad having her fall on him.

When Lily looks back at him, it's with an expression of almost giddy excitement from the jolt of danger. She starts climbing again, even faster than before.

Ryan's heart pounds in his chest, his adrenaline on full force.

He watches Lily throw her leg over the side of the building and disappear onto the rooftop. His feet scramble to find the next rung on the thin, shaky ladder.

When he reaches the highest step, the rooftop finally comes into sight.

The warmth of the day has settled and held at the top of the Maramount Hotel, a barren expanse only populated by a few worn-out chairs. It's dead silent, except for the gentle howling of the wind.

Across the rooftop, silhouetted against a brilliant pastel sky, Lily stands statuesque with her hair and skirt fluttering in the breeze. She has her face turned toward the setting sun. With such striking beauty, Ryan wouldn't be surprised if she were to suddenly float into the air and fly away.

Truth is, she will fly away soon enough, and as the day goes on, it seems less and less likely that Ryan will grow his own set of wings. But he keeps telling himself - the day's not over yet.

"If this was the last view you ever saw, it wouldn't be so bad," Lily says.

Ryan moves toward the figure outlined by the light, and notices that her feet are only inches away from where the 10-story building drops off into the abyss.

He rushes toward her, but she doesn't turn to look at him. His eyes fall to the cobblestone street below that's lined with ornate French architecture. The intricately carved doors and iron railings are bathed in the last tranquil rays of the day. The streets bustle with the contagious energy of hundreds of tourists, who have no idea they're being watched from above.

"You wanna experience a little fear?" Lily says.

Ryan doesn't respond. Closer to her now, he's even more aware that one step would send her careening toward the unforgiving asphalt. She's tossed her flip flops aside and stands there wearing no shoes, and strangely calm.

"Grab hold of the back of my dress," she says. "Hold me by the belt."

Ryan's nervous, but he moves the fabric of her dress aside to take hold of her thin belt.

"When I say grab it, I mean grab it like you've never grabbed anything before," she insists. "Fear's not always a bad thing. It can have its benefits."

"What are you gonna do?"

Lily's bare toes are wrapped over the edge of the building. She slowly and deliberately leans her body forward and lets herself hang over the side. Ryan clenches tighter to her belt as she entrusts her weight to him. Now, she's barely holding herself upright.

"Don't go any further," he says. "Stop there."

"No talking," Lily says.

Ryan's fingers slip. He wraps them around and pulls with all his might.

"Lily, stop."

It's him and Lily facing off against the unyielding force of gravity, with a steady wind challenging his strength. Lily holds her arms outward as if they're wings, her back arched against the elements.

Knowing it's a hundred-foot drop to the ground, Ryan's muscles are tensed.

And then he feels the belt give a little in his hand. Lily's no longer pulling him forward. She slowly takes over and stands under her own weight.

As soon as she finds her footing, Ryan protectively places his hands on her waist and pulls her off the ledge onto the rooftop. A wave of relief rushes over him now that Lily's okay.

Right away, she turns around to face him. She grasps his shoulders.

"Now it's your turn," she says.

Ryan's eyes are questioning.

"You wanna live on the edge? Let's live on the edge," she says. "You've gotta learn to face your fears. You've gotta learn to face that precipice. Most people just turn around and run for safety. Unfortunately, most of the time, safety is the one thing holding them back."

Ryan's shaking his head.

Lily looks down at his feet. "Take off your shoes."

Ryan tries to block out all the thoughts in his head as he follows her instructions.

Before he realizes what's happening, Lily has him perched on the ledge facing out over the side of the building, his feet scrambling for balance.

He's hovering above the vast landscape of the French Quarter. If this is his time to die, at least it'll be in Lily's hands.

"I'd be lying if I didn't say I'm a little scared here," he says.

Lily tightens her grip on his belt. "You know what, I wake up scared."

Ryan turns his head, the words ready to form on his lips - what do you mean? Before he can get them out, Lily inches him closer to the edge so his feet stop right at the precipice.

She cinches her hand around his belt and lets him know, "I'm ready."

Ryan takes a deep breath. Even though every bone in his body screams that this is something only a crazy person would do, he lets himself slowly lean forward.

He's immediately struck by a strong updraft of wind pushing against his chest.

His whole face tightens, his eyes almost closing, as his entire body reacts to the lofty emptiness of the drop beneath him. But it doesn't stop him from leaning further out over the abyss.

He's suspended over the edge with only the touch of Lily's knuckles on his back to assure him he's secure from falling.

He slowly opens one eye, then the next. His eyes shoot to the sidewalk far below, and his heart pounds almost painfully in his chest. Then, it's like everything goes numb.

Ryan's soaring effortlessly 10 stories up from an historic street packed with tourists. He's intoxicated by pumping adrenaline that courses through him, but he surrenders to the experience in every way. Nothing exists except this dreamlike moment where he's mastered even gravity itself.

He almost doesn't realize when Lily yanks him backward.

They fall with great force into a pile on the rooftop, both laughing and screaming in complete exhilaration.

"It felt like you were flying, didn't it?" Lily says. "Adrenaline's pumping. You're high as a kite right now, aren't you?"

"Absolutely."

She looks at him with a new intensity, her eyes aglow. "Me, too."

For what seems like forever, Ryan and Lily lay there staring up at a sky where dozens of stars have begun to emerge in the darkness.

"Seriously," Ryan says, "if I ever fall back into being some nine-to-five schlub again, you need to come find me and slap some sense into me."

Lily kind of laughs. "Are you kidding? I will hunt you down and knock that computer mouse right out of your hand. I'll throw a bag over your head and whisk you away to Mexico."

Ryan glances over at the woman who not more than five minutes ago had dangled him over the abyss, and whose eyes still reflect exhaustion as she comes down from the adrenaline high.

"Believe me," he says, "I'd like nothing better."

She gives him a little smile. "And hey, if you ever find me on a Saturday afternoon on my knees in the garden pulling up crabgrass in some suburban yard, promise me you'll rip those gloves off my hands and burn them."

Ryan smiles to himself. "Promise."

"I'm dead serious." Lily turns on her side to face him.

They share a look that's more like pleading, more like a contract of some kind.

Ryan turns to face her. "I'm serious, too."

As the sun casts its last rays on the murky water of the bayou, Crystal primps her fledgling tomato plants, misting the leaves with a spray bottle. Satisfied with their progress, she moves on to water a batch of onions growing in the fresh, fertile soil of her little garden.

It was only over the past few years that her garden finally came to fruition, and she was able to use the home-grown ingredients to prepare her signature post-swamp-tour meal of a crawfish po' boy, a genuine kosher pickle and homemade cajun chips.

As she checks on her onions, Crystal feels the ground suddenly rumble under her feet. It's like the slow build of an earthquake. Then comes the loud roar of car engines.

She stands up and turns her eyes to the dirt path that leads out of the brush and into the small swath of swampland she and Charlie call their own. In the soft light of a descending sun, she can see two professional-grade pickup trucks hauling trailers that carry big, metal boats with fans on the back.

Too much for the small, unpaved road, the trucks barrel through the landscape, carving their own forced path as if they're an invading army. The cavalcade comes to a stop in front of a stunned Crystal. She stares on in silence.

Hanging from the back of one of the truck beds is a large, corporate sign that reads: "Southern Tours and Adventures Inc."

In this section of the city known as Little Italy, the immigrants who laid down roots a century ago still proudly speak their native language and honor their imbedded traditions.

Not that the passage of time hasn't brought about some noticeable changes. In the modern world, other cultures have moved in and brought their own food and traditions. Some of the younger ones in the community have ventured off in search of something new and different.

But every year, the remaining residents of Little Italy gather in the streets to celebrate the same festival as their grandparents and great-grandparents enjoyed.

It all plays out to the soundtrack of Italian crooners who set a comfortable, relaxed mood.

With the sunlight a fading memory, fireworks explode across the sky as Monica leads Pokorski through the noisy, colorful party in the streets. The Italian festival consists of rows and rows of carnival games like the ring toss and bean bag throw, and countless food booths where Italian cooks create the most delicious homemade delicacies that scent the air with oregano and onions.

Pokorski might actually be enjoying himself if Monica wasn't constantly pulling him from place to place. Every time something catches his eye, she grabs his arm and drags him in another direction. And she never stops talking.

"Every year I miss this," she says, "every year. All because of that stupid place. All because of those douchebags and their red ties. If I see one more pink box, I'm gonna throw up. But tonight, just this once, I'm doing my thing. To hell with them."

Pokorski awkwardly clutches a massive, bright purple stuffed dog with huge, plastic eyes that Monica won for him after she masterfully tossed rings over seven separate bottles rigged to repel them.

"Can we just slow down a little?" Pokorski asks.

"No, I want you to taste one more thing," Monica says, "I've got a million things to show you."

Pokorski's patience has just about worn thin when Monica suddenly comes to a halting stop.

"Shh," she says, her face stoic.

Surprised by the change in momentum, Pokorski turns to see a slow procession of men, women and children marching down the street with solemn expressions and bowed heads, carrying a small statue of St. Joseph on a gold-plated float. They're draped in red, and reverently followed by a huge crowd of spectators.

Monica lowers her head, closes her eyes and says a silent prayer.

With a glance at his foam-filled canine, Pokorski bows his head, too, but only because he's trying to remember the identity of this particular awe-inspiring Biblical figure. His great aunt once dragged him to CCD class, but they only covered the "Blessing of the Throats," which totally freaked him out.

The procession passes, and Monica and Pokorski raise their heads.

"Maybe St. Joseph can help Jennifer in I.T.," Monica says.

Pokorski gives her a questioning look.

"She just got notice," she explains, ominously dragging her finger across her throat. "St. Joseph is the patron saint of the unemployed. We say a little prayer for those who got sadly tossed on their cans. I'm even gonna say a little prayer for myself. That relocation bonus would sure help me get out of a pile of debt. You should say a prayer for anyone who might be getting a pink box in your department. Can you even imagine?"

Pokorski's cheeks flush. "You know what? Maybe we should just go home. I'm not feeling very good."

Monica's gut sinks. This isn't the first time she's seen that expression on someone's face. This is how it usually goes with nice guys. They never say why, but for some reason they just suddenly want to leave. She's quickly beginning to realize what's going on.

"I'm sorry," she says. "I know, I know, I come on too strong. I'm loud and pushy and I get all caught up, but I just get excited. You've been such a good sport. Can I just have five more minutes, then I promise I'll take you home?"

"Yeah," Pokorski says, "sorry, I'm just not feeling great."

A tinge of guilt strikes him as he watches this poor woman's face.

Suddenly, a loud voice booms from across the crowd.

"Monica!"

Out of nowhere, a broad Italian man rushes over and wraps his arms around Monica, planting a big, fat kiss on her cheek.

Although deflated, she puts on a brave front. "Alessio!"

Suddenly, there's a whole group of people standing around them who bear Alessio's same lush, dark hair and robust voice. There's more hugging, a lot of hugging. Then, the strangers turn their attention to Pokorski.

"This boy good to you?" Alessio says in a thick Italian accent, eyeing Pokorski's massive stuffed animal. "He a good boy? No funny business?"

Monica's slightly embarrassed, and doesn't want to admit that this new man she's just brought to them has already been scared away.

"Actually," she says, "he's a really great guy. He's very patient."

"Okay." Alessio wraps his arms around Pokorski.

"Is this your family?" Pokorski whispers to Monica.

"We're Italians," Monica says, "everyone's family."

Pokorski watches as the affectionate group fawns over Monica, thrilled to see her as if they raised her themselves. For a moment, she's a content little girl being nurtured by the big Italian brood she always wished she had.

"Get this boy a zeppole," Alessio announces.

Pokorski has no idea whether a zeppole is a hammer, a pastry or a poke in the eye, but he says, "Sounds great."

He just hopes it doesn't contain spinach, because the last thing he needs is swollen lips.

"Zeppole! For Monica's boy!" Alessio shouts as he heads toward his food booth.

"Sorry about this," Monica whispers to Pokorski.

Alessio soon returns holding a plate of hot pastries covered in powdered sugar. Pokorski stares at the perfect, fried delicacy. He sets down his ill-stitched, knock-off Snoopy, and bites into the honey-and-powdered-sugar-covered donut infused with the flavors of apple, raisin and rum. The amount of flavor in the small treat catches him completely off guard.

"That's always been my favorite since I was little," Monica swoons.

Pokorski looks up to see that the entire group's wide eyed and waiting with bated breath to see his reaction. It's clear that what they've handed him is more than just sugar and fruit.

"It's amazing," he says. "Really unbelievable."

Everyone lets out a cheer of relief and delight. Alessio throws his arm around Pokorski and pulls him into the huddle like a lifelong friend. For the next few minutes, it's like Pokorski's been a part of this generous, gregarious family forever, as they swap colorful stories punctuated by bursts of robust, heartfelt laughter. But when Monica speaks, they quiet and listen with interest, gazing upon her with overwhelming pride.

Soon, it's time for them to return to their food booth and serve their hungry customers. Everyone bids farewell with enthusiastic hugs and kisses. As Monica's squeezed to the brink of not being able to breathe, Pokorski catches a hint of sadness flash across her face, one she's clearly trying to hide. It's like these people have been granted visitation rights with her for a few minutes, and now she has to go off into the big, cold world without them. For those brief moments, she found love and belonging among people who really understood her. She found her place.

Then, it's gone.

Monica turns to Pokorski. "Okay, let's get you home."

She notices something, and stops.

She reaches over to gently brush something off his cheek. "You've got a little powdered sugar right here."

To her surprise, Pokorski suddenly leans forward and gives her the most delicate of kisses. It takes Monica a moment to get over her shock, but then her surprise turns to a sense of calm and warmth. She leans in closer and succumbs to the unexpected connection.

With the festival bustling around them, the two stand there with their lips locked like a couple of 14 year olds sharing their first kiss. Monica's face now wears the same white sugary powder as Pokorski's, and if his eyes were open, he'd be able to see that her cheeks are slightly pink and she's almost glowing with the subtle aura of happiness.

Although no one wants to admit it, they're all waiting for magic to happen. Create enough mystery, and you can convince anyone that it has.

Rule #1: Don't use "I" or "we." It destroys the idea that the postcard came from some mystical source.

Rule #2: Never give them a specific solution. That's for them to figure out. It's your job to tell them to take a look.

Rule #3: Everyone has the same basic problems - their jobs, their health, they've never seen the world, they need to appreciate their loved ones more. Don't make things up, and don't blame them for their problems. Everyone gets stuck.

Ryan scans through Lily's all-important guidelines, which he's scribbled on the back of a crumpled flyer. He glances over to see that Lily's still tinkering with the heavy chain that secures an ornate, iron gate.

He looks down again. Next to the final rule, he's drawn a large star to mark its significance: Never, ever sign your real name.

A noise at the gate draws his attention, and he shoves the paper into his back pocket, where he's already storing a few postcards he's addressed. The last thing he wants is to miss a moment of his adventure with Lily, or that contagious spark in her eyes.

Lily suddenly grabs his hand and pulls him through the narrow opening she's created in the gate. She leads him past tombstones and down the barely lit path that runs through Saint Louis Cemetery No. 1.

The scattered lights cast long, misshapen shadows across the dark graveyard, whose grounds seem lost in another time. Ornate mausoleums bear old Southern names.

During the day, they're beautiful stone tributes topped with crosses and angels. At night, eery gateways between life and death.

Lily firmly grips Ryan's hand. She moves with energy and excitement, turning around from time to time to flash him a devious grin.

She finally stops at the foot of a simply shaped, white tombstone that towers above all the others. She kneels down in front of it and quickly rummages through her purse.

"Now I would've had a drink with this broad," she says with a bit of mischief in her voice.

Ryan reads the few words he can make out through layers of grime. "The 'Voodoo Queen'?"

He kneels down at Lily's level and studies the stone that's been marked with multiple sets of triple X's and adorned with beaded necklaces. The hand-carved X's vary in size and style, some formed with careful, perfect lines, others large and crudely drawn. For generations, people have hopped the fence, snuck between the walls and eluded security guards under cover of darkness to carve their little marks, or leave their beads, or maybe just to put a hand on the stone.

Without warning, Lily pulls a pen knife out of her purse, holds it to the solid rock and begins to carve her own mark.

Ryan's alert eyes scan the expansive graveyard for signs of lookers-on, but his excitement draws him right back to Lily.

With a glance over at him, she notices his eyes are engaged and his face full of energy. She reaches into her purse again.

"Here, see if you can find a blank spot," she says, handing him a sharp, metal nail file. "Get yourself some wishes granted."

Gripping the file, Ryan searches out a small swath of stone that's free from graffiti. He has to fight all his natural instincts that warn him - stop, don't do it!

"Andale," Lily prompts. "Get to carving."

Ryan presses the file to the surface and feels his adrenaline really kick in, as Lily struggles to carve precise lines in the dense rock. Her eyes are wide with focus as she bites her lip in concentration.

Ryan diligently creates the stubborn indentation. He's made a wish at almost every birthday, and like most people's, none of them have ever come true. But somehow, being here with Lily makes him think he might actually have a shot at this one. He sends out a silent plea: "Okay, Voodoo Queen, you know what my wish is."

Finished, Lily wipes her hand across the stone to clean it of dust and dead leaves. The absence of debris reveals its full inscription: "Marie Laveau (1794-1881)."

"She had everyone thinking she was magic," Lily says with obvious delight.

Ryan's intrigued by the tombstone, but even more so by Lily's undivided attention to it.

"What did she do?" he asks.

"She got in with the richest people, the hotshots in town, and she put on a great show for them," Lily says. "She'd do these over-the-top seances where 'the spirits' would reveal all this personal information about them. They were amazed."

Ryan's impressed. "So you're saying maybe there is a chance my wish will be granted?"

"No," Lily says, "the thing is, she was really just this nosy hair dresser who overheard all their gossip. She heard everything they said and then threw it back at them in these seances that were delivered from 'the great beyond.' They thought she was a 'voodoo queen,' but it was all smoke and mirrors." She reaches behind Ryan and pulls out the stack of postcards he's tucked in his pocket, shaking them in front of him. "Smoke and mirrors."

Ryan's shocked at Lily's ability to lead him down a magical path, only to throw reality right back in his face.

She hands him his postcards and returns to wiping off the striking white gravestone.

"People come here and draw these X's," Lily runs her hand over the stone, "hoping Marie's spirit will grant their wish. Everyone knows she's a fraud, but they still show up looking for magic. The power of believing in something is more seductive than the facts."

She pulls herself to her feet and wipes grass from her knees, then stands there face to face with a tombstone that's covered with the desperate wishes of strangers.

"But just because she has the power to make you smile, doesn't mean she can actually make all your dreams come true." She looks to Ryan. "Don't go chasing ghosts."

Ryan examines the unfinished one-and-a-half X's he's now permanently engraved in the stone. Then, his eyes meet Lily's.

"Your seven hours are up," she tells him. "Your lesson's over. It's time for you to go talk Charlie out of chasing ghosts."

Ryan nods, knowing what he has to do. But he can't deny that something's nagging at him.

"Charlie asked me something the other day," he says. "He asked me, if I had to choose between the librarian or the books, what would I choose?"

"And?" Lily prompts.

"What's the right answer?"

"Well, there is no right answer," Lily says. "Your instincts will tell you. If the library was burning down and you had to decide whether to save a single person - the librarian - or centuries of knowledge and wisdom, which would you save? Your answer to that will help you answer a lot of questions. What did you choose?"

Fully aware of the implications, Ryan admits, "The librarian." He pauses. "What did you choose?"

"What do you think?" Lily says.

Ryan gets a knowing look. "The books."

Lily can sense that he's a little embarrassed that his instincts seem to betray him at every turn. She gives him a sympathetic smile, like she's comforting a child.

"It's all right. That means you're a caring person. You're loyal, and you do what you're supposed to do, and you'll stick by people through thick and thin. The only reason the world works is because of people like you."

Although Ryan appreciates the sentiment, it doesn't comfort him.

"Yeah, well sometimes that feels like more of a curse than anything. And, to be honest, when it comes to loyalty, I'm not sure if I'm really good at it, or really bad. I guarantee if you asked the guys back home, they'd have something to say about it right now. And, geez, I know my mom would give you an earful."

"Oh," Lily says, "family dirt?"

"Let's put it this way. The first trip I've taken in nine years is to see you, not her. Not exactly loyal."

Lily nods. "Well, maybe that says more about her than it does about you."

"I guess. She did run out on me and my dad."

Even though Ryan's skilled at masking his emotions, Lily can see in his eyes that there are some serious scars, the kind that only reveal themselves in the subtlest of ways. The kind that never truly go away.

"Truth is, it's kind of an ongoing theme with me," Ryan says. "I guess you could say women never stick around for very long."

Lily kneels back down next to him and examines the heavily marked stone.

"You know, maybe it's okay to make one little wish before you go," she says. "For all I know, maybe I'm completely wrong, and Charlie's completely right."

Ryan gives her a slight grin, which she returns.

He goes back to diligently finishing off his second X.

Although he knows it's futile, he sends a half-hearted wish out into the universe - to the Voodoo Queen, to some magical force, to whoever might be inclined to make it come true.

Chapter 6:

"Fortune favor da bold"

Around the French Quarter, dozens of gas lamps have flickered on at once as the boisterous sounds of old-school New Orleans jazz burst out of every club and bar. Hearing the wild siren song, visitors and locals alike have filtered out into the streets to become a part of the undeniable electricity in the air, the spark of something they can't put their fingers on. There's adventure lurking behind every voodoo shop and centuries-old dwelling, in a city thick with history, but infused with the immediate energy of right here, right now.

"What do you mean you sold it?" Ryan's heart's pounding. "It's already done?"

Charlie stares out the dirty front windshield of his truck as they pass through the wild, unruly country of New Orleans.

"It all good, brotha," he says in a calm voice that's not entirely convincing. "Ya best get yerself packed an' ready, else ya gonna get left behind."

"You don't understand," Ryan says. "Lily's gonna completely freak out."

Charlie pulls into the parking lot of a wooden shack of a restaurant perched on the edge of the swamp, that makes Rusty Harpoon's look like Chili's.

"Lily da reason I doin' dis," Charlie says dryly. "She ain't got no right ta be surprised."

Miss Mabel's is an aging establishment without the slightest hint of plastic surgery. The paint's chipping. The parking lot's filled with modest to crappy cars. The crowd's feisty and loud.

"Now, I gonna go inside an' enjoy myself a meal," Charlie says as he exits the truck.

Ryan can feel his stomach doing somersaults. He's not sure whether to be terrified for his friend, or furious at him.

He finally hurries out of the truck.

"Charlie, I'm not gonna let you do this. You have no idea how bad this is. I know it seems exciting, but you don't understand the consequences."

Charlie's hand's on the door, but he pauses and turns around. Something Ryan's said has grabbed his attention.

"I get it, I ain't worldly. Sometime what I do seem perty simple ta some folk. But don't go tinkin' I stupid. I wrestle critter twice yer size, an' a hundred time more mean, an' I come out on top ev'ry time, so I wouldn't go implyin' nuttin'."

He pushes open the door. It's a rare subdued Charlie who turns again to face Ryan.

"Ya know, it like we both realize we in prison," he says, "but I been doin' ev'rytin' I can ta bust out. Seem like you jus' sittin' dere helpin' ta secure da lock. Heck, it like you pickin' out wallpaper an' hangin' up pictures in yer cell."

With that, he disappears inside the dim interior of Miss Mabel's.

As soon as Charlie walks in, it's like the whole place is making a simultaneous toast - beer bottles raised and conversation erupting from every table.

"I here fer suppa," Charlie announces like a performer putting it on for the adoring crowd.

"What else you be here fer?" a hostess yells out.

She waves him over to a wooden table that looks like it's meant for picnics - the only one in the room not packed with customers.

"Charlie La Bouche!" A middle-aged waitress with a name tag reading "Jackie" saunters over to the table, not afraid to flaunt her full hips in her painted-on jeans. "I ain't seen you in weeks. Dis place gonna go outta business you stop showin' up."

Jackie's crow's feet give her the hard-won wisdom of a woman who's always waiting on someone.

"Shoot," Charlie says, "ya'll need a breatha anyhow."

That's when Ryan finally enters the room. At the door, he pauses to take it all in.

Miss Mabel's hangs its history on the walls, along with everything from sports memorabilia to alligator skins. Pictures of swamp-weary fishermen with catfish the size of surfboards dangling from their lines. Photos of patrons swigging beer in some kind of contest, the same patrons who can be seen at the tables right now. Pictures of the aged waitresses who carried the very first pots of crawfish out of the kitchen.

But the glue that holds this place together is the absolutely heavenly smell of the local catch being broiled in the kitchen.

Ryan spots Charlie across the room, and begins a nervous walk in his direction. Charlie's also on edge as he approaches. The two men face each other in awkward silence.

It's Charlie who finally breaks the tension.

"Dis here my good pal, Ryan," he tells Jackie. It's clear he's struggling with his emotions. "He da kind o' friend ya do jus' about anyting fer. Da kind dat, no matta how mad ya get, you'd neva hurt a hair on dey head."

He meets Ryan's eyes, and Ryan's demeanor softens. He takes a seat on the hard bench across from Charlie.

Jackie fluffs her jet black hair with the ruddy brown roots. "Hey, cutie."

"Nice to meet you," Ryan says, putting on his best manners.

Jackie sticks her pen behind her ear and pulls up a chair. "Hey, how Crystal? How she been?"

Charlie almost flinches at the question, but forces nonchalance.

"She good," he says. "Been good."

Jackie doesn't even pull out an ordering pad when she says, "Da usual, Charlie? And make 'em cry?"

Charlie nods. "Dat right. Make 'em cry real good."

Jackie looks over at Ryan, and gives the stranger from out of town a little wink.

"Lemme take care o' everytin'," she says. "You gonna taste stuff so spicy - yer mama gonna need a drink."

Normally, this would raise all kinds of red flags for Ryan, but he's too distracted to pay it much attention.

Charlie gives him a couple of friendly nudges. "Dis here real cookin'. Dis a bowl full o' love. Ya won't be da same after ya had dis. All dat worry goin' on inside yer head, dis make it all go away."

There's so much Ryan wants to say, so many frantic thoughts about the damage Charlie's inflicting on himself and Crystal, but it all feels futile. Nothing can change the fact that Lily will never speak to him again.

Jackie shows up with a huge pot brimming with what look like tiny lobsters. She sets it down, and brings over two more buckets - one containing skillet cornbread, and another full of bell peppers, corn and onions that are well dusted with cajun spices and seasonings.

Charlie begins scavenging through the overwhelming bounty of food.

"Ya only live once, right brotha?" he says.

"Once all ya need, if ya do it right," Jackie pipes in.

Charlie glances over at Ryan, and holds up a finger. "Only once, brotha. Fortune favor da bold."

Ryan's gaze falls to the floor.

Jackie positions herself behind Charlie and pulls a bib around his neck, tying it in the back. She does the same for Ryan. They sit there looking almost childlike in their over-sized bibs decorated with cartoon crawfish - Charlie with the expression of a kid who's about to go on a roller coaster, and Ryan looking like he just wants off this ride.

Charlie grabs one of the little creatures and breaks it in half. Tail in one hand, head in the other, he sucks out the contents of the head, grunting with pure delight.

Ryan reluctantly picks up a crawfish and dangles it over the pot, but the grimace on his face has more to do with a general feeling of misery than his opinion of the evening meal.

Charlie leans in closer.

"Ya know, podna, ya got a right ta take five minute fer yerself - five minute when y'ain't figurin' out ev'ryone else troubles."

Ryan pauses, and gives him a little nod. With a deep breath, he finally snaps the small, red creature in half. He quickly exhales, before sucking out the contents.

For nearly 30 years of his life, he's denied himself this taste because of some stupid fear, because of the little legs, because of a perception of how it would taste. Now, his mouth fills with complex, savory flavors, maybe just a hint of sweet, and a slow, almost controlled spicy heat to finish it off.

Temporarily distracted from a million worries, he grabs another one and scarfs it down almost as quickly as Charlie, as if he's trying to make up for all those years of being a coward.

He finally gives Charlie a food-filled grin. Charlie tries to grin in return with his overstuffed cheeks.

With his mouth full of food, Charlie manages to get out, "Let finish dese li'l buggas off. Den we see 'bout gettin' you straighten up. Ol' Charlie here be yer guide."

Ryan nods, but Charlie knows he doesn't mean it.

"Yer worried 'bout Lily," Charlie says, "but ya know what she doin' right now? She packin'. She fixin' ta leave." He looks at his defeated friend and shakes his head. "Darnedest ting. I never saw someone paint a picture so perty, den tell everyone not ta look at it."

Ryan leans forward in his seat and rests his head in his hands.

"Ya know what," Charlie says, "it don't matta what Lily say no more, or what she tink, 'cause Charlie La Bouche gonna have himself an adventure. She can tink I too stupid all she want, but I goin' out ta see da world, even if it mean I gotta go alone."

He looks to Ryan.

"I promise ya dis, podna, if she don't want ya around, yer sure as hell not gonna be alone. You can come along wit me," he says. "But I don't reckon ya gotta worry 'bout dat, 'cause she got a twinkle fer you. No way she lettin' ya go witout her."

Ryan wishes he shared Charlie's rosy view of the situation. He looks up to see a roomful of happy patrons enjoying the ambience of Miss Mabel's. The place is abuzz with activity and energy. Everyone's huddled around pots of crawfish and mugs of beer. Messy, home-cooked food passes freely between them as they laugh out loud and hold nothing back. It might as well be a family reunion.

Ryan picks up a crawfish and starts eating again, trying to lose himself in the surprisingly complex flavor.

As the contents of the large pot disappear, he slowly begins to come to a quiet acceptance. Charlie's right, he is stuck in a cage. But there's nothing he can do about it.

The truth of the matter is, he doesn't have the skills to pull off any of what Charlie's suggesting. It's just not in his makeup. He's missing that intuition, that spark, Charlie's all-important juju. Any twinkle Lily may have had in her eyes, it's quickly fading.

The two friends empty the pot, and Ryan removes his bib and uses it to wipe a thick layer of butter from his hands.

As they lean back in their chairs, bellies full, Charlie reaches into his jeans pocket and pulls out a large stack of postcards. Although they're written in his best penmanship, they're still sloppy.

He surveys all the familiar faces gathered around the picnic tables.

"Ya tink folk all ova da world jus' like dese folk here?" he says. "People in Egypt chew da fat an' share some good ol' grub after dey do whatever dey do all day?"

"Good question," Ryan says.

He pulls out his own impressive stack of postcards, which were scribbled in a messy, slap-dash manner as he tried to keep up with Lily. Some of the handwriting's barely legible. He's not even sure how well he adhered to Lily's rules. He slaps them down next to Charlie's on the table.

Charlie laughs.

"Yeah," Ryan says, "but no one's ever gonna read these."

Just then, a table full of partiers in jeans and t-shirts let out a loud toast that kicks up the noise level several notches. Charlie smiles.

"I gotta b'lieve dey all like dis, good hearted an' such. Look at dese folk. Nuttin' fancy. No coastas 'neath dey drink. No napkins on dey lap. Dey wear bibs. Dey all com-f'table wit it. Gotta give ya a good feelin'. Sometimes I wish I could jus' pack 'em in my bag and take 'em wit me."

He adjusts his gold teeth in his mouth. "But, we ain't gonna know what otha folk like unless we get out dere. It all 'bout ta start, buddy."

Ryan sighs. "Maybe you're right, Charlie. Maybe you're right about all of it. But there's one problem."

"What dat?"

"Whatever you and Lily have, whatever spark, I don't have it. Whatever it takes, it's not in me."

"My eye!" Charlie says. "Ev'rybody got magic in 'em. It just most folk don't know dey got it, and even if dey know, dey got no idea how ta use it. But believe me, we all got it, and brotha, I tink we just findin' ours."

Ryan again looks into Charlie's eyes. There's no malice, no hidden agenda.

Then, his gaze falls to the tables full of people caught up in the communal merriment and the complete joy of the feast - the crowd that's an organism of its own, one that ex-ists without him, that he can only watch from the outside.

His eyes drift to individual faces. His ears pick up the subtle nuances of conversations.

He laughs. "Now see, if Lily was here, she'd be reading every single person in this room." He glances around. "Like that guy over there, sitting by himself with food all over his face and a wrinkled shirt. She'd tell me that he's single, and not exactly self aware. She'd say he's so impatient for the future and what's coming next that he hasn't even finished one beer and he's already signaling to the waitress that he wants another."

Charlie's watching Ryan with interest.

"Or that table over there," Ryan says, "Lily would notice that they're opening their bill and doling out mints, but the one lady on the end is the only one who didn't get one. She's looking around for the waitress, then hoping her friends will notice, then looking back at the waitress. Lily would say her whole life is about, 'I'm gonna be the one who's left out.' The future's nothing but a lurking worry for her."

Charlie gives Ryan a funny look. "But Lily ain't here, is she?" He pauses. "What about dat fella ova dere?"

Ryan follows his gaze.

"Him? New father. Tired eyes, not drinking, a little disheveled. He's not here to party. Probably just wanted to get out of the house."

He looks over to see Charlie's broad smile.

"Oh my god," Ryan says. "Oh my god."

"I knew it," Charlie says. "Dat juju workin'."

With a bit of excitement, Ryan remembers the wish he made on the tomb of a woman everyone believed was

185

magic. He stands up and starts to hurry off, but Charlie grabs him by the arm.

"Yer postcards, buddy!"

"You know what," Ryan says, "mail 'em!"

Charlie almost whispers, "We goin' ta see us da world, ain't we?"

Ryan whispers back, "We're going to see the world, Charlie."

"Well, go den, go!"

As Ryan rushes across the room, Charlie yells out, "Dat boy goin' ta get him a girl!"

A room full of enthusiastic customers holler and pat Ryan on the back as he hurries past.

"Go get it, brotha!" Charlie shouts. "Go work dat juju!"

On a modest stage near the dance floor, the Psychedelic Moondogs belt out classic rock ballads to the rowdy crowd at Salty Jim's Sea Shack.

At a back booth, all alone, sits Lily. Her face is dimly lit by a candle in the center of the table, and there's the subtle reflection of fire in her eyes. She has the long stare of a person who still relives years' worth of decisions over and over in her head.

"Excuse me, miss …" the waiter says.

Lily snaps out of her daydream.

"Oh, yeah." She gives him the bill folder with her credit card.

"Thank you," he says, "but actually ..."

He hands her a crisp, clean New Orleans postcard.

She takes it, initially confident it's one she dropped, until she notices that the handwriting isn't hers. From the tight, abrupt letters, it was clearly written by a man.

In the dark room, she has to hold it close to the candlelight to read what it says.

"You're sitting all alone at a table for two, but what you really need is someone to drink with, someone to dance with, someone to travel with."

Lily gets a slight tingle after she reads the words, knowing exactly who wrote them.

A devilish grin crosses her lips, and her engaged eyes scan the long bar and surrounding tables. Through the crowd, across the dance floor, she's meticulously searching.

She zones in on a familiar face at a booth across the room.

Ryan's sitting confidently with one arm strung over the back of the seat. With the other, he's holding a menu that he's deliberately perusing at the complete exclusion of everything else. Without a hint of concern about his surroundings, his eyes are aloof and focused.

Lily gathers up her belongings and begins the slow walk in his direction. She makes her way straight through the chaotic mass of people dancing and partying in the center of the room. Her eyes are glued to Ryan as she maneuvers the crowded dance floor.

For a second, Ryan looks up and gives her just a hint of a smile. She flashes a coy grin - you sneaky devil.

She steps up to his booth, postcard in hand.

"Oh, I'm sorry." Ryan cuts her off to motion for the waiter. "How are the jalapeno poppers?" he asks.

"Greasy," the waiter replies.

"Ooh, that sounds good. I'll take those."

Lily's frozen there as she waits for him to acknowledge her. Ryan finally grants her eye contact.

"Did you write this?" she asks with a playful tone.

"I did."

"Why me?"

Ryan tries to contain his smile as he toys with Lily by putting on a false smug attitude. "Oh, I write them to a lot of girls in bars. Make a change. Make 'em think."

Lily's trying to play offended, but she's enjoying every moment of the game. She takes a seat across from him in the booth.

"Okay, wise sage," she says, "what am I supposed to be thinking about, or changing?"

Ryan's not prepared with an answer, and realizes he's not very good at this game.

"Uh, dancing," he says.

He waits for Lily to stand up, then leads the way out onto the dance floor where they have to maneuver through a wild, intoxicated crowd.

The beat's pounding and contagious, and almost irresistible as the floor vibrates along to the music under the dancers' feet. This time, Ryan immediately falls into the strong beat with Lily at his side. He's giving in to what's coming more and more naturally to him.

He and Lily can't hold back a growing sense of fun as they succumb to the party, and it's as if some kind of wall or barrier has vanished between them and they're just two friends out for the night, enjoying each other's company. Lily's eyes are wide and her smile bright, not from alcohol or anything else, but from the sheer enjoyment of a moment where she can effortlessly be herself.

But just when the party's at full force, a power riff on the guitar signals that the energy of the room is about to shift to something else. Judging by the melodic chords that begin to emerge, it's something far more personal.

Lily immediately makes a break from the dance floor. Suddenly, she feels a tug on her hand, as Ryan pulls her toward him.

"One dance," he says.

She's cautious. "I have sensitive toes. If you step on them once, you're out."

Ryan pauses for effect. Then, he slips off his shoes and tosses them to the side of the dance floor, now on equal terms with a barefoot Lily. They both look down and wiggle their toes, then back up at each other with a grin.

Lily carefully wraps her arms around Ryan's shoulders for support. He places his arms around her waist, and can sense that she's waiting to be led. And he does, gently finding the pulse of the music as Lily follows suit.

From his place of distinction on stage, Randy Sparkles leans into the crowd, belting out high notes that barely land, playing straight to every groovy lady in the place. His crow's feet strain as he emotes about the heartbreak and loneliness of doomed love in "Freebird."

Ryan's right there with him, Lily in his arms and the drum beat matching his racing heart.

But Lily has something on her mind. "How did your talk go with Charlie?"

Ryan gets a bit of a devilish grin. "Actually, surprisingly well."

"Good," Lily says, looking more than a little relieved.

She allows herself to settle back into the dance.

"So," Ryan says, again faking smugness, "there was this small country in Europe where the guys would hand carve these amazing wooden spoons for the girls they liked."

"Oh, do tell," Lily says.

"I read about it," he says. "They'd put in a crazy amount of detail, and spend weeks carving these spoons, hoping the girls would fall in love with them."

"Wow, I've never heard of it."

"Really?" Ryan says with a touch of humor. "I thought you might have gotten one during your travels."

Lily examines his face, trying to understand the new man standing before her, but liking what she sees.

"Okay. How did you find me, smarty pants?"

"I had a good teacher," Ryan says. "You've been dropping hints all week."

"Oh really?" she says with a sparkle in her eyes.

"Well, how about I'll call them clues. You love this band. You mentioned it several times, and they perform here on Tuesdays and Fridays. You mentioned oysters this morning. The last time you were here, you wore flip flops and danced barefoot. You were wearing flip flops all day today."

"Wow." Lily gets a broad smile. "What have I unleashed?"

Instead of feeling proud, Ryan has a serious look on his face.

"And I also know that you're leaving for Spain in two days," he says.

Lily's smile disappears, and there's visible shock in her eyes.

"I'm right, aren't I?" Ryan says.

As if she's been caught red-handed, Lily slowly nods.

"Okay, how?" she says.

"First off, you mentioned I should buy espadrilles, and those are Spanish shoes. You keep using random Spanish words. Then, when we had lunch, you let slip you'd love to see that festival on Bourbon Street later this week, but you looked a little sad like you'd have to miss it. And I remembered you said …"

"Okay, okay."

Lily meets Ryan's unflinching gaze. Peering deeper, it's as if she's trying to read what's inside him, to see into his heart and his most private feelings.

Ryan struggles to convey his every wish and desire through his stare - how much this week has meant to him, how much he needs this moment.

"And I'm embarrassed to tell you about the other things I've noticed, too," he says.

Lily looks a little nervous.

"Like the small freckles just across the bridge of your nose," he says. "That you always sneeze in twos. You put ketchup on your eggs but not your french fries, and you hate when your hair falls in your face. And I get the sense that you're starting to discover that traveling alone isn't all it's cracked up to be …"

Suddenly, with one loud, jolting chord, the song abruptly comes to an end.

Randy Sparkles falls to his knees, wrought by the pain of unfulfilled dreams and lost love. He looks up at the sky, feeling it for a long time, until his band mates start to glance around. Show's over, right?

Lily steps back, her head down and her emotions suddenly guarded. Ryan looks to the stage with disappointment.

A roadie with a bandanna around his forehead comes out to lead the belabored singer off stage, but the Dollar Store version of Bret Michaels, having not yet exhausted his troubled tale, looks back longingly at the microphone.

The roadie shakes his head no. There's always another show, Mr. Sparkles. Save your strength. The guitarist with the frizzed-out hair helps the aging, wanna-be rock god safely off the stage.

"Don't move," Ryan tells Lily. "Don't even blink."

He rushes over to where the tired members of the Psychedelic Moondogs sit carefully disassembling their stage and instruments.

"Hey, you guys gotta play one more song," he says. "Just one more. Come on."

"Nah, man." The guitarist shakes his shaggy head. "I got dental school in the morning."

Ryan notices the pathetically empty tip jar sitting on the edge of the stage. On impulse, he pulls out his wallet and begins taking out ones and fives, which he stuffs into the jar. Now, it's half full and gives the appearance that the aging rock band has had a semi-successful show.

Ryan looks to the scruffy guitarist, who says, "I don't know, man. Randy's peaked."

The band exchanges glances, then huddles together to confer about the decision over the $17 tip.

When Ryan looks back to the dance floor, Lily's gone. He frantically searches the room, and finally catches a glimpse of her over by the bar in a heated dispute with the waiter.

"One song, guys," he tells the band. "Just one."

He takes out another $10 and shoves it into the jar.

With that, he hurries over to where Lily's holding her ground with her hands on her hips. Besides arguing with the waiter, she now has another person to contend with - the stern manager with the 1970s plaid tie and poorly matched toupee. Ryan's a little concerned when he sees her troubled expression.

"Everything okay?" he asks.

"Do you have $18?" Lily says. "They won't take my credit card."

Anxious to pick up where they left off, Ryan immediately opens his wallet, but he's interrupted by the crashing of a symbol and a drum roll.

"This goes out to all the lovers out there," says the guitarist, who's now the temporary singer of the leaderless band. He gives Ryan a little wink of acknowledgement.

"It's only $18," Lily says. "I'm good for it."

Hearing the sappy love ballad kick in, the absolute last one of the night, a distracted Ryan pulls a credit card out of his wallet.

The waiter shakes his head stubbornly. "Listen, no offense, but it's cash only now."

Ryan takes a regretful glance back at the band's half-full tip jar that's padded with his money. Then, he looks down at his wallet to see his last $15. His eyes shoot back to the jar.

He walks with shame toward the stage, his head down.

The guitarist watches him approach and greets him with a nod, until Ryan's hand goes for the jar.

"Sorry," Ryan mouths before grabbing three dollars back.

In between lyrics, the guitarist angrily forms the words, "Not cool, man."

Ryan rushes back toward the bar and is immediately confronted by the manager.

"Did you just steal from the tip jar?" he says.

"No, I ..."

"Listen, I don't want any more trouble from you two."

Ryan throws all his cash on the bar, including the three dollars he just de-gifted. "I've got it. We're good."

He motions for Lily to follow him back to the dance floor.

The manager disdainfully counts the money.

"Now, I don't want to see your faces in here ever again. Get out of here."

"What?" Ryan says. "Just because of this?"

Lily's defiant. "Why should we leave? We paid the bill."

Whatever softness Ryan saw in her eyes when he had her all to himself has been erased by this idiot and his erratic temper.

"My god," Lily says, "he cut up my card. Let's just get out of here."

Ryan looks back at the stage to see that the entire band is glaring at him, longing to get him alone in a dark alley right about now.

When he turns back toward Lily, she's grabbing her flip flops and heading for the door. He rushes over to retrieve his own shoes from the dance floor, and hurries after her, shouting, "Wait a minute!"

Outside, Lily's already signaling a cab.

"I need to take care of this," she says.

"I'm going with you."

"No," she says, obsessively sifting through her over-stuffed bag. "I'll see you tomorrow."

"I'm talking about Spain," Ryan says. "I'm going to Spain with you."

"What?"

"There is magic, Lily, and I've been touched by it. I've felt it. And you can't tell me you haven't felt it, too."

Ryan moves in closer, and stops Lily's frantic rummaging.

"You're the only person I've ever let suspend me by the belt over the side of a building," he says. "The only one I would ever think of doing that with. And I get the feeling that, for whatever reason, I'm the only person you've ever let do the same to you."

"Oh my god," Lily says, "you didn't talk Charlie out of it."

"This has nothing to do with Charlie. I'm talking about what's happening between us. And you know that at this point, if you deny it, you're just a liar."

Ryan now has Lily's complete attention. Her eyes are unflinching, and she obviously can't deny what he's saying.

As she stands there shell-shocked, a cab pulls up to the curb. Ryan opens the door for her.

"It sounds like we both have some loose ends to tie up," he says as she climbs in, "but as of tomorrow morning, it's you and me, and we're taking on the world."

"I just can't believe you built this thing for me." Monica's clearly choked up.

On the floor of Pokorski's small den sits a work-in-progress computer surrounded by stray parts and empty boxes. It's been assembled right there in a tedious, technical process that's created a kind of virtual life, with all of Monica's data and pictures already loaded on it.

"It's got four gigabytes of ram, a Radeon HD video card," Pokorski tells her, "a Quad-Core processor ..."

As Monica struggles to take it all in, Pokorski looks deep into her eyes.

"You're my muse," he says.

"Your what?"

"My ... muse. Like Kira."

He points to the wall where there's a huge poster of Olivia Newton John's character from the movie "Xanadu" dressed in leggings, roller skates and big 1970's hair.

"They're creatures of rare mythical beauty," Pokorski says. "They inspire mortal men to achieve great works ..."

Suddenly, Monica pulls him close and surprises him with the kind of kiss that should have him weak in the knees.

She backs off when she senses that he's not fully in the moment.

"What's wrong?" she says.

"I prayed," he says. "I prayed and prayed that day at the fair."

"Yeah," Monica says, confused.

"St. Joseph didn't answer my prayers," Pokorski says. "But, you know what, I've never been a guy who prayed much, so I probably didn't do it right."

"What are you getting at?"

"I'm not going to Phoenix," he admits. "They didn't ask me to go."

"Oh." The news hits Monica hard. "Oh, my poor baby." Then, her natural fire comes out. "Those friggin' idiots! Are you friggin' kidding me?"

Pokorski shakes his head.

"This isn't fair to you. Phoenix is gonna be your new home, and I don't want to start something we can't finish. I feel it's only right to tell you this now, so you don't go down a road where, in a few months, you have to choose between me and this great new adventure."

Monica's resolved. "I don't give a crap about any of that. I'm not stopping my friggin' life now because of what may or may not happen in the future. I'm gonna live it. If it means you and I can live it together for the next three months, then that's what we'll do.

"But it doesn't matter anyway, because those Red Tie freaks have hit on me more times than I can count, and you better believe they're gonna get an earful from me. They're gonna hear how friggin' amazing you are. They're gonna be sayin' a lot of prayers of their own before I get done with them, and you mark my words, you're going to Phoenix."

"Sorry, buddy." Charlie gazes remorsefully into the huge, sagging eyes of his trusted hound dog, Rufus. "I gotta leave ya behind."

His truck sits parked in a dark recess of the woods, an overgrown back corner he's known about since he was a youngster mastering this terrain. He's one of a very small group of experienced outdoorsmen who even knows this spot exists.

A makeshift fort created from small logs and branches sits not far from the truck. It looks like it's been part of these woods forever, like it just sprung up out of the swamp.

Its simple structure would be just enough to protect an explorer from the elements, or any critters who might want to take them on.

Charlie constructed the fort before he was even old enough to shave. Now, in a one-person pan, he fries the frisky catfish he easily overpowered 20 minutes ago.

Rufus has found the perfect spot near the fire, his eyes admiring the fresh catch from under heavy lids. As soon as the fish has reached crispy perfection, Charlie removes it from the fire and lays it in front of him. Rufus' expression doesn't change, even as he digs in.

"I goin' ta see dat monument in Washington. Dat my first stop," Charlie says. "Now, I jus' gotta convince dat stubborn woman what best fer us."

Rufus drops his head and lets out a tired groan.

"I know, buddy. Y'aint da only one havin' dose doubt."

Charlie has an old, rusty ammo box open on his lap, containing trinkets from his childhood. His first gun shell he used to clobber a beanie weenie can. A note from his 3rd grade teacher in which she referred to him as "not such a wild bore."

The box is solid metal with a busted latch. He carefully fills it up with his granddaddy's Swiss army knife, a lucky rabbit's foot, a youthful picture of Crystal, whose discarded frame has been tossed in the fire, and lastly, a substantial wad of $10,000 in cash from the sale of a business he inherited from his granddaddy, who accidentally started it when he did a favor for friends and took them out on the water.

When Charlie's grandfather passed, his daddy took it over. It wasn't long before he discovered that whether it was his crooked smile, his quirky delivery or just his sincere love of every little swamp critter, people started specifically asking for Charlie as their guide.

Pretty soon, Charlie's daddy was running the business from behind the scenes, and Charlie was the one doing all the tours.

On what seemed to the rest of the world as just another Tuesday evening, Charlie's beloved daddy held tight to his hand as he savored his last bayou sunset. Charlie inherited a business, but not the business sense to run it. He struggled for awhile, which really tore him up inside, but the family business finally found its footing again when he met a young girl who happened to wear an eye patch, and who knew her way around the books and such, even without any training.

It was Crystal's idea to introduce the home-cooked meals to cap off each outing, and that's when the small swamp tour business really took off. Soon, it grew to the point where it afforded them a nice life on the edge of the bayou they loved so dearly.

His emotions pulling him in so many directions, Charlie locks eyes with his droopy hound dog companion one more time.

"But da ting is, Rufus, I goin' ta see da pyramids. Cleopatra 'n all. Life just one big adventure waitin' ta happen, boy. Ya just gotta know where ta find it."

Betty Parks peers over the massive stack of paperwork on her desk to the corridor outside her office. It's dark and deserted. That's what happens when you're the last holdout at Redding for the night.

"I think you wanna sleep on that," she says into the phone. "This isn't what I was expecting to hear. I thought I'd have your candidate list by now."

Ryan carries a few more shirts from his dresser drawer to the suitcase that's open on the bed.

"I know, I know," he says, "but I just don't see it happening. I've decided to cash out my 401K and take a different path."

He grabs his well-loved backpack and begins rummaging through all his brochures. He finally locates three glossy booklets advertising the sweeping seaside views and lush, jagged mountains of Spain.

"Besides," he says, "Bradley Michaels told me that list was pointless, or maybe it was Trent, I don't know. All that matters is he was wearing a red tie."

Betty's almost too exhausted to address the issue, but she rolls her eyes at the reference.

"First rule you need to learn," she says, "everything's negotiable."

She looks to the documents in front of her. "You know what, I'm dealing with stacks of pink slips as it is. Why don't you sleep on it, and we'll talk tomorrow."

As Ryan continues packing, phone to his ear, he glances up at the TV. It plays a black and white movie from the golden era of cinema, when men were dashing and women always seemed to have a certain regal affectation to their voices. A handsome leading man passionately kisses his beautiful leading lady on a bustling Manhattan street corner.

"Tomorrow morning, first thing," the man proclaims, "we're off to the courthouse to pledge our love and join together as husband and wife."

"Absolutely, my darling." The woman stares at him with wide-eyed adoration.

Remembering where he is, Ryan snaps back to reality.

"Actually," he tells Betty, "I think I've been sleeping for years."

He hangs up the phone and carefully folds another shirt. But his eyes immediately drift back to the romantic scene playing out on the small TV screen, where a cab pulls up in front of the amorous couple, and the charming man chivalrously opens the door for his bride-to-be.

"Sleep well," he says, "and tomorrow we'll begin our exciting future together."

Ryan smiles as the old-time movie so perfectly mirrors his own life. He stands a little taller, suddenly thinking himself clever and debonaire just like the handsome leading man who's won the heart of the lovely enchantress.

As the movie cab pulls away from the curb, the driver turns to the young beauty sitting in the back seat.

"To the Regency Suites Hotel, ma'am?"

Her demeanor suddenly changes. "No, to the airport. I need a plane to take me out of this nowhere town."

They speed off into the dark night, the leading man none the wiser.

Standing there holding a pair of hole-y socks, Ryan slumps back down to his normal posture.

Your gut twists and turns at the thought of any big decision, but it's even worse when a postcard has found its way into your life with the express purpose of disrupting it. A man holding his third cup of black coffee reads his postcard amid huge skyscrapers. A woman on a bus switches from reading her textbook to studying her postcard, her eyes unsettled. A couple of teenage girls who have yet to perfect the subtle art of appropriate makeup application giggle over another. The name on the card: Dixie Normous. They share a look that only they understand. A guidance counselor with tired eyes eats a frozen dinner he's heated in the microwave, a postcard tucked under the edge of the plastic container.

A woman in her mid 20s sits in a grey cubicle, a single picture of a far-off land tacked to the wall.

Into her phone headset, she recites her usual, "Hi, I'm Chloe with Tradewinds Properties. Congratulations, you've been invited to try one of our ..." She's cut off by a dial tone.

With the sound of rejection blaring in her ear, the woman pulls the postcard off the wall and again devours the words on the back. They speak to her of possibilities, adventure, something more. She smiles with tears in her eyes.

In a beat-up trailer at the center of a crowded mobile home park with a sign that's fallen off the hinges, a man in his 60s uses a bottle cap to scratch off the last number on a lottery ticket. Wearing a tattered old work shirt bearing a logo for Leonardi and Son's Auto Repair and Body Shop, a company that employed him so briefly that the shirt's seen more ketchup stains than car grease, he peers through his cracked eyeglasses to see that it's another dud.

After so many hours without moving, his body's almost melded to his old recliner with the gaping rip along the back. He tosses the disappointing ticket on the table and studies a postcard that just came in the mail. He scans the words on the back: "Sometimes life just gets so busy that you have to step away, and you know better than anyone when it's your time." He pours himself another strong drink.

Ryan takes off his backpack that's filled with brochures and sets it on the bar stool. He pauses for a moment to steady his nerves.

The first ding to his confidence comes when he sees that Lily's not at her usual table on the back patio. In fact, her regular spot's occupied by an older couple whose novelty t-shirts and slightly bewildered expressions peg them as tourists.

Ryan checks his watch - 11:14 a.m. His eyes shoot to the front door. When Marcus sets a Diet Coke in front of him, he shakes his head.

"No," he says. "I'm just here to settle my tab. Lily and I are getting our swamp tour, then we're out of here. Adventure awaits."

He's not entirely believing his own words. He again checks his watch, then the door that hasn't budged.

"Who?" Marcus says.

"Lily."

"I don't know any Lily. If you mean your little girlfriend, I'm guessing she's run off."

Ryan's immediately alarmed, but he tries to stay calm, not wanting to acknowledge his own fears. "Wait, what? What do you mean 'run off'?"

"Yeah," Marcus says, "because she's a thief."

Ryan lowers his voice and leans in toward him. "What are you talking about?"

"She's screwed me out of a month's worth of bar bills," Marcus angrily whispers. "She tried to pay with a stolen credit card."

Ryan's voice drops even more. "Did you say stolen?"

"Yeah. I see her face in here again, I call the cops," Marcus says. "I'm a hair and a whistle away from losing this joint, and I'm not about to go under because of some crook in a skirt."

Ryan's rendered completely speechless. He looks down at his watch - 11:17. He checks the door again.

Marcus is less than reassuring. "I'm telling you, that little bird's flown the coop."

Ryan's feeling a little nauseous now. It's as if that nagging worry in the back of his head now has a voice. And a harsh, gruff one at that.

He tenses when he hears the female tourist from the back patio suddenly shout, "Oh my gosh, is that her?!"

His eyes instinctually shoot to the door, where he sees Lily standing there looking straight at him. She lets out a deep breath as if she's been holding it in ever since the night before. In her hand is Ryan's postcard.

"Shockingly," Marcus says, "that is her."

The cheerful tourist, normally a simple piano teacher, wears her summer attire that's been on moth balls all winter, and an overstuffed fanny pack. She rushes over to squeeze Lily's small frame with a Midwestern dose of love. Her excited husband follows behind.

Ryan turns back to Marcus, and sees that he now has the phone to his ear.

"Wait!" Ryan says. "I'll cover her bill, I'll cover it!"

A confused Lily's wrapped up in the bear hug of a complete stranger. She looks to Ryan for help, but can only see his back. She turns to Marcus, whose eyes shoot lasers in her direction.

Ryan pulls from his wallet the crisp $20 bills he's just withdrawn from the ATM. He counts the cash and finds that it only comes to $80. Marcus shakes his head that it's not enough. He starts to dial the phone.

"Just give me a second," Ryan says in an insistent whisper.

He's clearly conflicted, but finally pulls his watch off his wrist.

He stares at it for a moment. Although only a couple of years old, it was distinctly designed to look vintage, as if from a much more distinguished era. He polishes the face before hesitantly adding it to the pile of cash.

Marcus gives the well-made timepiece a once-over, trying to determine if it's actually worth what Ryan's suggesting.

He hears a woman's voice on the phone. "New Orleans Parish Police Department."

"I promise I'll get you the rest," Ryan pleads. "I swear."

Marcus hesitates, but finally tells the dispatcher, "False alarm."

The piano teacher's gushing to Lily. "This is just such a thrill. I can't tell you how much we loved your postcard. It was just what we needed. We've been in such a rut since the kids moved out."

Ryan watches a scowling Marcus deposit the money in the register. He starts to turn toward Lily, but Marcus firmly grabs his arm. The strength of his grip sends a chill through Ryan's body.

Marcus pulls Ryan toward him.

"Listen, you seem like a nice guy, but you're being played for a chump," he says in a clenched whisper. "I guarantee you ain't the first, paying for all her stuff in hopes of getting a piece of ass. And, let me guess, you haven't gotten a thing off her. You guys are like love-struck teenagers. She's got you hook, line and sinker, and you just put out another 130 bucks on her."

Ryan studies his face, not at all sure what to believe anymore. Marcus pulls him in closer.

"Man to man," he says, "no bullshit. You know what she said to me? 'People just want to spill their guts to somebody. If you pretend you care, they'll pay up.' The words of a con man."

Ryan slowly turns in the direction of Lily, who's being barraged by the two tourists. Her hand's being enthusiastically shaken by the piano teacher's husband, and she looks a bit like a cornered animal.

"I can't believe you're real!" the piano teacher squeals. "The bartender didn't even think you'd show up."

Lily's clearly uncomfortable with the interaction, and Ryan can see that she's putting on a friendly facade for their benefit.

"Wow," she says with a guarded voice. "Great to meet you."

"I feel like we already know you," the woman tells her. "You were the only one who knew we needed a good kick in the pants. You're a special, special person."

Marcus lets out an angry chuckle at the compliment. Lily tries to ignore him.

"Henry was like … Oh my gosh!" the piano teacher says. "We're Sarah and Henry."

"Lily," comes the taut response.

She looks to Ryan for support, but his eyes are fixed on his now-bare wrist with the visible tan line, which he gently rubs.

"Oh, you mean 'April Showers' isn't your real name?" Henry says with a chuckle.

Sarah laughs. "Yeah. Your last name's not Stems or Blossoms, is it?"

Ryan's eyes shoot to Marcus, who gives him a wink - I told you so. And with that, Ryan abruptly walks out of the bar.

Lily's confused as she watches him go.

"We've just stewed and stewed about this for weeks," Sarah says.

Lily looks at Marcus questioningly - where's Ryan?

"I don't think he likes Diet Coke with lemon so much anymore," Marcus says.

"What?"

"So anyway," Sarah continues, "we've got so many questions. I can't wait to sit down with you and get it all sorted out. Should we keep the house, or should we move into something smaller, like a condo, so we can travel?"

Lily's mind is elsewhere, her eyes locked on the door.

"I gotta go," she says.

The bewildered tourists stare after her as she exits the bar. Then, Sarah's cheerful demeanor resurfaces.

"They seem like such a cute couple," she says.

Marcus angrily slams the cash register shut.

"What the hell is that getup?" Larry stares at his wife through the bathroom mirror.

"You're asking *me* that question?" Janet snaps.

Perched in front of the sink so he can perfect his look, Larry's wearing his big boy suit that's hung in the closet for almost a decade. Lucky for him, men's styles haven't changed very much. His hair slicked back using Janet's products he found under the sink, he resembles a nervous child on picture day.

He's examining his wife's light blue, knee-length dress with the frilly apron around the waist that makes her look like something straight out of Mel's Diner.

"This is an official waitress uniform," she says.

"Do you have any idea what I'm going through right now, Janet? Today's my meeting. Do you understand what's at stake here? I find it horrifying that I'm the only one who's invested in this."

Janet smooths out her skirt and fixes her collar. "No, I'm the only one taking this seriously. I figure I can pull the shifts after you get home from work for now, and we'll figure it out from …"

"You need to wake up!" Larry says. "There are two options - Phoenix, or we move an hour and a half to the city so I can get a job at one of the big startups. Pull your head out of the sand and face reality. We're not staying here."

He brushes past her on his way out the door.

Chapter 7:

"There's a fine line between mysterious and just keeping secrets"

When Lily hurries out of Rusty Harpoon's, Charlie's already yelling at her, "C'mon, get in da truck!"

Ryan's in the passenger seat. Lily attempts to read his face as she heads in that direction, but he's staring straight ahead with no visible expression.

"Let show some enthusiasm," Charlie shouts to her. "Dis here da very last La Bouche swamp tour. Dis a historic moment."

Lily stops dead in her tracks. "Shit."

Down a bumpy dirt road, they're jostled and shaken by the truck's sputtering movements. The cab's filled with Charlie's nervous energy. He doles out nuggets of bayou information that would thrill most tourists, but Ryan's blankly fixated on the front window, and Lily's so put-off by the distance in his eyes and his stoic demeanor that she doesn't even hear Charlie's anecdotes about "'gaters, swamp rats and reeds as tall as you 'n me."

"Dis gonna be da best one eva," Charlie says. "I gonna pull out all da stops. I show ya tings y'aint neva gonna believe."

Lily nervously adjusts in her seat.

"Charlie, it's never too late to rethink things," she says.

He's not listening. "Hand down da most God-darn beautiful ting ya'll ever see. Critter da size o' yer devan."

"Don't you have a girlfriend at home?" Lily says. "You can't just leave."

Charlie nods. "Da juju tellin' me she gonna come 'round. She a smart lady. She probably packin' up her bags as we talkin'."

Lily again adjusts uncomfortably in her seat, trying her best not to bump into Ryan. In her maneuvering, her foot accidentally kicks something solid and hard on the floorboard - Charlie's old, rusty ammo box.

She uses her foot to gently lift the lid. It opens to reveal a Swiss army knife, a small picture of Crystal and, confirming Lily's worries, a rather large bundle of cash. Ten thousand dollars in fresh bills.

Suddenly, the lid's slammed shut by Ryan's foot. A shocked Lily turns to see him staring right at her. She's taken aback by his unflinching glare.

The noisy vehicle rattles up to the small dirt patch in front of Charlie's trailer.

Charlie jumps out, slams his hand against the hood of his truck a couple of times and announces, "Let get goin', you two!" He focuses in on Lily. "Today we see da swamp, tomorrow da world!"

Ryan and Lily cautiously climb out of the truck. What they see when they get out stops them in their tracks. Ryan stares in stunned silence, while Lily's hands shoot to her mouth.

Charlie doesn't notice their shocked expressions. But when he finally turns in the direction of "ladies' row," where he has lined up his small fleet of wooden boats, he freezes.

With his back facing them, Ryan and Lily can't see his reaction to the fact that his simple boats with hand-painted titles like "Swamp Princess" and "Reed Warrior" now sit in the overpowering shadow of two aluminum goliaths with flat bottoms and huge, metal fans on the back.

This is no longer an abstract idea, something Charlie's going on about. It's not something that's happening in a week, or even in a month. It's happening now, and it's happening fast.

What's worse, Charlie's homemade swamp tour sign has been carelessly tossed to the side and replaced by a large, industrial-sized corporate sign that reads, "Southern Tours and Adventures Inc." An attachment at the bottom proclaims, "Coming Soon!"

Saying nothing, Charlie pulls on a pair of dirty hip waders and stoically gets to work preparing one of his boats.

Just then, the front door of the trailer swings open with a hard smack, and Crystal comes marching out holding a cracked shotgun. She cinches her bathrobe, then loads two shells into the weapon as she marches toward the group gathered in her front yard.

Both Ryan and Lily freeze like statues. Ryan hasn't seen many guns in his lifetime, and most of them have been on TV. He never realized they looked so solid and intimidating in person.

Crystal's a mess - her hair ratted from a terrible night's sleep, her eyes sunken and deranged like a woman having a nervous breakdown.

Charlie doesn't even flinch.

"For someone who leavin', you sure doin' a shitty job," Crystal yells at him. "You trespassin' on private property. I shoot you dead, Charlie La Bouche. I shoot you graveyard dead."

Crystal slams the shotgun closed and holds it up to her one good eye, aiming straight at Charlie.

The gun's shaky under her unstable grip. If she shoots, there's no telling what she'll hit. She cocks the gun with loud determination.

Ryan and Lily try to maintain their solid, steady pose, not wanting to reveal that they're terrified their friend will get his brains splattered all over the swamp.

Crystal holds the gun like a wanted criminal, but her whole body's shaky.

Boom! The sound of the weapon firing suddenly cracks through the air. Crystal's warning shot has done its job. The new corporate swamp tour sign explodes into several pieces and crashes to the ground.

Charlie's unshaken, while Ryan and Lily are a blink away from needing a change of underwear.

Crystal's facade quickly crumbles. She lets her arm, and the shotgun, drop to her side.

"What I do, Charlie? What I do dat drivin' you away? I fix it. I mend it. Please. Tell me what I gotta do."

Without looking at Crystal, Charlie lifts the front of his boat and lugs it all the way to the edge of the swamp.

That's it. Crystal's vulnerability turns to fire. She and her shotgun charge straight toward Ryan and Lily, who back up into the side of the truck.

"You two done all dis," she yells. "Ya filled his head wit dem crazy idea. Now look what he gone 'n done. Dis whole ting on you two. Who da hell you tink you are?"

Lily's like a deer in headlights. Ryan steps in between the two women.

"I'm sorry, Crystal," he says.

With Ryan standing in front of her, Lily manages to squeak out timid words.

"I didn't tell him to do anything. Charlie should just stay in the swamp. That's where he belongs."

"What dat s'pposed ta mean?" Crystal says. "I ain't likin' her tone. Dis here my home! His home! Who da hell you to judge?"

"That's not what I mean," Lily says.

"Dis our life! It take t'ree generation ta build dat business, but ya tink dat a waste o' time just 'cause we doin' it in some 'swampy corna o' da world.' Now, he gone and pissed it away, all 'cause o' you two."

"Oh my god," Lily says under her breath, "I can't believe this is happening."

"Listen," Ryan tells Crystal, "we're gonna talk to Charlie, and we're gonna get this sorted out."

"First off, I gonna sort her out," Crystal says.

She throws the shotgun to the ground and decisively pushes up her sleeves, ready for a bare-knuckle, knockdown brawl. From Lily's frightened expression, it's clear she's never even come close to having to defend herself from a physical confrontation.

The look in Crystal's eyes is dead serious and focused. She's moving in for the kill.

At the last minute, Charlie's hands appear on her shoulders and he pulls her away.

Lily bends over and takes several fast, deep breaths.

"Wow," Ryan says, "who almost got the bloody nose this time?"

Charlie's led Crystal to the edge of the swamp.

"Ain't you heard her? She insulted you home," Crystal shouts. "No. She insulted you, Charlie. You is da 'swamp.' Y'ain't gonna change dat, no matta where ya go. A bird don't change it color by flyin' somewhere else."

Their eyes lock, hers conveying every moment of the toil and hard work that's gone into their lives together. The daily struggles and triumphs that have created their home, and sustained something that was merely a glint in someone's eye a couple of generations ago, but that now defines who they are.

Charlie grabs her by both wrists, his eyes almost begging her to understand.

"Come wit me," he pleads. "We see da Nile."

Crystal looks deeply into his eyes, then turns to leave.

"Cleopatra," Charlie says, "da Nile."

Crystal keeps walking. "I got chips ta make."

At the truck, Lily finally regains her composure and stands fully upright. When she looks to Ryan, she sees his cold, distant eyes. Whatever's brewing inside him, it's big.

She turns back to see Crystal heading into the trailer. Crystal notices her watching, and glares angrily in her direction.

Lily moves Ryan's backpack out of the way in the cab, handing it to him before grabbing her oversized purse.

"This is on you," she snaps. "I'm getting out of here."

"I know you'd love to drop this on my shoulders," Ryan says, "but, let's face it, he was always doing this because of you. It was all for you, just to even get a hint of your approval. I just made a convenient scapegoat."

Suddenly, Charlie comes barreling in their direction.

Ryan locks eyes with Lily. "Once you explain to Charlie how you manage to live this way, maybe he'll change his mind." He looks back at the trailer, where he can see Crystal in the window. "Maybe he can salvage what's left of his life."

"Tour boat leavin'!" Charlie shouts, raising up a baggy that looks like it's loaded with old wood chips. "I got da complimentary rabbit jerky!"

As she signals her assistant to let in another one, Betty Parks' eyes show clear signs of fatigue at a process that's draining her energy from the time she arrives in the morning until late in the night.

She's aware of the long line of employees standing outside the conference room with knots in their stomachs and their eyes aimed downward.

Inside, the executives seated around the long, rectangular table wait stoically as the next employee takes a seat. Three of them wear blazing red ties, and a little too much cologne.

Betty sees the intense stress on the man's face as he enters, and knows she's about to add to it.

"Have a seat, Larry," she says.

Larry's cheeks are slightly flushed and, for the first time since his hiring interview all those years ago, he's wearing his best Sears suit. He has to do everything in his power to hide his disgust for the three men at the table - with their perfectly coiffed hair, their indifferent eyes and their crimson ties with the symmetrical windsor knots.

The room's so silent that everyone can hear Larry's taxed breathing.

"Boy," he awkwardly squeaks out, "those Phoenix Suns need to shape up if they're gonna get any new converts from this place …"

Betty manages a courteous grin, but everyone else ignores his quip.

One of the men, Trent or Bradley or … Larry realizes it doesn't even really matter at this point … cautiously slides a small, manila folder across the table. With his unsteady hands, Larry opens it and reads.

"We've put together a really great recommendation letter," Betty says. "Of course, you'll get the full severance. You've really been a great part of the …"

She's interrupted by someone's cell phone ringing. All the men with red ties check their phones. It's the one in the middle. He shuts it off. Betty looks to see that Larry's frightened expression has now changed to stunned realization.

"I'm really sorry," she says. "To tell you the truth, this is not necessarily a fair process. There are more politics happening in this room than procedure." All heads turn in her direction. "But I know you have a strong family and a lot of support, so you'll get through it."

Down Redding's back hallways and little-used corridors, the "War Room"'s a hidden oasis tucked away behind a nondescript door.

The once-abandoned closet's been transformed over the years into a guys' sanctuary complete with a card table, a few old chairs and a mini-fridge stocked full of Larry's favorite sugar water. It's a safe room where Larry, Ryan and the gang can speak freely without middle management watching on.

Larry hurries around corners and past nosy coworkers, his face flushed and his heart pounding in his chest. He avoids the many sets of eyes glued to him as he leaves the executive offices.

It's amazing the great sense of relief he feels just opening the door, until he's confronted with a small room - *his* small room - completely emptied out except for a few new boxes along the wall, and the mini-fridge with its door swung carelessly open. It's like a deserted home right before the family takes its last load to the moving truck.

Three workmen stand there taking a break from their job, each of them holding one of the last bottles of Larry's prized Old Time Sarsaparilla.

When they see Larry, they don't want to be rude.

"One left if ya want it," a worker tells him.

At the opposite end of Redding, a woman steamrolls her way past dozens of workspaces, on a path straight toward the executive offices. High heels pound on the carpet and a tall, teased poof of hair passes by the cubicle walls.

Monica's a woman on a mission. She's not the type of person you want to wrong, especially when it comes to someone she cares about.

She knows exactly where she's going. As she passes one of the members of the Red Tie Brigade, who's standing outside his office surveying his territory, he gives her the usual sneer that makes most employees cower as they walk by, but Monica's not having it. Her eyes meet his, and the game of chicken quickly ends with the man looking away.

Down another hallway, Monica's at the office of Bradley Michaels. She knocks on the door that's half closed.

Bradley's at his desk with the phone to his ear.

"I apologize, you called during some stupid meeting," he's saying. "Yeah, let's schedule that massage for 3:30. Deep tissue."

His eyes shoot to the door, where Monica's now standing.

"We need to talk right now," she says.

Bradley looks her up and down, annoyed. He hangs up the phone.

"Yeah," he says, "fine, let's do this now. As a matter of fact, we do have something we need to talk about."

Charlie stands at the helm of the small swamp boat like the proud captain of a naval vessel. He's swallowed his complex emotions and is now at the top of his game, in his element as the resident authority on the beauty that surrounds him. He's strong and dignified, with loyal Rufus manning his usual spot in the boat.

"Dat dere a bald eagle nest," he says. He lays his hand over his heart and clears his throat until his passengers do the same. After he feels they've given proper reverence, he's back to business. "If ya'll had a fishin' pole, you be eatin' some bluegill or flathead catfish tonight."

Right away, it's obvious this isn't one of those commercial swamp boat tours that have become popular, where tourists are raised safely above the water in a large, comfortable vessel that allows them to take pictures from a distance.

In Charlie's old, rickety boat, you feel like you're almost in the swampy water, caught up in the moss, at jaw level with the alligators that can grow up to 18 feet long. You're surrounded by the twisted cypress trees and noisy swamp life.

On Charlie's insistence, Ryan and Lily have squeezed their grown-up bodies into child-sized foam life jackets from 1978. Once bright red, the vests have now faded to a diluted shade of pink. The two passengers look like children who've been pulled away from the playground on a Saturday and forced into hard labor.

Next to Ryan sits Rufus, who has no visible opinion of the situation, but wears his own faded, pink life jacket.

Ryan's had to lay his precious backpack, containing all the knowledge that will fuel his travels, on the dirty floor of the boat.

He and Lily sit across from each other on two planks of wood that work for seats. Lily finally makes eye contact with Ryan. His expression says - well, what are you waiting for?

Knowing she has no choice, she reluctantly speaks up.

"Charlie, the life I'm leading isn't easy. It can be difficult." She pauses, her eyes turning to Ryan. "And to be honest, the world's not always pretty, or friendly. As much as I hate to admit it, it does get pretty lonely out there."

For a moment, Ryan flinches. His anger softens a bit, but he knows he can't be taken in by a con woman.

Charlie's doing everything in his power not to have to engage in the conversation. He's a man who's not ready to face any stark realities.

He doesn't veer from his usual script. "If we was in Honey Island Swamp, just up dataway, we be on da lookout fer Big Foot," he says. "Dey call him da 'Honey Island Swamp Monster,' but he Big Foot. My buddy saw him takin' a whiz in da bushes 'bout a mile from here."

Ryan once again looks down at his now-bare wrist.

"Yeah," he cuts in, "your life's so hard that you've had to resort to some pretty clever tactics to get by. Why don't you tell Charlie about them?"

Lily turns to look at him, and she's surprised to see anger behind his stare.

"What do you mean?" she says.

Ryan rolls his eyes. In his inhibited state of movement, squeezed into his life vest like sausage in a tube, he struggles to lean in for emphasis. He finally unfastens the buckles and removes the jacket.

"I hate to break it to you, Charlie," he says, "but what Lily's after is what you've got in your gun box."

Lily's eyes go wide. "What?"

"Huh uh," Charlie says, "all dis happenin' tanks ta Lily. She da reason I doin' it all."

"No Charlie," Lily says adamantly, "you did this on your own."

Ryan refuses to let up. "Did you know she's been paying for everything with stolen credit cards?"

"Are you serious?" Lily snaps. "That's what all this is about? Because of last night? I told you I'm gonna pay you back. Jeez, I've never seen someone get so riled up about 18 bucks."

Suddenly, the boat's jolted. Something has violently knocked it from the side with the power of a small truck. With a Bam!, a massive alligator takes another slam at the wooden vessel, which creaks like it's about to fall apart. They're under attack by a creature with small, dead eyes perched atop its bumpy head, and a gaping jaw that's armed with saw-like teeth.

Rufus musters up a bark that sounds more like an old man wheezing.

Lily's been thrown to the floor of the boat.

Charlie glares fiercely at his reptilian nemesis. This isn't their first battle. Rufus peers over the side of the boat, but Charlie pulls him back.

"Yer gator days are done, ol' boy," he tells him. "You sit dis one out."

Charlie stomps three times in answer to the gator's threat.

"Take me on, ya slimy bastard! Today a good day to die!" he yells. "You took a piece outta old Rufus here." Rufus' damaged ear hangs low. "But now you goin' down!"

Remembering his passengers, Charlie's professional. "Hang on, folk."

That's exactly what Ryan's doing. He's picked up his backpack off the ground and wrapped his arms around it.

When the gator pops out of the water, it looks 10 feet long with its enormous jaw snapping. Forget Big Foot. This thing's the real monster.

Ryan and Lily watch their brave captain curse at the creature in a jumbled mix of English and French, wielding his oar like a Samurai sword.

"Scaly, toothless, piece of merde, le cervau d'un sandwich au fromage!"

Charlie lets out a wild battle cry and gives the alligator one more tremendous whack with his paddle. With a moan, the gator disappears under the water.

Quiet is restored to the swamp.

Ryan's still clutching his backpack so tightly his fingers hurt, as Lily struggles to get up.

Charlie's triumphant. Tall and proud, oar raised above his head, he's the reigning captain of his vessel and the keeper of his passengers. He's in his element, until he notices that Lily's having trouble.

He leans in to help her.

"One o' da many exciting tings out here in da bayou," he says.

That's when he notices Lily and Ryan watching him with confusion and concern. He comes to a sudden realization, and his hands shoot to his mouth.

"My gold teeth!" he yells.

He drops the paddle and leaps into the water, advising his passengers to, "Hang tight, folk!"

Ryan and Lily don't listen. They rush to the side of the boat just in time to see tiny bubbles surface above their submerged friend. The water's the murkiest greenish-brown they've ever seen. Charlie comes up for a second.

"Rufus," he announces, "dis vessel under you command."

He raises a finger to indicate he'll be right back, then with a deep breath, submerges again.

"I can't believe you were gonna scam me ... scam Charlie," Ryan says.

"What?" Lily says. "I wasn't gonna scam anybody."

"Please, I know everything. If it wasn't for me, you'd be in jail right now."

"What are you talking about? What do you mean? Who's gonna put me in jail?"

"Marcus," Ryan says. "I can't believe you let me tell you all that stuff just so you could take advantage of me. You let me spill my guts just so you could get a few bucks out of me."

"Are you crazy?" Lily snaps. "I know Marcus is definitely crazy."

"Yeah, I guess I am," Ryan says. "I guess I'm a sucker."

Lily's repositioning in her confining life vest.

"You think I lied to you, all over $18? I'm gonna share all these vulnerable moments with a guy just for some pocket money?"

"No," Ryan says, "I think that's how it starts. Now I know why you're so scared, because deep down inside, you're just a little girl who doesn't know what you're doing, who's been faking it the whole time, and now the well's running dry, you're running out of options and you've just laid eyes on a couple of perfect marks."

Lily's caught off guard. Looking unsteady and vulnerable, she glances at the water to see that Charlie's nowhere in sight, then back to Ryan.

"I'm right, aren't I?" Ryan says.

"I'm not a thief." Lily turns away.

Charlie suddenly pops up out of the swamp.

"Dis ting goin' down!" he yells.

Ryan looks at his feet and notices a trickle of water bubbling up from the bottom of the boat, where the gator attack has left a small hole.

He quickly places his tennis shoe over the hole in a desperate attempt to plug it. Water's rushing in faster now, and the flood's growing.

"Holy shit!" Charlie yells, rushing over with his gold teeth firmly planted in his mouth. "Dis bateau sinkin' quick. Abandon ship!"

Ryan looks straight at him. "Are you serious?"

He glances over to see Lily's reaction, but she still has her back to him.

Ryan examines the dirty, green liquid that's engulfing his shoes. Even though Lily's flip flops and exposed feet are now slowly succumbing to the mucky water, she shows no signs of life.

Charlie reaches into the boat and grabs a bottle of whiskey from under the bench. He then grabs the oar with one hand and wields it like a sword, ready for battle.

"C'mon!" he yells to Ryan and Lily. "Half mile trek and you be back on dry land. Rufus and I handle any critter get in our way."

Charlie takes a swig of whiskey. He offers the bottle to Ryan, who accepts and forces down a bit of the hard liquor.

When he hands it back, Charlie motions toward Lily - what's going on with her?

Ryan mouths the words, "We'll talk later."

Charlie nods. He scoops up a floppy, emotionless Rufus with his free arm.

Ryan leaps into the cold water, which only comes up to his waist.

He has the sudden, disgusting sensation of his shoes sinking into the cold, slimy mud. Even through the rubber soles, he can feel the sharp rocks and jagged roots of trees. He reaches for his backpack that's stuffed to the brim with travel brochures, which is only inches away from submerging.

Then, he looks to see Lily sitting there with her back to him, her bare feet now completely submerged in swamp water. She hasn't made a move.

His eyes return to his backpack. After a moment of hesitation, he defiantly reaches for it.

Without warning, the small boat lurches, losing all stability now that it's overwhelmed with water, and sending Lily heading straight for the swamp. Just before she hits the water, Ryan's hands are firmly planted on both her arms.

He looks at her, but her red eyes don't make contact with his.

"Come on," he says, "get on. It's either that or the bottom of the swamp."

Lily reluctantly maneuvers out of the boat and onto his back. It takes everything he's got to hold onto her and keep his footing on the unstable swamp floor. He struggles not to slip and fall.

Charlie has a tight hold on Rufus, who's laying his head on his shoulder.

Ryan sees Charlie turn around to look back. He follows his gaze, as Charlie watches the boat that's carried hundreds of passengers over the years, and that his father and grandfather probably built with their own hands, succumb to the swamp. Ryan can tell it's taking his breath away as he watches it sink.

The thick, murky water slowly engulfs the vessel, and with it, Ryan's once-pristine and cared-for backpack containing 20 years' worth of small, crisp mini encyclopedias that perfectly detail a world of extraordinary experiences.

Charlie and Ryan pull themselves and their soggy rescues out of the water onto shore.

"I see what clothes I can find ya," Charlie says. "Ya might wanna check yerselves for leaches and other vermin."

Ryan lets go of a water-logged Lily.

"Let me help you to the truck," he says.

"I'm fine," she says, pulling away from him.

She walks barefoot across the gravel in the direction of the truck.

Ryan stands with his feet planted in the mud looking cautiously up at Charlie's rundown trailer. The corporate swamp tour sign lays in broken pieces on the ground, next to an abandoned shotgun that, only an hour ago, had been fully cocked and loaded. The small trailer's menacingly still and quiet.

A dozen feet in front of him stands Charlie.

When Ryan slowly approaches, he sees that Charlie's staring at a tray of food that's been nicely laid out on the weathered picnic table next to the trailer.

It's just as the brochure promised: three crawfish po' boys, genuine kosher pickles and homemade cajun chips.

"Ya know, 15 year back, I almost had ta give dis whole ting up, 'cause I ain't got a head fer books an' numbas an' such," Charlie says. "But den Crystal come in an' fix it all, make everytin' work. She real smart." His eyes haven't left the tray of food. "Ya know, she ain't got no peripheral vision."

Ryan pats his friend on the back.

Chapter 8:

"Sorry, but I think I'm all out of answers"

Lily pulls off her damp sweater and tosses it to the floor, phone held tightly to her ear. She wipes away a steady stream of tears. She's wearing Charlie's old, flannel shirt, which is short enough to make her a little uncomfortable, but just long enough to cover her where she needs to be covered.

The room's cluttered with dirty clothes and stacks of postcards. The bed's not only unmade, but completely disheveled.

"I don't understand what's going on. I'm in a world of shit here," she says into the phone. "Those credit cards ..."

"You need to come back and deal with this," Mike says. "It's gotten way out of hand."

Lily reaches into her purse that's thrown open on the bed and pulls out a miscellaneous mess of papers, hair ties and receipts. It's not what she's looking for, so she continues her search.

"What do I do?" she says.

"Get back here before this blows up into something bigger than it is."

Lily's pulled out more items and discarded them. "Isn't there something legal you can do? Doesn't your office deal with stuff like this?"

"No. We deal in estates, settlements," Mike says firmly. "Listen, there's a ton of paperwork you need to handle to get this stuff straightened out. I'll send you some money in the meantime, but this is not gonna go away." He pauses. "I expect you to do what's right. I'm not telling you this as a lawyer. I'm telling you this because I'm genuinely concerned about you."

Lily gives up on her purse and heads over to her suitcase, which she begins carelessly rummaging through.

"So you're gonna get me some money?" she says.

There's silence on the other end of the phone.

Mike's defeated. "Where do I send it?"

"I'll email you the address."

As Lily hangs up, she shuffles through the miscellaneous items in her suitcase with more focus. Her eyes scan the hodgepodge of random junk.

She finally pulls out a small, beige purse with a large, gold buckle on the front that clearly belongs to a much older woman. It's a simple, dignified handbag. She opens it and pushes a bottle of cholesterol pills and a calcium supplement out of the way. Inside, the ID of a woman in her late 50s, and some credit cards and cash. Lily takes the cash, counts it and slips it into her own wallet.

She rummages through again. This time, she comes up with Ryan's postcard from Salty Jim's. She flings it across the room.

Reaching back inside, she has her hands on a well-worn leather wallet that a man has carried in his hip pocket for a good decade. A hurried search reveals that it contains more cash, which she also stuffs into her wallet.

"To making stupid decisions!" Ryan announces.

At an open-air, sidewalk bar in the French Quarter, he's ridiculously attired in Charlie's stretched-out, button-down shirt that's survived years on the swamp. Underneath, he's wearing one of Charlie's favorite t-shirts, with the armholes stretched wide.

He pulls up the baggy jeans with the holes in the knees.

The group of inebriated co-eds surrounding him doesn't seem to notice or care that he's wearing someone else's clothes. As far as they're concerned, it's a retro hipster outfit - hillbilly chic.

"My mom says I should be going back to college," says a pretty girl who's tattooed a butterfly on her neck. "What do you think I should do?"

Ryan gives her a disinterested shrug. "You're not gonna make yourself happy, and you're not gonna make anyone else happy."

The girl gives him a flirty smile. Despite the fact that he's looking like a downtrodden hobo right now, he's still a young, well-proportioned guy with a fresh haircut and what he's been told are "nice eyes." Ryan's oblivious to her interest, and after a couple of drinks, he's feeling more lethargic than anything. His indifference makes him all the more attractive.

Ryan lifts his beer and decisively chugs it.

When the phone rings, he looks at the number and starts to walk away from the group.

"Don't forget to come back!" shouts the girl with the butterfly tattoo.

"I need you back here," Larry says when he hears Ryan's voice. "You've gotta come back now."

Ryan pulls his fingers through his hair.

"God, Larry, you have the worst timing. I can't handle this right now."

"Buddy, I am not kidding around. You're gonna blow up your whole life with this. How long do you think you can be gone before they don't think you care about this job at all?"

Ryan looks over at the group of co-eds still listening to his every word.

"Calm down, Larry," he says. "Don't get all freaked out."

"Listen, I know you're bummed about the break-up, I know it hurts, but we all lose sometimes. Running away is not the way to handle it."

Ryan can't hold it in anymore. "No, Larry. That's not why I left." He takes a deep breath, and another big swig of beer. "I left because they wanted me to take over the whole damn department, okay?"

"What did you say?"

"Yeah, Betty Parks asked me to move to Phoenix and run the whole department, which I don't want to do, so my only real option is to quit."

"Holy crap," Larry says.

"Right, so we're all in the dumps here," Ryan says. "They've screwed us all."

Larry's not buying his spin. "Wait, so you were offered a promotion, and the opportunity to run the team? Our team?"

"I guess you could look at it that way."

"And to choose who's on the team?"

"But Bradley Michaels, or whichever of those idiots it was, made it very clear their plan was to get fresh blood in Phoenix."

Ryan hears nothing but silence on the line.

"Larry, you know I had no choice. Like my dad's been saying …"

"I gotta go," Larry says. "Stay as long as you want."

When the phone goes dead, Ryan slowly slides it back into his pocket. He looks back to the group of strangers staring at him with voyeuristic interest.

Just then, a young man with a nose ring raises his glass in the air.

"To bad decisions!" he toasts.

Ryan makes a beeline for the bar and slams down a wad of cash.

"Next round's on me," he says.

He turns and starts to walk away, but the pretty girl with the neck tattoo yells after him, "Hey, where ya goin'?"

"To see the world," he replies.

Slamming his phone on the table, Larry looks down to see a small face with sleepy eyes staring up at him.

"Daddy, are you mad?" asks his five-year-old son.

"No." Larry quickly tries to shift gears and quiet his anger. "Let's head back to bed, buddy."

He gently leads the boy back into his bedroom and helps him crawl into a bed that's covered with pillows that look like Mater and Lightning McQueen. It's his own perfect, little boy sanctuary, with Nascar heroes lining the walls, a race car bed and the perfect dark blue paint.

Larry takes a seat on the edge of the bed and waits for his son to close his heavy eyes.

Like he has so many times before, he tries to figure out how to freeze this simple moment for his boy. In 20 years, this child will be a man dealing with all the inevitable insecurity and conflict, but Larry would love to hold that off and lock in this moment when, despite financial worries, the kids are safe, the family's together and his boy's fears can be easily quieted by Lightning McQueen.

People talk about "savoring" a moment, but Larry's never figured out how that works. Life only stays happy and stable for about five minutes, and memories become hazy no matter how precious.

His son quickly drifts off to sleep, his face serene.

All because of a few well-placed decals of adorable cartoon cars, and a careful paint job with impeccable edges. Janet spent an entire weekend wearing her old t-shirt splattered with dark blue stains.

Larry would give anything to go back to that moment when, after hours of working to get the room ready for a tiny baby, he and Janet just sat on the back porch sipping wine and talking.

He can't remember a single word of what was said, or if it was cold outside, or the label of the wine they were drinking, but he clearly remembers the warm feeling of contentment and happiness that enveloped him like a blanket on that peaceful night. He would do anything to get that back.

After a half hour, Larry slowly rises so he doesn't shake the bed and wake up his now-contented son. Heading down the dark hallway, he stops two doors down to peek into the simple, tasteful master bedroom, where Janet's fast asleep with blankets pulled up all the way to her chin.

From her placid expression, it's obvious she's temporarily free of the persistent worry that's always a part of her consciousness these days. She's been going to bed earlier and earlier, in search of this kind of escape.

Larry quietly heads into the kitchen, dialing his phone.

"Hey," he says, "you up for getting a drink?"

"I tried ta jus' light it all up, burn it ta ashes, but I couldn't do it," Crystal says, packing some of Charlie's well-worn t-shirts into a box. "Is it okay if I come stay wit you, Mama?"

She stops when she hears a soft knock on the door. When you live in the isolated depths of the bayou, it's never a good thing to have a visitor at 11 p.m.

Crystal excuses herself from the phone and pulls a small .22 pistol out of the drawer. With caution, she discreetly approaches the door.

She has the gun firmly gripped in her hand as she opens just slightly. There stands a man with a freshly scrubbed face and hair slicked back with Brill cream.

"Ain't ya done wit me yet, Charlie?" Crystal says with pain in her voice.

From behind his back, Charlie pulls out a small bouquet of lilies tied with string. He presents it to Crystal as if he's offering up his deepest dreams and desires.

Crystal eyes the flowers skeptically.

"I don't give a crap what you say, just taking off like that makes the guy nothing but a selfish jerk." Pokorski pushes open the glass door that leads into the Chili's restaurant, which within an hour will go as dark as the rest of the dormant shopping center it anchors.

Almost in unison, Pokorski and Larry freeze as soon as they take one step inside the familiar building. Beyond the hostess stand, the bar's packed with customers as if it's the Super Bowl on a Saturday.

Larry has a visceral reaction to the herd of other humans. "Oh hell no, I'm out of here."

But as soon as he turns toward the door, he catches a glimpse of a face that's vaguely familiar to him. Someone he could never put a name to, but who somehow shows up in his life on almost a daily basis.

He scans the bar and notices that the room's full of people he's definitely seen before.

Blevins from Accounting, the tall, skinny guy from Systems, Mindy from HR - who always snags the microwave mere seconds before he's ready to heat his Hot Pocket. The unhappy zombies who wander the halls of Redding, rarely looking up to make eye contact, but sharing the same life, day in and day out.

Pokorski's concerned eyes suggest he's noticing exactly the same thing.

He and Larry don't necessarily know these people's identities or job titles, but they do know one thing. Within the past week, each of them has received their very own pink cake box.

Perched at the edge of the dark bayou, just a dozen feet from the shattered corporate sign that lies on the ground, Rufus has his eyes fixed on a small boat that floats serenely in the middle of the still, murky swamp water.

Charlie and Crystal sit face to face on two pieces of wood that work for seats. Crystal's stiff posture says she's not at all sure about any of this. Not ready for whatever new bombshell she might have to endure.

Charlie's fidgety, unnerved by the frightened expression on the face of someone he's always strived to protect above all else.

The swamp's nocturnal activities have kicked into full swing. As the moon reflects on the water, the joyful dance of fireflies and the rhythmic croaking of frogs feel like a serenade meant to soothe the uneasy couple. A chorus of crickets sings from the trees. Charlie tries to calm his nerves by breathing in the familiar, earthy aroma.

Some people find it hard to call the swamp "beautiful" because they view Louisiana as backward compared to places like Paris or Rome. They think they have to leave the good 'ol U.S. of A. in order to find something worthy of snapshots in the photo album.

Truth is, these tranquil waters rank right up there with the most exotic rivers of the world in terms of being just plain pretty.

Nothing's ever seemed more peaceful, more removed from everything and everyone else, but where the tranquil setting would normally comfort Charlie and Crystal, they're caught up in a moment that feels tentative and charged with emotion.

Charlie's a gentleman in his dated suit and bow tie, topped off with newly polished swamp boots. Crystal's primped in a flowery dress with a matching eye patch. On her feet, she sports the same swamp boots as Charlie. They sit with straight backs and hands in their laps, their nerves jittery.

Through her trepidation, Crystal finally gets out the words, "Okay, Charlie, why ya ask me ta put on my Sunday finest?"

Charlie gathers himself for a moment, a catch in his throat.

"I come ta realize I gotta blossom where I planted, an' when I do, I wanna be right here next ta da pertiest flower I ever saw."

A bit of hope flashes across Crystal's face.

"Ya mean dat, Charlie? 'Cause dis ol' heart can't take no more."

Charlie nods. "I mean it."

As Crystal slowly absorbs his words, her eyes drift back toward the small, tilted trailer perched on the shore, whose windows emanate a soft glow.

Her next words are tinged with sadness. "But I tink it too late now."

That hits Charlie hard.

"We ain't got no place ta blossom no more," Crystal says.

Charlie shakes his head, but within a moment, a look of determination overtakes him.

"Don't matter," he says. "We gonna make our way. Long as you willin' ta have me."

Crystal cautiously meets his gaze. "Charlie, I always got you. Ya know dat."

Charlie slowly reaches into his pocket. Although she doesn't show it, Crystal's drawn to the small, velvet box he pulls out.

She watches as he nervously pries open the lid. His eyes are sincere and heartfelt, well aware of what he's lost, but trying to hold onto the one thing he has left - the most precious of all.

In the center of the box rests a shiny glass eye. Crystal gives him a little smile, and a nod.

"Forever?" Charlie says, a touch of moisture in his eyes.

"Forever," Crystal says.

Just out of their sight, along the hidden edge of the swamp, Charlie's droopy, emotionless hound dog watches the scene unfold. Rufus doesn't even flinch when Ryan, who's been standing next to him for some time, takes a seat on the muddy ground. Behind them, a city cab idles in the background.

"I guess she was right about one thing - Charlie's staying put," Ryan says. "And I'm guessing you don't have any deep down urges to go see the world."

When Rufus grunts, Ryan shakes his head. "I didn't think so."

The subdued hound dog sticks out his tongue to give Ryan a sloppy, heartfelt lick on the cheek.

Ryan appreciates the affection, but his hollow expression remains unchanged.

It's funny how events in your life come and go and you barely remember the details, but when it's a regret, when it's a moment you'd give anything to take back, you remember every single insensitive word, and every tinge of pain on the face of someone you'd never want to hurt. You'll remember it until the day you die. That horrible feeling is always right there just under the surface, waiting to rear its ugly head from time to time, waking you up in the middle of the night to contemplate it at 4 a.m. You'd give anything, anything, to get a second chance at that moment.

The conversation pauses as the Chili's waitress sets down a party-sized tray of potato skins, boneless chicken wings and cheese sticks. The activity, and the aroma of fresh food from the kitchen, barely interrupts the flow of stories and laughter coming from every table.

With 15 minutes left until closing, the rowdy group - who've rearranged the tall bar tables to form a circle into the middle of the room - show no signs of calling it a night.

The tight-knit band of coworkers have never formally met each other until tonight, but they share a common daily routine, the same worries, similar memories. Through tears and cathartic laughter, they swap stories of meetings gone wrong, unfulfilled promises, and that feeling of being relegated to the no-man's land that exists just under the radar. And then there's that unbearable odor in the break room ...

At times, Larry lets out a belly laugh almost like a release valve has been turned, venting tension from every pore.

But inevitably, the light-hearted tales of corporate struggle lead back to three people everyone knows based only on the color of their ties. That's when the mood turns dark.

They begin to speak of orders barked without the courtesy of eye contact, hard stares that sear right through them. A common dread, the drudgery of being held down and pushed to the brink of despair.

And they talk about something else, too - they complain about bright pink boxes that contain crappy cake picked up in haste from the grocery store down the street.

The pit in Larry's stomach grows, and it's only the knowledge that everyone else gathered around these tables has suffered the same indignity and humiliation that makes it a little more bearable. The reality is, most of these people have it much worse than him. Many have no savings accounts. Some are single or divorced. Others have endured personal tragedies to accompany the gut punch at work.

And all the while, three pathetic, undeserving jerks have been living it up on their yachts while they vacation together at island resorts.

The stories fly from table to table, and there's a cleansing effect that comes from purging something painful to people who not only understand it, but intuitively feel it themselves.

"Last call!" comes the announcement from the manager.

She has to say it a few times to get through. "Last call, everyone! We're closing in 10 minutes!"

All sound suddenly stops. The newly bonded coworkers glance around at their neighbors, filled with overwhelming disappointment. A somber mood descends on the group as they realize the significance of the manager's words.

Without warning, Larry's up and on his feet.

"Hey, who wants to have a little fun while our key cards still work?"

At first light, Lily watches the rotating glass doors that lead into the hotel. A few guests trickle into the lobby, making sure to stuff themselves to the point of indigestion on the complimentary breakfast in the front room. Lily stops a hurried woman in a concierge uniform.

"Did FedEx come?" she asks. "Is there a package for me?"

"Sorry ma'am," the woman says. "Nothing's come in yet this morning. Maybe in a few hours. What's the name again?"

"It's ..."

"Excuse me," a male voice interrupts.

Lily turns around to see a man standing there with desperation in his eyes. He has a backpack thrown over his shoulder, and his normally groomed head of thick, dark hair is scruffy and unkempt. Although the bags under his deep-set brown eyes are a genetic trait, they're now puffy and pronounced as if he's coming off a restless night's sleep.

Jack, the troubled guidance counselor from Ohio, who's usually found crushing the grandiose dreams of scruffy high school kids in faded Rush t-shirts, printing out their dim futures on his barely functioning printer, grips a postcard that's aged and worn from constant reading and analysis.

"You sent me this?" he says.

"I did," Lily stoically acknowledges.

"I have so many questions for you."

"Sorry, but I think I'm all out of answers."

Jack takes a good, hard look at the beautiful but clearly emotionally exhausted woman standing in front of him, and breathes a slight sigh of relief.

"Your hair's gotten long."

"Let me help," Jack says.

"No." Lily's on the floor of her hotel room struggling to squeeze another pair of flip flops into her disorganized suitcase.

"People are worried sick about you," Jack says. "The sooner I get you home, the better. We just want what's best for you. What you've been doing is wrong."

"Did Mike give you money?" Lily says.

Jack notices that the desk and dresser are covered in postcards. Some lay face up to reveal breathtaking images of vacation paradise.

He picks up a few and notices they're addressed to names he's never heard of.

"What are you doing? Who are these people? Do you know them?" he says. He carefully reads through the words, and slowly shakes his head. "I guess I wasn't the only one, huh?"

Lily doesn't respond.

"Have you heard anything I've said?" Jack asks.

In exasperation, he drops an envelope full of cash on the desk. Lily immediately grabs it and heads for the door.

He stands there and watches her go, a man hurt in more ways than he ever thought possible. Finally, determination takes over. He tosses the postcards back where he found them, and follows Lily out the door.

At the top of the stack he tossed sits a fresh new postcard with crisp edges and a message clearly written in the simple handwriting of a man: "Someone to drink with, someone to dance with, someone to travel with."

Ryan's labored steps lead him down the hallway toward the familiar hotel room where he'll finally get a reprieve for his aching, sleep-deprived body.

Without much thought, his tired eyes fall to a man with dark hair and a plaid shirt standing all the way at the end of the corridor.

He barely gives the man a second look, until he notices that he's holding a big, pink bag.

Ryan's gut sinks. When he turns the corner, his suspicions are confirmed by the sight of Lily standing at his door with her hand raised to knock.

He ignores her as he gets out his key.

"I'm guessing that's not your brother," he says without making eye contact.

Lily shakes her head no.

Ryan glances up to see that even at this early hour, Lily looks just as frazzled as him. Her hair's matted and her eyes pink and puffy with exhaustion.

"Are you okay?" he says. "Do you need to come in?"

Lily shakes her head again.

Ryan's eyes shoot to the well-groomed, 30-something man who's watching them from the end of the hallway. He makes eye contact with Jack, whose disgust is palpable. Jack sizes Ryan up, then turns and disappears around the corner.

Lily pulls an unorganized wad of cash out of her pocket and shoves it in Ryan's hand.

"It's all there," she says. "$130."

Ryan stares at the crumpled bills.

"I'm sorry," Lily says, "it's just a complicated ..."

"Don't worry about it," Ryan says. "I just wish I wasn't so stupid. I should have known more lies were coming."

Lily stares straight into his eyes. "I'm not a liar, but you're a jerk."

"I'm a jerk?" Ryan holds up a finger for emphasis. "Don't move."

He turns around and heads into his room, on a mission.

Alone in the hallway, Lily's hard facade breaks down for a moment. She fidgets nervously as she searches the corridor, locking eyes with Mila, who's giving her a stern dressing down from her cleaning cart.

Ryan returns to the door and holds his postcard in front of Lily's face. "Dear Ryan," he reads, "I write to you because we both know something - something neither of us would admit to our best friends, not even to ourselves. We …"

Lily yanks the card from his hand and tears it in half.

Ryan watches the pieces fall. He's too tired to fight.

"I really thought everything you said to me was real, every moment was real. I really believed that. Now, I know you're just as phony as those postcards."

Lily's eyes well up with tears, her lips tightening with emotion. She looks to the end of the hallway, and lowers her voice.

"If you believe those moments weren't real," she says, "then you've got bigger problems than I can fix."

"I guess I really came here to prove my dad wrong," Ryan says, "to prove there are still decent and good people in the world, who aren't just out to take advantage of me. But instead, all you did was prove my dad right."

Ryan notices that the solitary man has reappeared at the end of the hallway, and stands there solemnly staring at the ground.

"You've got someone waiting for you," he says.

With that, he shoves the wad of money back into her hand.

Lily wraps her sweater tightly around her like she's trying to disappear into a cocoon. Her tears flow freely down her cheeks now.

Defeated, she walks off down the hallway toward the man who waits to put his arm around her shoulder and lead her away.

Ryan helplessly watches them round the corner out of sight.

Suddenly, he feels someone place something in his hand. He looks down to see half a dozen mints in his palm, then glances up to find Mila standing in front of him offering a kind, nurturing smile.

She says a phrase in Russian. It's clear from Ryan's face he's struggling to make sense of it all.

Mila leans in closer, and in her broken English clarifies, "Love precious with correct person."

She closes his hand around the mints, and holds on for a second.

Ryan's silent, but his eyes reveal that there's so much going on inside his head.

"There's something I have to go do right now," he says.

Three sleek cars pull into the parking lot almost in unison, heading straight for their designated spots right in front of the building.

Three well-dressed men in fitted suits get out, and confidently push open the glass doors of Redding Corp.

Each holds in his hand a double-caf, grande latte with cream. Every word they share is either a condescending remark or an inside joke designed to exclude and demean.

They barely bother to glance toward the vast landscape of the cubicle maze on their way to their gated community of offices nestled behind protective glass.

As they chuckle over a joke that would barely even land in any other friend group, Trent suddenly stops dead in his tracks. The other two men slam into each other, caught off guard by his sudden lack of movement.

"Holy crap!" Bradley Michaels' eyes go wide. For a second, an amused smirk begins to cross his lips.

All eyes are aimed at Trent's office.

Stacked in tall towers all over the floor, desk and chairs are dozens, if not hundreds, of pink, rectangular boxes. They've been carefully, meticulously piled everywhere. Even the lampshades wear pink boxes as hats. With the door flung wide open, it's obvious that everything's pink except for a narrow pathway that winds through the office in the direction of the sturdy desk in the middle of the room.

Bradley's smirk fades when he glances across the way to his own office, and sees that it's suffered the same fate - a pink cardboard nightmare!

"Oh god!" Lorne rushes off toward his own office down the hall.

Trent slowly steps closer to the workspace where he usually finds escape and solitude, a deep feeling of dread washing over him. This was definitely, undeniably personal.

He walks the narrow pathway between boxes as if there very well could be a bomb waiting for him at the end.

Suddenly, he stops. With a disgusted groan, he picks up his foot to see that sticky frosting and smashed cake have leaked out of the boxes and become embedded in the carpet.

He's not even thinking about the fact that Bradley and Lorne are suffering the same horror, as they follow their own winding paths toward the desks they've adorned with their personal photos and chotskies.

Trent finds that his desk is strangely clean, except for the large cake box positioned perfectly in the center. He cautiously pulls open the lid.

Inside sits an entire ice cream cake that's almost completely melted into a puddle of goo. All that remains is a carefully crafted message written in baker's frosting on the top: "We know you've been cooking the books."

Next door, Bradley nervously approaches the box that rests in the center of his desk. He finds an intact ice cream cake that's also oozing and melted, with its own message written in large, sugary loops: "Insider trading is a crime."

Lorne stares at the large, rectangular box that leaks colored liquid from every corner. He slowly pulls back the lid until he's faced with a cake saturated in melted ice cream, and he can't escape the message someone really wanted him to receive: "You're just an asshole."

He removes the handwritten note that's taped to the inside of the box, and can't stop himself from reading:

"The problem isn't Phoenix or moving to a new city. The problem's not overtime or cramped cubicles, and it's not meetings that go on forever, or equipment that never works. The problem is when management loses sight of the fact that a company is more than just walls, cubicles and computers. It's a group of people who came together to create something new and exciting because they cared, hoping to maybe leave their mark on the world and build a legacy bigger than themselves. Your employees are the soul of your company, and without a soul, innovation is replaced by nothing more than maintenance."

The three men barrel into Betty Park's office and simultaneously unleash a stream of complaints. They're dressed alike, and over many years of working and playing together, they've become strangely like triplets.

In the swell of voices, Trent manages to emerge as the loudest.

"Heads are gonna roll," he says, handing Betty the handwritten note.

She carefully takes hold of the edges, dumbfounded as she tries to avoid the goo and cake smeared all over it.

She reads the words written with heartfelt emotion on yellow stationary. Then, she glances up at her three furious visitors.

"Actually," she says, "this is something I wanted to talk to you about."

Several massive trucks barrel down the narrow path that leads through the brush and shrubbery of the bayou. Branches snap in their wake, and they send water flying everywhere from the puddles they decimate.

Soon, they reach a large clearing that frames a simple, white trailer with chipping paint.

Charlie has a horrified expression as he watches the noisy vehicles clamber in.

"I still got two more week!" he shouts, rushing toward them. "I's promised two more week!"

Crystal comes running out of the trailer ready to join the cause, but she's sad to see that Charlie's fighting spirit has been replaced by a quiet acceptance. The trucks drive past him and park in front of the massive, metal boats with fans on the back.

A burly man jumps out of one of the vehicles.

"All right, boys. Let's do it."

A more subdued Charlie walks over to him.

"Dey say I got two week left," he tells the man.

The stranger hands him a stack of paperwork, and says, "You got as long as you want, buddy."

Charlie looks down to see that it's the deed to the property.

"What happened to our sign?" the man says, referencing the bullet-ridden metal strip reading Southern Tours and Adventures Inc. that's destroyed on the ground.

Charlie has other questions. "What goin' on?"

"Someone thought this business should be in your hands," the man says. "They must think very highly of you, 'cause they put out quite a lot of money on this place."

Charlie scans the paperwork that's full of complicated language, and his eyes fall to the last line: "Co-signer: Ryan Davis."

Sometimes it's when you think you have it all figured out that life throws you a curveball you never saw coming. Sometimes things happen that make everything worse, but sometimes change brings about good. Sometimes justice is actually served, and you find out someone's been paying attention to your struggle all along.

The embattled employees of Redding Corp. pause in their packing up of desks to rush toward the windows that overlook the parking lot.

They watch three men in bright red ties exit the building with their heads hanging low, carrying large cardboard boxes filled with office supplies and picture frames - with everything they've accumulated during their many years at Redding. Each of the men is accompanied by a dire-looking security guard who's braced to react should they make any sudden moves.

It's a view none of the employees has ever seen before - the Red Tie Brigade looking so deflated and helpless. A murmur of excitement begins to spread through the room.

People wonder if they're really seeing what they think they are. If their eyes are deceiving them.

Smiles break out, and a bit of nervous laughter.

Outside, Trent opens the door of his Lexus and drops his heavy box on the backseat. His door accidentally grazes the black sports car next to him. Bradley unleashes an unfiltered stream of obscenities at him.

Now the employees take in another new sight - two members of the legendary brotherhood of the Red Tie Brigade gesturing angrily at each other.

When Bradley glances over at the building and sees dozens of eyes aimed in their direction, he abruptly drops his head and jumps in his car.

Three luxury vehicles speed off across the parking lot toward the exit, as the sound of applause erupts from the building behind them.

Sometimes life's biggest curveballs end up bringing you right back to where you started in the first place. You find yourself standing on familiar ground, but seeing it through eyes that have changed somehow.

Like when Betty Parks called an emergency meeting of the board of directors of a company where she'd spent the better part of a decade climbing the ladder toward success. A success everyone told her she could never achieve.

It's a company where Betty's now responsible for the hiring of half the employees and most of the current procedure and protocol.

With the full attention of the Redding board, she stood there holding up a letter that was visibly smeared with cake frosting. Each of the board members read the letter and passed it along, leaving everyone's fingers sticky and gooey.

And then Betty presented another letter - this one announcing her immediate resignation unless some big changes took place at the company, ASAP. From the look on her face, it was obvious she meant what she said.

Charlie carefully hangs the solid wooden sign that's engraved with the words "La Bouche Swamp Tours" in its rightful spot, marking the small fleet of weather-beaten boats lined up and ready for service. He lovingly straightens the sign, then steps back to check it, adjusting it until it's just right.

As Crystal opens a crisp, new tablecloth and spreads it across the picnic table, Charlie pulls one of the boats into the open area so he can meticulously scrub it of any swamp muck that's latched on during its outings.

Crystal watches him move a towel across the boat to restore the luster of the paint.

This was his daddy's favorite swamp boat, built by hand as a young Charlie watched on to learn the ins and outs of construction.

Crystal approaches Charlie and gives him a pat on the back, offering him the homemade cajun chips he loves so much. Charlie smiles, but his attention's diverted by a modest sedan with a rental sticker in the window that's slowly coming down the path toward them.

Crystal straightens Charlie's shirt a little.

"Look like you got yerself a customer," she says.

Charlie gets an excited grin as a couple in their 60s, whose novelty shirts and fanny packs peg them as tourists, anxiously exit the car.

"Are you *the* Charlie La Bouche?" the woman asks.

"Da one an' only, ma'am."

She's relieved. "There was this man at a bar called Rusty Harpoon's who said you're the best person to talk to - about swamps," she pauses, "and life in general."

Charlie nods.

"What say we take in a li'l scenery on da swamp, an' indulge ourself in some good ol' bayou philosophy," he says.

The tourists can barely contain their excitement.

It's a peaceful evening as Larry steps onto the familiar back porch of the home he's shared with his family for almost a decade.

He stands there watching his kids, who seem happily oblivious to everything that's been going on, throw a ball around the grass.

His blank expression doesn't change when the back sliding door opens and Janet slowly makes her way across the patio.

Their eyes meet and ... he's surprised when she wraps him up in a heartfelt embrace that squeezes him from the inside out. He follows her lead and tightly engulfs her in the safety of his arms.

She leans in to whisper in his ear, "I heard about death by cake. Wow."

Larry shakes his head at the reminder. "Well, you don't have to worry about going to Phoenix anymore. I definitely took that option off the table, didn't I?"

Janet pulls him in closer. "Larry, home is where you are, and wherever that takes us, I'm willing to go."

"Honestly, I would die if it was any other way. Whatever you want is what I want."

They stand there in the comfort of each other's arms, in the backyard with the tiki lamps and modest pool that they took out a second mortgage to create as their own personal Hawaiian paradise. Deep down, they both know that no matter what path they choose, reality will soon set in. This intimate sanctuary will probably only be theirs for a little longer.

The kids play, undeterred by their parents' emotional embrace. The couple seem like they'll never let the other one go. Just holding each other. Wishing they could meld into one.

Thanks to circumstance, they know life will now change forever. Friends will be lost, and new ones gained. This home will soon be relegated to memories, the children too young to have any real knowledge of their times here. The events, both good and bad, will only exist through photos and stories told by Mom and Dad about days gone by.

The sun sets on the young family, who's gripping onto a past that's quickly disappearing, and a new, unforeseen future that's rushing headlong toward them.

Sometimes you try to outrun or avoid the curveballs coming toward you in life, but at a certain point, when you've exhausted all other options, you have no choice but to face them head on, for better or for worse.

A housekeeper matter-of-factly wipes down the mirror, disinfects the toilet and runs a vacuum across the aged carpet of a fifth-floor hotel room. With the single female occupant, a woman people called Lily, checked out and gone, the next guest will soon be arriving. She quickly swipes her arm across the top of the dresser to knock dozens of forgotten postcards into the trashcan. They fall on top of a few ornate tea bags she's already thrown away.

Down the street, the third-floor hotel room still feels like something out of a romantic movie from the 1920s, with its bronze bed posts, lacy pillows and extravagant armoire. There's a quaint breakfast table next to the bay window, and that love seat fit for Cleopatra.

When Ryan first arrived in this room, it felt foreign and intimidating, but as the days went by, it felt like he was coming home each time he put the key in the door.

"Housekeeping!" Mila knocks. "Housekeeping!"

Using her own key, she pushes the cart into the room and finds it empty and quiet, its occupant clearly gone.

In the trash can, she spots a pair of once-pristinely white sneakers that have now been sullied by a thick layer of grime. Then, something on the bed catches her eye.

She lifts the envelope and finds that it contains a healthy tip, along with a note: "You'll get more use out of this than I will. Thanks."

Mila unfolds the paper that accompanies it. It's Ryan's complimentary airline ticket, which reads: "one free, round-trip ticket to anywhere our airline flies."

Chapter 9:

"Sounds like you really screwed things up"

Ryan stares down at his wrist, where his faux-vintage watch is now safely fastened again. He looks to Marcus, who's behind the bar wearing a t-shirt that reads, "Don't pee down my back and tell me it's raining." Somehow, Ryan understands Marcus' shirts a whole lot better now.

He picks up the suitcase at his feet and turns toward the door.

"Hey," Marcus stops him. "Sorry, I know it's rough."

Ryan's surprised to hear the gruff voice expressing a halfway friendly sentiment. He nods, and gives Marcus a conciliatory look. "It's okay. I probably could have been …"

"All right," Marcus says, "let's not turn this into a make-out session."

Ryan smiles, and laughs to himself.

That's when his eyes drift past the bar, out the doors swung wide open, to the tranquility of the back patio.

It's almost a compulsion that leads him in that direction, to a table under the branches of the big tree that's made quite a mess as it's shed almost all its pink blossoms. Especially all over the table where he first met the woman in the big, floppy hat.

Ryan tries to scrape off the tiny, adhesive flowers, but finds that they're sticky and attach to his hands. Rubbing his fingers together to clean them, he takes a seat at one of the chairs that have become as familiar to him as the ones around his kitchen table back home. He pulls an ornate little packet of tea from his pocket.

The delicate lace pouch gives it the appearance of something that could have been served at a royal tea service in some exotic country, to aristocrats of great importance in an era gone by.

He opens the fragile sleeve, and slowly pulls out a single tea bag. Hanging from it is a tag that reads, "Lipton."

Just then, the opening of the front door casts light on the few drunks sitting inside at the bar. Ryan glances in to see that a young woman has entered. She's wearing an understated skirt and top, and definitely doesn't look like she came here to drink herself under the table.

She approaches Marcus, who offers up his usual sarcastic smirk. After a brief conversation, she pulls something small and rectangular out of her purse. Ryan's gut sinks.

Marcus' arm shoots in his direction.

Ryan's completely unprepared as the stranger heads onto the back patio and approaches his table with a tentative, "Hi." He can't even come up with a simple greeting in return.

"Avoid it at all costs," the woman says.

"What?"

Ryan looks down to see that the brochure advertising the desert metropolis of Phoenix, Az. is sticking out the front pocket of his suitcase.

"Oh," he says, "trust me, I've been trying to."

The woman smiles. "Maybe I'm giving it a bad rap. Actually, the desert in Phoenix can be really pretty. It's just my view of it for the past few years has been four grey walls."

"I know what you mean. Unless, of course, you're referring to prison?"

She shakes her head no and they share a laugh.

"Third cube in at Tradewinds Properties, the leader in luxury timeshare experiences," she says.

But without wanting to seem too desperate, she's staring straight at Ryan as if braced for answers.

"My name's Chloe," she says. "I got this in the mail."

Ryan jumps right in. "I'm so sorry. I know the person who wrote that, and, well ... to lay it all out there, it's a lot of bullshit."

Now tapped into his every word like he's about to reveal the meaning of life, Chloe pulls up a chair next to him.

"You know Richard Hurtz?" she says. "I've got so many questions for him. This thing has really opened my eyes. It's like he already knows me. How does he know me?"

Ryan winces. "Did you say Richard Hurtz?"

"Yeah, it's like we've lived the same lives."

Ryan takes a deep breath.

"It's a fake name," he says, "a joke name."

Chloe's processing the information, and Ryan's now in competition with a flood of thoughts and questions going on in her head.

"Dick Hurts?" he says, twirling his hand around to encourage her to understand.

"Oh." Chloe puts her hand to her mouth. "Oh god!"

She looks inside to Marcus, who shrugs his shoulders.

"Not to make this worse ..." Ryan points to himself. "Dick Hurts."

Chloe's clearly struggling to process this information.

"So wait, you wrote this?" she says. "How do you know so much about me?"

Ryan wouldn't even be able to describe the twisting and turning going on in his stomach at having this young woman sit right where he once sat and ask the same questions he did.

When she makes eye contact with him, it's obvious in her intensity that she's laying all her hopes and dreams right at his feet - not much different than how he laid them at Lily's that first day in New Orleans.

His face flushes with humiliation. "Listen, I'm really sorry. I didn't think about - Okay, I wasn't thinking at all. I'm sorry."

Chloe looks down at the postcard, then directly at Ryan. "I don't understand. Why did you pick me?"

The question came out of Ryan's own mouth not so long ago, and the response was philosophy and riddles that, in the end, only led to more questions. But he's starting to realize that maybe the situation wasn't that much different for Lily than it is for him right now, and it's much scarier than he ever imagined.

"I'm suddenly feeling shitty in more ways than one," he says. "I'm sorry, but this is probably not what you want to hear."

Chloe holds up the postcard in front of him.

"I spent two years saving up to go to Australia, and now I've spent that money to come here. I traveled 1,500 miles for this," she says. "I need this not to be bullshit."

Through the bar, there's the faint sound of a honking cab outside. Ryan's eyes shoot to the front door, then back to Chloe, whose intense stare isn't letting him go.

"Please," she says, "tell me this is not bullshit."

Lily glances over to find that Jack's watching her. With a nod, he gently but adamantly encourages her to keep looking for her overstuffed bag on the crowded luggage conveyor belt.

In the busy airport hub, travelers crowd around the belt waiting for their suitcases or duffle bags to appear. Lily's barely even noticing. Her eyes have drifted upward to the bright screen positioned just over the ticket counter, which displays an assortment of travel destinations: Flight 425 to Albuquerque, Flight 710 to Denver, three separate flights to Mexico.

A piercing shriek suddenly breaks Lily's focus.

She looks to the other side of the luggage carousel to find a red-faced little girl throwing herself on the ground in a full-fledged temper tantrum. Things didn't go the way she wanted and she's making a big scene, screaming out her frustration to a bunch of strangers.

Her embarrassed father looks on, his cheeks flushed with helplessness. He tries to console the girl, but it's just no use. She's out of control.

Lily's startled to see that Jack's now standing behind her.

"I need to ask you," he says, "and I want the truth. Was there more than just friendship between you?"

Lily doesn't have the energy anymore. She turns her tired gaze in his direction, and their eyes silently meet.

"Please, wait!" Ryan shouts as Chloe rushes down the tourist-filled street.

He has to push and shove his way through the crowd to try to catch her.

"No," she says, "this is so embarrassing."

Her cheeks wet with tears, she can barely contain the crushing emotions - the silliness of the journey, the money wasted.

"You know what my friends are going to say when I get back?" she says. "Oh my god, I look like such an idiot."

Ryan works hard to close the gap between them.

"Believe me," he says, "I know exactly how you feel."

"Susan is never gonna let me hear the end of it. She told me this was a scam. She's never right about anything, never. But now ..."

Ryan finally catches her and blocks her path, forcing scores of people to flow around them.

"I understand every word you're saying. I understand more than you know, okay?"

She finally looks into his eyes, which are genuine, and filled with pain.

"Except I kept lying to myself that it was real - probably screwing myself in more ways than I know how to fix, all because of something somebody wrote on a stupid little postcard," he says. "And my advice is to throw that thing away as soon as you can. It was just me shouting to the world because I was angry and frustrated, and, unfortunately, you're the one who got shouted at, and I'm sorry about that. The woman who wrote mine was probably shouting at me, too. But I've realized that just because someone's pointing out all the problems, doesn't mean they have the answers."

He looks to Chloe, and there's a deep sadness in her eyes that unfortunately reminds him of that moment in the hallway, and the unbearable hurt so visible on another woman's face. A sadness that's stayed with him every moment since.

What he doesn't reveal to Chloe is that deep inside his suitcase, carefully reassembled using several strips of tape, is the postcard he received in the mail so many months ago, signed by Wendy Breezes.

"Okay," he says, "I'm being harsh, I'm sorry. It's just, if she didn't have the answers I was demanding, I definitely don't have any to give you. I'm just trying to save you from the disappointment."

Chloe's not sure whether to keep walking, or to give this jerk any more of her time.

"And how are you gonna do that?" she asks.

"I have no idea. I'll pay for your trip. The whole thing. Every penny. That's a start, right?"

Annoyed tourists flow around the two, who have become a bottleneck on the crowded street.

Chloe reluctancy pulls a pen from her purse.

"Every penny," she says.

She scribbles her name and address. Before she hands the paper to Ryan, she stops. Although she's a little afraid of the answer, she asks anyway.

"There are millions of names in the phone book. Why mine?"

Ryan pauses for a moment, then takes the slip of paper from her hand.

"Honestly? Because your name was attached to the one place you told me to avoid - Phoenix." He kind of laughs. "Stupid, huh?"

Chloe finally manages a chuckle. "Yes, very stupid."

She looks into his eyes, which plead for forgiveness. There's no malice, nothing to gain, just a simple guy who's trying to fix a wrong.

"But I kinda get it," she says.

Ryan finally feels like he can take a breath. He holds up the piece of paper.

"Every penny, I promise."

Chloe also takes a deep breath, wiping her cheeks.

"You don't have to do that," she tells him. "I just … I just need to process all of this."

"Let me show you around. There's this awesome graveyard. Oh, and a restaurant with this dancing waiter …"

"No," Chloe says. "I think I'm going home."

Ryan nods, trying with all his might to avoid saying something stupid.

"And from what you've told me, so should you," she says. "Sounds like you really screwed things up."

Ryan's a little surprised by the comment, but finally nods, knowing she's right.

The crowd continues to flow around them, now almost indifferent as if they grew out of the sidewalk years ago, or have just always been there. The two look at one another, both confused about how to feel about the other, or where to go from here.

Ryan holds up the small piece of paper with her name and address on it.

"Every penny," he says.

Jack pulls into the familiar driveway almost by rote, his mind clearly elsewhere.

"So there was nothing more to it?" he says. "I have nothing to worry about?"

Lily shakes her head. "Jack, you need to let this go. I already answered you."

Her eyes stare out the front windshield to the neglected older home with the overgrown brush that seems like it's from another lifetime.

Jack nods that he understands. Realizing he's pushing the issue too hard, he accepts her answer, and gets out of the car.

Now briefly alone, Lily gazes up at the empty suburban tract home. In an oddly defensive way, she cinches her purse closed.

"Come on," Jack yells.

Lily nods okay, but she grasps her bag a little tighter.

Before she gets out, she takes one quick, deep breath. Little does Jack know that before they left her hotel room for the last time, she managed to retrieve from the pile of card stock in the trashcan one single postcard. It was crumpled and bent, and covered with some food stains. She now keeps it buried deep in the bottom of her purse, hidden from view.

It reads: "What you really need is someone to drink with, someone to dance with, someone to travel with."

The cookie-cutter metallic building stands in a cookie-cutter industrial park that's marked by a large sign reading "Redding Corporation." It's decorated with a few strategically placed trees to heighten its "green" image.

Every day, hundreds of employees have to maneuver around a bulky, silver piece of art that was unveiled a few years back with balloons and cake, but has since attracted every annoying bird in the area.

In the early morning sunlight, a jet-lagged Ryan stops just outside the large, perfectly polished glass doors that lead into Redding. It used to be at this point that he would always pause and pretend to entertain the idea of turning around and just driving as far away as he could.

He heads inside just like he has a thousand times before, passing the receptionist, who throws out, "Welcome back," as he passes. He travels a hallway that's stripped of its framed awards proclaiming "Best Local Business" and "Chamber of Commerce Bright Star."

Passing faces that seem dismayed or, at best, confused, he reaches the heart of the cubicle maze, where dismantled computers clutter the walkway.

He finds Larry, Pokorski and Monica loading their belongings into the empty boxes that have been provided to them. There's something strangely jovial between them, a lighter mood than he would have expected. Even as they lug their belongings, they're joking around and teasing.

Ryan sets down his suitcase, and when that doesn't get their attention, subtly clears his throat. Everyone looks at him, and their laughter stops. The gravity he had expected now seems to overtake them.

"Did something happen I don't know about?" Ryan asks.

"Yeah," Larry says, "you could say that."

No one moves to greet Ryan. Instead, they go back to loading their boxes and cleaning out their cubes.

"So," he says, "I'm gonna go talk to Betty Parks, see if there's something I can work out."

"Good for you," Larry says.

"I'm gonna talk to her about the team, as well," Ryan says.

The group chuckles.

"I don't think she's gonna be too receptive to that, buddy," Larry says.

"What does that mean?"

Another voice comes from behind. "Excuse me, sir ..."

Ryan doesn't hear it. He's just noticed that hanging from one of the sprinkler heads on the ceiling is a limp, listless red tie.

"Um, I think you're being beckoned," Larry tells him.

Ryan turns around to see a man standing there.

"Excuse me, Ryan, but Ms. Parks would like to see you."

Ryan nods, and follows Betty Parks' assistant down the hall.

As they approach the executive offices, he begins to see something odd up ahead - a splash of color where it shouldn't be.

"What the hell?" he says.

"Yeah," the assistant says, "you missed a lot while you were gone."

Ryan stares into an office window that's almost entirely obscured by bright pink cardboard boxes smudged with gooey cake frosting.

Betty Parks settles into her high-backed executive chair and gives Ryan a long, thoughtful look.

"I was told you cashed out your 401K," she says. "I didn't think I'd be seeing your face in here again."

Ryan nods. "I guess you could say I'm diversifying a little. You're looking at an investor in a small business in New Orleans." He pauses. "Why do I get the vibe that I've missed out on a few things?"

Betty gets a slight smile. "A little. There's been a reorganization of staff. Bradley, Trent and Lorne will no longer be with the company. Those seats are now empty, and will remain that way. Each department head will report directly to me from now on. No more middle men."

Ryan takes a second to process the information.

Betty holds up some documents.

"I have two offer letters for Phoenix here for the members of your team. Since I was under the impression I wasn't going to see you again anytime soon, I was about to go out there and present them myself. But I have a feeling they'd much rather hear it from you."

Betty slides the papers toward Ryan. She can already sense his hesitation, and her face flushes with a bit of frustration.

"You know, I spent nine years struggling for everything I have at this company, fighting tooth and nail to get where I am, and here you are just getting it handed to you, and I can't for the life of me decipher why someone would possibly turn that down."

In the sunlight of late afternoon, Lily and Jack stand on the front porch of a simple home with a gable roof that's surrounded by overgrown trees. Old newspapers clutter the steps.

Lily looks out on the dead, brown grass with the distant stare of a kid who's been pulled away from playing with friends to have Sunday dinner at her great aunt's house.

When Jack unlocks the door, it unleashes an awful stench. He scrambles to open the windows, but it really doesn't help. Lily's attempts to flip on the light switch don't work either, thanks to an overdue electric bill.

But the filtered light from outside reveals a house that clearly, to a family, was a home.

A brown, leather couch bears permanent dents from where a mother, father and daughter would spend Sunday afternoons binge-watching their favorite shows. The door jam's carefully marked with pencil lines that measure years of a child's growth.

It's not a perfect place by any means. There are papers stacked here and there, shoes on the floor, a rug that's a little tattered from foot traffic. Look closely and you might find a few potato chip crumbs on the old TV tray next to the couch that stands out because of the bright red flowers all over it, that a 4-year-old insisted they buy more than 20 years ago.

The fireplace mantel's lined with a hodgepodge of frames that never quite went together, but it doesn't matter, because it's what's inside that's important. A rustic wooden frame holds a picture of a middle-aged couple with a young girl standing between them, a giant waterfall in the background. Next to it, inside a simple gold frame, sits a more professional portrait of an adult woman alongside the same couple.

Looking around, it's obvious this is the type of place in which we embed our memories, and over the years become scared to change, or worry the changes will cause our memories to fade. So we hang onto the tacky umbrella lamp Mom inexplicably loved, or the clumsy coffee table Dad built himself in the garage. They deemed them important, so we deem them important.

Lily stares down at a button on her sweater.

Jack's already moved into the kitchen to shove old casseroles and spoiled milk into a trash bag, in a desperate attempt to ward off the disgusting smell. On the door of the fridge hangs a child's drawing that dates back almost 20 years. It's held on by mismatched magnets, some shaped as letters of the alphabet.

Lily slowly makes her way into the room that's locked in time. A moldy burrito sits half eaten on the counter and grimy dishes clutter the sink. Open on the kitchen table is a real estate magazine in which she's circled pictures of several houses. The caption under one reads: "Starter home - cozy but needs work. Perfect for a young couple."

Lily finally looks to Jack. As he pulls the engorged garbage bag closed, he returns her gaze.

"You're doing good," he says.

Even though he's trying to remain optimistic, he's frustrated when he sees no emotion on her face. She doesn't say anything, but she nods.

Pokorski moves with more speed than he's mustered in a long time. Through the cubicle maze, around the executive offices, past the office supply closet and down the hall. He bursts into accounting, out of breath but all smiles, only to find an empty chair where Monica usually sits. When he looks to the other women, they all shrug their shoulders.

Pokorski can't hide his huge grin as he finally reaches the break room and finds Monica at the counter with her back to him.

"Holy cow!" he says. "You're never gonna believe this twist!"

Monica turns around, and her expression says that she wants to scoop him up in her arms. "What is it, baby?"

Before he can get it out, he notices a subtle pink hue to her normally vibrant eyes. There's the slightest smudge in her blush, and a tissue she conceals in her hand.

"What's wrong?" he asks.

"Don't you worry about me," Monica replies. "I wanna hear your news."

Pokorski looks right into her eyes. "Come on, spill it."

Reluctantly, Monica points to the long break room table, where a single pink cake box sits starkly in the middle.

"That's mine," she says.

Pokorski groans.

Monica tries to pull herself together. "You handled it like a man," she says, "so should I. Who wants to go to Phoenix anyway, right? At least we've got each other. Now, what's your news?"

Larry haphazardly shoves the offer letter into his pocket.

"Uh, how about a thank you?" Ryan says.

"How about a thank you?" Larry says. "You know what, that's your biggest problem. The whole time, you think you're doing this for us. Even if I were to take this offer, I'm not doing it for you. I'm not doing it for Redding, either. I'm doing it for me and my family, and all that matters is what's the best move for us. And you need to start doing the same. You've got a dead weight around your neck that you cling to like it's a life preserver, but all it's doing is drowning you."

Ryan knocks for the third time on the faded door of a trailer that stands out from all the others, not because of age or nature's wrath, but simply because of neglect. Because someone either didn't care or couldn't muster the will.

At the center of a crowded mobile home park with a sign that's fallen off the hinges, it's the type of trailer where no one bothers to stop by to borrow a cup of sugar anymore.

Ryan finally hears footsteps approaching the aged door, which opens to reveal the resident.

"You still need to get those glasses fixed, Dad," Ryan says. "I gave you money for that."

Still wearing his tattered old work shirt with the logo for Leonardi and Son's Auto Repair and Body Shop, a company that employed him for less than a month about 10 years back, Al adjusts his cracked eyeglasses.

"Welcome back, jet setter."

Ryan's not happy with his father's mocking tone. He enters the trailer that's cluttered with frozen food containers, failed lottery tickets and dirty laundry.

He sets down a bag of subs from an Italian deli down the street, as Al lowers himself into his worn 1970s recliner with the rip across the back.

"Have you taken out the garbage recently?" Ryan says, recognizing an all-too familiar smell.

With Al struggling to get his recliner to adjust, Ryan begins loading old wrappers and junk mail into a trash bag.

Al just watches him, almost a bit of disdain in his eyes. He grabs a postcard from the small table next to his chair.

With clear annoyance in his voice, he begins to read:

"Dear Dad, You might be a little surprised and concerned when I don't show up for my normal Tuesday evening visit. Honestly, I'm a little surprised, too. There's a part of me that says you may not see me on Tuesdays for a while. For years I've been convincing myself I'm taking a step forward, only to realize I've been going in circles. Sometimes I feel like I've been working so hard to fulfill two people's visions of my future, that I haven't even stopped to figure out what I want that to be. But when something came up out of the blue and led me halfway across the country, I think I might have found it - in New Orleans, sitting at a back table under a small tree, shaded and obscured by a big hat. Sometimes life just gets so busy that you have to step away, and you know better than anyone when it's your time. Maybe it's my time."

Al looks up at his son, his eyes unsympathetic.

"So I guess you came to your senses," he says. "A guy who's been swept away usually doesn't show up with crappy sub sandwiches on a Tuesday afternoon."

Ryan's unresponsive.

"Why so quiet?" Al prods.

For a moment, Ryan looks like an eruption is about to burst from deep within him.

"Aw," Al says, "don't let your emotions get the best of you."

"Dad, I just feel ..."

"Feel? We don't feel. We should be thinking."

Silently, Ryan cinches the garbage bag closed.

"Uh, the company I work for is relocating to Phoenix, Dad."

Al takes in the news. "So you telling me we're gonna be short on money for awhile?"

"No, Dad. They want me to go."

Al sits forward in his chair as if someone's directly challenged him.

"Good riddance to them," he says. "We'll take our chances here."

"It's a really good package," Ryan says.

For a second, Al examines his son. He's evaluating his demeanor, his concerning tone. He can't believe he has to teach this lesson again.

"You know they're just gonna pay you pennies on the dollar for your soul," he says.

"They offered me a promotion."

Al adjusts in his chair, and his eyes are more serious. If there's one thing he won't tolerate, it's his perceived corruption of his son.

"Wow," he says, "they really got in your head."

"I don't know, Dad. I just thought, I'm not getting any younger. This might be a good opportunity. It's not like I wouldn't visit you, and you couldn't visit me."

"You know I don't have that kind of cash to go around globe-trotting." Al's voice is strained. "Oh, they're always full of those pie-in-the-sky promises, aren't they? They know just what to say. Remember that start-up that tried to steal you away?"

"Google?"

"Yeah. Whatever happened to them?"

"They're actually doing pretty well," Ryan says.

"And that Texas one, too. You would've been lost in a company that big."

"Yep," Ryan says, "there was the one in Texas."

Al clearly has something on his mind.

"Now don't get all riled up about this," he says. "Don't freak out or anything, but I need some help. I need $1200 for some unexpected bills that came up."

He waits for Ryan's typical overblown reaction, signaled by the tightness in his face, but Ryan just walks over and starts wiping down the kitchen counter.

"Okay, Dad," he says, "I'll take care of it."

The voices in the other room are muffled, but Lily can just make out a few words here and there. While they're not mean, they're definitely not kind, either.

Murmurs of the spoiled little girl who ran away. The spoiled little girl who turned everyone's lives upside down.

Lily's trying to stall in the entryway of this all-too-familiar house as long as she can.

"This is too soon," she says.

Jack looks like he's struggling to get something out.

"Listen," he finally says, "reception was really bad out there that horrible night. I'll never stop being sorry about that. I wish I could have been there for your call, when you needed me. I'll never let it happen again. Ever. But … now it's time to move forward."

Lily just stares straight ahead.

"I'm not ready for this," she mutters under her breath.

Realizing she hasn't heard a word he's said, Jack gives her a look.

"It doesn't matter anymore," he says. "These people deserve better."

Heading into the living room, he announces, "We're here."

From the reception he receives, it's clear he's won the hearts of Lily's extended family - aunts, uncles and cousins.

Lily finally takes the few steps around the corner, and stands in full view of her family. They're almost immediately plunged into stunned silence. They quickly try to hide the fact that, for a moment, they looked as though they had seen a ghost. A woman whose appearance almost, but doesn't quite, match what they remember. Her hair slightly longer than she ever wore it, features slightly more mature. And a frame that's thinner than they've ever seen it.

Anxious to break the awkward silence, an older woman finally heads in Lily's direction.

"We're just pleased as punch that you're home safe where you belong," Aunt Jessica tells her.

For a moment, they stand face to face. Aunt Jessica finally moves in to embrace her wayward niece. While it's a loving embrace, it's one that also suggests some trust has been broken.

Once they've separated, the only thing that remains is the painful silence.

"Well, I've made some sandwiches and cookies," Aunt Jessica says. "How about we all have a bite?"

The group agrees, more to end the discomfort than out of any real hunger.

Sitting on the couch with a plate of half-eaten cookies, Lily tries to keep her eyes locked on anything in the room besides the other people - the faces she's known her entire life who almost feel like strangers now.

Jack is just the opposite. Even though it's only through whispers, everyone seems to console him, as though what happened a year ago doesn't excuse the actions of their runaway niece. As though their hearts broke right along with the brave young man who still wears his pain on his sleeve. The man who kept the family, not even his family, informed and hopeful as they searched in vain to find her.

Out the corner of her eye, Lily spots Aunt Jessica on her way over again. The woman with the kind eyes cautiously sits down next to her and hands her a glass of milk.

"You always had to have milk with my cookies, always." Aunt Jessica smiles. "You had such procedure. Dunk the cookie, bite the cookie, then a sip of milk. Repeat. You always had your little rules for everything."

Lily forces a smile, but those days seem very far away.

Aunt Jessica's smile disappears just as quickly as it surfaced, and Lily knows what's coming next.

"Everyone's had a hard time with this, most of all you," Aunt Jessica says, "so no one blames you for, well, for taking a break."

She waits for Lily's response, but the awkward silence suggests one won't be coming.

"That was the most dangerous road," Aunt Jessica says. "I swear, they should just close that part of the highway altogether. And you know them, they were off to help someone come hell or high water. They were such good souls."

Lily feels the sharp sting of an anger she's worked hard to suppress. Although her face doesn't show it, a turmoil brews inside. She nods in agreement, but the thoughts in her head say something very different.

Of course they were off helping someone - some pathetic person who should have been helping themselves. They wasted so much time worrying about strangers. Social workers who saw themselves as the guardians of the world. If only they had put themselves and their family first just one time.

If she's honest with herself, Lily would admit there's only one postcard she'd give anything to be able to write, but unfortunately, the recipients are already gone. She would have loved to hear the two people she cherished the most recount stories about some exotic adventure, where they overindulged on strange delicacies and explored quaint little shops full of foreign trinkets.

As Lily retreats into her head, Aunt Jessica puts on an understanding smile and gives her niece a gentle pat on the knee.

"I best go check on everyone," she says. "You never know who might need some milk."

Her aunt's departure disturbs Lily's thoughts.

Glancing around, the house remains exactly as she re-members it. As a kid, it was fun and filled with personality, but now, through adult eyes, it merely reflects her aunt's quirky, old-fashioned tastes in the old, painted plates that hang on the wall and the dozens of porcelain figurines that have their very own shelving unit.

"Sweetheart," a man's voice interrupts.

When he sits down next to her, it's the first thing that's actually brought an authentic, though slight, smile to Lily's face.

"Hi, Uncle George," she says.

She makes eye contact with the man who always had the best corny jokes to tell, and would humor her as a little girl with endless, obvious card tricks.

His face says it all. Sorry. Sorry for your loss, sorry for our loss. Life is not fair. I wish I could take away the pain.

"How are you?" he asks. "How you holding up?"

"I hear the Braves had a good year. Do you still have your annual seats?"

There's a little surprise on Uncle George's face. "They've held their own, honey. Thanks for asking."

Lily nods in a way that tells him there's not much more to say at the moment. He gives her the gentlest of kisses on the forehead, and heads back to the family gathered in the kitchen.

They make their way over one by one, trying to console, trying to empathize, trying to say magic words that will make the grief go away.

Each of them acting as if her parents were merely the victims of a bad situation, something that happened to them out of nowhere. When in reality, they didn't have to be out there at all.

Lily feels the pressure building again. Why did they take those chances? Why weren't they just content to live their lives as two retired people with a loving daughter and no more mortgage to pay?

They should have been spending that night eating popcorn and watching one of those stupid horror movies they loved so much, instead of recklessly driving off into the biggest storm of the year.

Lily's tears, and memories, can no longer be contained.

It was June and her mom was probably all emotional about the details of someone's personal quicksand, and Dad was listening to her go on and on when he should have been watching the road.

Around the dangerous curves of State Route 8, the winding road took them along the banks of the Cuyahoga River, what the Iroquois called the "crooked river."

But they probably weren't even looking at the twists and turns of the water, because, of course, they were talking. According to Lily, they were always talking. Meanwhile, she felt like she could never get a word in edgewise. She felt like she'd have to be on fire to get attention.

She always thought she'd have to be one of those sad souls who were losing their homes, or failing at marriage, or struggling with money. The ones who mattered.

But lately, she's starting to think that her memories might just be those of a spoiled little girl who got all the attention in the world, but it wasn't enough. Who was jealous to see them focus on anyone but her. The memory of a girl who had it better than any other girl she knew, and now has to sit here and know that they're gone.

State Route 8 was the worst road in the county and the rain was coming down in sheets.

Meanwhile, Lily was watching the clock at home. They said they'd be back by five.

What started as a small argument quickly escalated, as they often do, into a heated discussion that made her dad take his eyes off the road. It was one of those fights that both parties would deem silly the next day, or just forget about.

He wrestled the car back onto the road a few times. He probably didn't see the grove of trees through the foggy windshield that would soon become shards of razor-sharp glass piercing the car's interior.

Lily thought they'd be home by five. Instead, she got a call at one in the morning.

Right away, she tried to reach Jack. She called his cell phone for hours, but he was on a camping trip with his friends and there was no way to reach him.

Lily saw her parents' ashen faces and made the identification. She left the morgue with nothing more than a random collection of their wedding rings, cracked eyeglasses, her dad's weathered leather wallet, and her mother's small, beige purse with the gold buckle on the front, all of which she hastily shoved into her big pink bag.

After that, she never went home again. She never looked back, never drove the same streets. Never used her real name again.

Ryan shakes the computer mouse a little to prod it into functioning correctly, as he scans through so many reports and memos he missed during his "vacation."

As soon as he tries to move the cursor to the top of the screen, it freezes again. He curses under his breath and tries to force activity on the screen.

Lifting the mouse to check out its inner workings, hoping to see something shoved in there or some kind of obvious malfunction, he stops himself.

With an exasperated breath, his eyes turn to the hallway. If he ever returned to the life of a schlub, a cubicle jockey, he was given a sworn promise by a beautiful woman on a rooftop that she would slap the mouse out of his hand and whisk him away from it all.

He's a little jumpy when a figure appears in the doorway - Betty Parks holding a stack of paperwork.

"I know you have a lot on your mind," she says, noticing his distracted expression, "but we really need your signature on these documents. Without that, we can't move forward."

"All we need is your signature," the bank manager says. "You understand our system relies on habits and frequency of activity, and with several of them being joint accounts …"
Dressed in his usual suit and tie, Mike glances over at Lily, who's absentmindedly staring out the window at the bank parking lot.

He interrupts the manager. "I gotta imagine this is an easy fix."

That's the advantage of having your lifelong family lawyer do the talking. He knows the ins and outs of the law and doesn't scare easily. It was Mike who started Lily's first college fund, and talked her bleeding-heart parents out of falling for several charity scams over the years.

"Yes, of course, sir," the bank manager says. "It was just flagged as stolen. As a precaution, all the accounts were frozen. I apologize for the inconvenience."

The manager now directs his comments to Lily.

"In the future," he tells her, "use traveler's checks when you travel, or every time you get to a new location, contact the bank so we can make a notation on your account. Now, I'll just need to see some ID."

Lily doesn't move.

"Uh, you wanna pay attention here?" Mike prompts.

She distractedly shuffles through her purse, pulling out her wallet, brochures, pamphlets and keys.

"Is this it?" Mike says, holding up her license.

Lily shakes off her distraction and hands it to the bank manager.

The manager's reading her file. "Wow, miss. You're quite the jet setter. You've been everywhere. Hawaii, Thailand, the Mexican Riviera. Must be great to be so free to roam around like that. Nothing tying you down."

Mike's expression says he doesn't share this man's enthusiasm.

"So this won't happen again?" Lily asks.

"Not as long as you follow protocol."

As Lily follows Mike out of the bank, he leans in toward her.

"Listen, there's good news here. The house is settled, the estate is settled. There's no reason you can't get right back into your own life now, pick up where you left off."

Lily nods, and keeps walking.

With the trees trimmed and a fresh view of what used to be a fairly nice backyard, Lily squats down so she can begin the long, tedious process of removing all the weeds that have taken hold as if they own the place.

This has always been her least favorite household chore. Dad used to do it, except after the knee surgery that had him out of commission for awhile.

As she tugs at a particularly stubborn piece of crabgrass, her hand slips and pulls off part of her rubber gardening glove. From the skin that's exposed, she notices that her hands are worse for wear and dirty, despite the gloves.

But she was given a promise. A sworn promise on a rooftop that a young man with a kind smile would never let her end up in this situation. That he would show up to save her.

She rubs her sore palm, tired from a long day's work.

When she hears the screen door open, she sees Jack walking across the brittle, brown grass. She barely has time to think before he's standing in front of her.

"You know …" he starts. What's about to come out of his mouth isn't easy for him. He doesn't normally share his feelings. "Sometimes I'm a guy who wants to live inside the box. I like to live by guidelines, but you know what, my guidelines aren't necessarily your guidelines. My rules aren't necessarily your rules. That's why I found you so damn irresistible in the first place. You do things differently. And I have to be more open to your way of doing things."

A shell-shocked Lily doesn't react.

Jack pulls out a small box, and from it a ring with a Princess Cut diamond. It's taken him a long time to get up the nerve, but he tries to play it off calmly.

"I was hoping you would put this back on," he says.

Lily slowly pulls herself up from the ground and removes her remaining rubber glove. She rubs her hands together to make sure they're clean. Then, she takes the familiar ring from Jack's hand.

Rolling it around between her fingers, she can clearly see from the way the light sparkles off the diamond that Jack's had it cleaned.

"Two words," Jack says. "'I do,' and you seal the deal."

Chapter 10:

"And ya still don't believe in magic?"

A backwater version of "When The Saints Go Marching In" fills the air and drifts out over the twisted cypress trees that line the murky banks of the Louisiana swamp.

The late afternoon sun peeks between branches to create a dancing pattern across dark green water that's covered in lily pads. Serenading the scene is a chorus of croaking frogs and chirping crickets.

Someone's gone to a lot of trouble to string white Christmas lights from Charlie and Crystal's trailer to the surrounding trees. They've also lined up dozens of folding chairs that have already been filled with eager guests. Those who couldn't find seats are willing to stand in the back.

Crates have been stacked into a makeshift stage in the front, and there's a plastic Jesus propped up in the dirt, which prompts a passerby's emotional outburst of, "Dis a sacred day!"

Down the aisle comes rushing Charlie, distracted and concerned in his outdated powder blue suit.

"Come on, ya gotta get up dere," an audience member nudges.

"I know it," Charlie says. "I just got one more ting I gotta do."

On the stage stands Rev. Leonard, a laid-back man of the cloth in a concert t-shirt who normally gives his fiery sermons from a water-side shack of a church marked with a cross he nailed together himself.

"It okay, Charlie!" he yells. "She gonna love it!"

Charlie hurries toward the stage, still muttering, "I jus' wanna make it da best eva."

He steps up to take his place and gaze out on the smiling faces of his many guests. In a testament to his gregarious nature, the audience represents every race, creed and religion - ranging from Bob the mechanic to the polished bar owner from the French Quarter. But one face is noticeably missing. Charlie's contented smile fades a little.

With a tinge of disappointment, his eyes fall to Rufus, who wears his usual droopy expression topped off with a big black bow tie.

Suddenly, Charlie's eyes shoot to the back of the crowd and he breaks out into a huge smile. Framed by a simple archway, late but looking dashing in his tailored suit, Ryan straightens his tie and smooths his jacket as he surveys the scene.

Charlie nods to indicate a seat in the third row. Careful not to disrupt the moment, Ryan makes his way down the aisle, playing it cool even as he's keenly aware that several female guests have taken notice of the young city boy in the well-fitted jacket.

Realizing maybe he's slightly overdressed, he settles in next to a man with the same winning, slack-jawed smile as Charlie, who he assumes must be some kind of cousin.

"Ya'll ready fer da big moment?" the band leader yells.

The crowd breaks into an enthusiastic chorus of hoots and hollers.

A surprisingly skilled country guitar signals Crystal's march down the aisle on the arm of her father. Everyone turns to look, and someone whistles a cat call, in their world meant with the utmost respect. Crystal nods her gratitude.

She's a vision in her homemade white wedding gown and frilly eye patch, a thick layer of blue eye shadow to mark the importance of the event.

At Crystal's side walks a man with a genuine smile who's a product of this bayou and all that goes along with it. In his camouflaged baseball cap and worn, baggy blue jeans, he limps at his daughter's side with great effort, but nothing would stop him from making his way down the aisle. Nothing's ever been able to slow him down, not even the harsh realities of this Louisiana swampland where he's toiled for decades.

Ryan glances around at the crowd, then back at the stage where Crystal's Romeo awaits her, looking every bit the romantic lead in his 1970s, hand-me-down suit with the wide collar. Charlie and Crystal are beautiful in the most unconventional of ways, a perfect fit for their Southern-with-a-touch-of-blues surroundings.

As soon as they're within 10 feet of each other, the couple kick up sparks. They could break out in a make-out session or a fist fight, and either one would be evenly matched.

There's a truth and brutal honesty to their go-to-the-bathroom-with-the-door-open kind of relationship. Nothing hidden, nothing secret.

The band kicks in - three guys straight out of the deep, back woods wearing overalls, cowboy boots and straw hats. With the sophistication of a jug band, they strum a fiddle, steel guitar and harmonica in a down-home jig. It's a rag-tag group of old buddies who've learned a countrified version of rock-n-roll during post-church rehearsals in their bootleg cellars.

Crystal's daddy escorts her to her designated spot and sends her off with a sweet kiss.

Now, a young boy approaches Charlie with careful, measured footsteps. His suit and tie make him one of the most well-dressed at the ceremony. Delicately nestled in the center of the frilly ring pillow he's holding lies Crystal's prized possession, a sparkly glass eye. The crowd "ooohs" and "aawws," though several people cringe at the strange sight of the eye resting on top of the pillow.

Charlie, however, watches over it protectively.

The boy's obedient in his important duty, until his eyes get bigger and he's struck by something that seems to be out of his control. When his nose twitches, the whole audience holds its collective breath. Despite his best efforts, the ring bearer lurches forward in a sneeze that jolts him from head to toe. A visible mist falls upon the glass eye.

The audience squirms with discomfort.

Crystal's doing her best to maintain her polished, "It's-my-wedding-day-dammit!" smile. With a quick wipe from his jacket, the ring bearer has the situation under control, and the hand-off to Charlie is complete.

Crystal lifts her veil and turns away from the audience. The crowd's restless, waiting to see the bride in all her glory.

After some wiggling and maneuvering, Crystal turns back to face Charlie with two vibrant, green eyes. He's a man completely overtaken by love.

The crowd lets out a gasp suitable for Miss America, and Crystal's almost standing fully upright for the first time since an 11-year-old girl lost the sense of being a complete human being. With her better posture, her wedding dress smooths out like fine silk.

Crystal's young and pretty because her adoring audience sees her that way. Because Charlie has always seen her that way. Because, in this light, she can finally see it herself.

She gazes upon the crowd, beaming with pride and confidence. There's no eye makeup where her patch used to be.

The happy crowd's unleashed to celebrate the momentous day with some good, rowdy fun.

"One, two and a three," says the conductor as he attempts to lead the band holding the end of a fishing pole as his baton. The guys struggle to interpret his moves, swigging beer in between songs.

Charlie and Crystal greet the eclectic menagerie of guests. They all know each other, and have for years, and it's a comfortable family atmosphere complete with a spread of cajun cooking fit for an army.

Ryan's about to join the receiving line, but stops to allow two older ladies to cut in front of him. They awkwardly giggle like schoolgirls at the chivalrous gesture from the handsome newcomer.

"Why," one of them says with a put-on charm, "aren't you the perfect gentleman."

Ryan's distracted as he spots a large, floppy hat in the crowd. Everything else suddenly becomes background noise.

Whoever's under that hat has sophisticated movements that suggest she's not homegrown. She's moving easily through the crowd, greeting people with cordial nods.

So many times, Ryan's replayed his last moment with Lily - how he tried to hold it together in a hotel doorway while her eyes begged him for any hint of the former magic that seemed to be compelling them toward each other, but he withheld it.

He follows the woman through the large group. It's hard not to lose her with so many people bustling around and so much activity.

"I want ya'll ta encourage dis couple in dey first dance as man and wife." All eyes turn to the stage, where Rev. Leonard rallies the crowd in his concert t-shirt.

The spectators let out another long "aww" as they part to form a circle around the newlyweds. Charlie and Crystal stand facing each other, the air heavy with emotion.

"Okay, boys," the conductor shouts, "this time, give it some oomph, like a possum dun crawl up yer drawers!"

The three long-haired swamp rats on stage break into a twangy version of Bon Jovi's "Living on a Prayer." Charlie and Crystal kick up their heels and cut loose like they're the only ones in the room, the crowd cheering their approval from the sidelines.

Ryan watches the first of so many dances that are yet to come for these two, but he quickly finds himself scanning the crowd again in search of the big, floppy hat. What he finds instead is a familiar face - no hat, her hair nicely cut, vibrant green eyes that could look through anyone's soul, a spattering of freckles across the bridge of her nose. A woman who almost glows in her simple but elegant dress.

As Lily watches the couple playfully interact on the dance floor, the last thing Ryan wants to do is ruin the moment by drudging up old memories, but suddenly, her eyes land on him.

She gives him a subdued smile, clearly gauging his feelings about seeing her again.

Ryan pulls something out of his back pocket and holds it up - a homemade invitation with a picture of Charlie and Crystal glued to the front. He smiles at the sweetly amateurish work.

Lily's amused. She holds up a similar card that's been cut and pasted, the words drawn on in sloppy handwriting.

She and Ryan both laugh, releasing some of the tension.

Lily points to her own clothes to indicate his groomed attire.

"You look nice," she mouths.

With a big gesture as if he expects her to be amazingly impressed, Ryan mouths, "Suit Barn."

Lily feigns star-struck admiration.

On the dance floor between them, the newlyweds enjoy the music with carefree enthusiasm. Every once in a while, beer bottles clank and they have to try to kiss in the middle of their dance. Charlie's again the best swamp tour guide in the bayou, with his homespun princess at his side.

In its excitement, the thick crowd sometimes pushes Lily, but Ryan keeps track of her every movement. Her eyes fall to his face as he's watching her.

"Wanna dance?" he mouths.

She shakes her head and waves her hand - probably best if we don't.

Then, her gaze drifts to a group of young, eligible women who giggle and wave in Ryan's direction, anxious to catch his eye.

Lily flashes Ryan a coy smile. He's embarrassed, but smiles back.

With a perfect country chord, the rockin' song comes to a climactic end. The crowd erupts in robust excitement that's fueled by the truth exploding out of the band's instruments.

"If ya'll could fix yer eyes up here - dis Crystal's daddy, Mr. Grady McCoy. He got somethin' he wanna say." All eyes turn to Rev. Leonard on stage, as an older man straightens his camouflaged baseball cap and limps toward him.

Grady's gaze falls to the face of his daughter, who can now look back at him with two dynamic, green eyes.

"Dere no greater joy den walkin' my li'l girl down da aisle," he says with a raspy voice and an obvious catch in his throat. "I remember when you's li'l an' we barely got nuttin' at all, livin' in da deep swamp eatin' only what we could catch or hunt. You a girl who never, ever complain. Never ask why ya didn't have what dem others did. But once, I heard ya in yer bedroom and you was prayin' hard. You was sayin', I ain't one ta fuss, but someday, I hope ya send me a knight on a white horse ta sweep me off my feet." Grady turns with pride and emotion to his new son-in-law, who wears the worried expression of a man whose biggest fear is not living up to this man's hopes for his daughter. "Charlie," he says, "how it feel ta be da answer ta someone prayer?"

Charlie absorbs the words. He gives Grady a slow, respectful tip of the hat.

"Well sir," he says, "no girl could ask fer a better daddy, and I be lucky if I could give 'er everytin' you did, or if I could scarcely fit into one o' dem big ol' shoes o' yers."

Ryan turns to share his joy with Lily across the crowd, only to find that she's walking away.

"To da new couple!" the reverend shouts. He raises his glass toward the audience, which lets out a raucous cheer of excitement that's accentuated by whistles and shouts.

With a heartfelt twang from the guitar, the musicians kick in with a slow ballad. Ryan's eyes frantically search the party for Lily. Suddenly, he's grabbed and pulled out onto the dance floor.

Jackie, the waitress from Miss Mabel's Kitchen, has a firm grip on the cutie from out of town. She's wearing a short skirt with frizzed hair and an apron that says Miss Mabel's, which is catering the earthy ceremony. Her heavy eyelids betray that she's had more than a few drinks.

She wraps her arms tightly around Ryan's neck and immediately begins a steady stream of chatter, but he's preoccupied with finding Lily in the thick clump of people.

"Boy, I knew dere sometin' betwixt us when we locked eyes at Miss Mabel's," Jackie says with a slur. "People said a country girl like me an' a city boy like you wouldn't never make it work, but I say ..." She takes a second to steady herself. "I say go ta hell. Dat what I say. 'Cause we can do it. I can wear high heels an' eye paint."

"I'm sorry," Ryan says, his panic growing as it looks like he's lost Lily for a second time. "I gotta go."

Jackie struggles to understand. "Oh hell. I's worried 'bout you heart-breakin' city boys."

Someone grabs her arm and utters the ominous phrase, "A lady o'er dere puttin' ketchup on her crawdads."

"Lord, no!" Jackie rushes off to prevent travesty.

Ryan hurries through the crowd with a singular focus. He moves through groups of partiers, offering quick apologies as he pushes his way past strangers.

At the edge of the packed dance floor, he scans the surrounding wilderness and the dirt field that serves as a temporary parking lot. Just as he fears he may already be too late, out the corner of his eye, he spots a figure headed for the woods.

Ryan takes off toward the thick grove of overgrown trees and unruly brush that runs along the swamp.

The sun sneaks its last fading rays through the grove of cypress trees. Ryan enters with care, feeling the moist ground under his feet and a little unnerved as the happy sounds of the party fade into the background.

He pushes past underbrush that leads him in the direction of a large clearing. His eyes struggle to search the shadows that swallow up everything.

In the distance, he spots a massive, old cyprus tree whose branches twist and weave toward the sky. Its canopy of thick moss hangs downward, as if it's struggling to stay grounded. At its base, a demure figure stands on one of its twisted roots.

Lily's facing the swamp water that perfectly reflects the orange hues of the sky.

Nothing about her has really changed, other than her haircut, but Ryan's gut tells him that something's been lost. He's not sure if the change is in her or in him, but it's clear that Lily's not about to fly away anymore. She's firmly earthbound now, and the aura of the mystical or magical has been replaced by the modesty of simple humanity.

Ryan looks at her feet and sees that she's shed her shoes and stands barefoot on the rough wood.

Lily's transfixed by the still water that's flanked by tall, sweeping trees whose branches reach down to touch it. The frogs and insects of the swamp create a background serenade.

"If this was the last view you ever saw, it wouldn't be so bad," she says.

Something about the tone of her voice doesn't exactly fill Ryan with confidence.

"That cake looks delicious back there," he says as he slowly approaches. "I don't think we're gonna want to miss it."

"No," Lily says, "you go ahead."

She lowers her toes down to the water and pushes around the green algae that floats on top.

Ryan takes a deep breath and swallows hard.

"You know, when I was 8, my dad won big at the track," he says. "He took us on this amazing trip to Six Flags and we had the best summer of our lives. After that, he was obsessed with recapturing his lucky streak. We lost everything. We actually lived out of our car for awhile. My mom worked two crappy jobs. When I was 13, she'd had enough. She moved us away to Florida to live with relatives."

Lily's foot still hovers over the murky water, nudging a lily pad that's serenely perched on the surface. The motion doesn't even phase a tiny bug who's scurrying around the outer edge of the pad.

"But you know what I did?" Ryan says. "On my 18th birthday, I bought a one-way ticket to fly back to be with my dad, because he needed me and I wasn't about to abandon him. I now realize the person I really abandoned was my mom. I haven't been back to see her in 11 years. She had the world turned upside down on her, and she dealt with it the best way she could. I was just too dumb to see it."

Ryan struggles with a storm of emotion.

"I'm the one who ran away. And honestly, even with my last girlfriend, I told you more on the rooftop than I told her in six months," he says. "So whatever brought you here, whatever you did, I know you had a good reason. And again, like an idiot, I was just too dumb to see why."

Lily stares down at the small insect who's still obsessively following the edge of the lily pad.

"It's funny," she says. "This little guy here just keeps running in circles. He thinks he's going somewhere, but he's really going nowhere, ending up at the same place over and over. The joke's on him. You can never find the edge of a circle. Sometimes I think we're all stuck in our circles."

Ryan's eyes follow the bug's movements. "You definitely helped me break my circle."

"Mine was shattered a year ago," Lily says, "when I was sitting in the city morgue at 3 a.m. I swear it was the same little bug, this little guy, except he was on a ceiling sconce going in circles over and over again, just trying to find that edge."

Thinking he was really getting somewhere, but always ending up in the same place. That's when I realized, we're all just going around and around."

"Who was in the morgue, Lily?"

She hesitates for a moment and again disrupts the lily pad with her foot, but she can't break the bug's repetitive motion. She pushes harder. His head's still down to the grindstone.

Lily pulls her foot away.

"Mom and Dad," she says.

Ryan's struck by the words. In all his complaining, at least he still has a mother and father.

"I'm so sorry," he says.

Lily's thoughts drift back to the night when she would never go home again. When she would pack her things, including the personal items the coroner gave her from the couple in the car that ended up wrapped around a 100-year-old oak tree. A man's leather wallet and a purse with a gold buckle that belonged to a middle-aged woman.

"The sad thing is, all I could think was, who's gonna be proud of me now?" Lily says. "All my life I was planning to build this beautiful treehouse, and before I could even cut one piece of wood, someone ripped the tree out by the roots."

Ryan watches her foot move toward the swamp again. This time she shoves her foot down into the lily pad with quite a bit of force, completely submerging it and giving the small bug no choice but to desperately leap off. Spreading its wings and in a bit of a daze, it struggles to find its bearings. When it finally gathers itself, Lily and Ryan watch it flutter off and vanish over the horizon.

As Lily stares after the bug, she feels Ryan step up onto the large root of the tree and stand next to her, staring out across the unique backwoods landscape.

"You know what, I think you're absolutely right," he says. "If this was the last view I saw, it wouldn't be so bad."

He takes her hand and they stand there in silence for a moment.

"How about that piece of cake?" he finally says.

Lily's eyes are filled with apprehension, and maybe a hint of concern.

"I'm gonna be honest with you," she says. "I'm a little scared to go back in."

"It's okay," Ryan says. "I'll be by your side the whole time. I promise, just a whisper away."

Lily looks at him reluctantly.

The jug band on stage has kicked into full swing with songs of celebration and love. Ryan watches couple after couple take off arm in arm toward the dance floor.

"Is that the cake?" Lily asks.

"Uh, yeah," Ryan says.

He picks up two platefuls of homemade cake crafted from a recipe passed down through many generations. He hands one to Lily, who offers him a small smile in return.

He and Lily carefully maneuver through the dense crowd. When Ryan finally gets a chance to take his first huge bite of the sugary confection, his face twists into a strange expression. He looks to Lily, who's making the same distorted face.

"Oh my god," he says, "this is the worst cake ever."

"I know," Lily says, "I think I just bit into a Skittle."

They both laugh, and covertly drop their plates into the nearest garbage can.

Ryan's eyes again drift to the crowded area where couples sway in time to the music, hand in hand, cheek to cheek.

Out the corner of his eye, he catches a glimpse of Jackie waving wildly in his direction.

"Come on," he tells Lily, "you have to save me."

He pulls her out onto the makeshift dance floor. Wrapping his arm around her waist, he can sense her tension and hesitancy. He knows he has to do something to lighten the mood.

"Good thing you were here," he says, "or else there might have been a second wedding by the end of the night."

Lily doesn't even crack a smile. Ryan tries to meet her gaze, but her eyes evade him.

"Listen," he says, "I never officially apologized to you. I shouldn't have accused you of those things."

Lily shakes her head. "I'm the one who should be sorry."

Ryan's struggling to read the look in her eyes.

"There's something else, isn't there?" he says. "What …"

Suddenly, he and Lily are swallowed up in a big, three-way hug.

"Dis here a sight fer dese ol' eyes," Charlie shouts. "I happy ta see you two, but da misses won't take so kindly." He leans in toward Lily. "If she go fer da trailer, run."

Lily smiles at Charlie's half joke, but she gets the hint. She'll stay on her best behavior. She offers a deeply apologetic wave to Crystal. With a crooked smile, Crystal lets her know that she may not get her shotgun just yet.

"Charlie!" A large, 70-year-old woman comes barreling through the crowd. She's the thickest woman Ryan's ever seen, and could probably split a log with her bare hands.

"I best go cut a rug wit' da mother in law 'fore she get riled up," Charlie says. Out the corner of his mouth, he whispers, "Da stars out tonight fer you two. Better make some sparks."

As soon as he hurries off, Ryan's attention returns to Lily.

"You know, I just want …"

"I'm gonna stop you there," she says. "Thank you for everything. Thank you for tonight, but I really do need to go."

She starts to make her way across the dance floor. Ryan's a little shell-shocked at first, but doesn't waste any time hurrying after her. When he catches up, he struggles to understand the strangely panicked look on her face. He finally gets close enough to grab her hand.

"Where are you going?" he asks.

"I told you this was a bad idea."

"I'm not letting you go again. I made that mistake once, but there's no way I'm making it twice."

Lily's eyes are filled with desperation.

"You want to know why I didn't want to come back here? You want to know why I'm scared?" she says, her voice cracking with emotion. "I'm scared of you."

Her words hit Ryan like a ton of bricks.

"I'm scared of you. I'm scared because of how I feel when you look at me, like I'm somebody, like I'm someone important. To you, my words have meaning, and the look in your eyes when I talk … Most people are just waiting for their turn to say something, but you're actually listening to me. No one's ever done that before. I'm scared to see you look at me that way again."

Their eyes connect, and Ryan's at a complete loss for words.

"Just tell me, are you here to take me away?" Lily says. "Is that why you came? Did you come here to whisk me away from everything? Is there a plane waiting to fly us off somewhere?"

As Ryan tries to process what she's saying, Lily opens her hand to reveal a perfect, Princess Cut diamond engagement ring. Tears come streaming down her face as she's overcome by emotion.

"I took this off the moment I saw you," she says. "Tomorrow, are we gonna find ourselves on a beach somewhere, thinking our real lives don't exist?"

Ryan gently takes her hand and brings her in close. Gazing into her eyes, he can feel this poor woman's conflicted emotions welling up with force inside her.

He softly squeezes her hand, struggling to suppress his own overpowering rush of feelings. But he quietly utters the word, "No."

He picks up the small bauble she's holding and examines it to see that it's an older ring, the type that's been passed down from generation to generation, from grandmother to granddaughter, and most recently, to great-grandson. Then finally, presented in a tiny velvet box to Lily.

Ryan carefully places the ring back in Lily's hand, and she wraps her fingers around it.

"And that's not what you want either," he says. "All I want is to dance with this beautiful girl on a starlit night. The one person who understands me. The one who shook up my life over thousands of miles because of a simple postcard. I just want to dance under the stars and forget that everything else exists, even if it's only 3 1/2 minutes of a corny love song." He's almost afraid to ask, "Will you give me those 3 1/2 minutes?"

He reaches out to Lily, who cautiously places her hand in his and allows him to lead her back onto the dance floor.

He wraps his arms around her waist and lets his fingers rest against the small of her back. Lily places her arms around his neck, too, one hand holding the ring. Her cheek rests against his.

Pressed so close, Ryan can feel every curve of her body as he's in synch with her breathing, and the strong, rhythmic beating of her heart in her chest.

Lily moves in closer. She's surprised at the strength of Ryan's solid frame - unwavering, holding her so tight. Her fingers brush the small, thin hairs at the nape of his neck.

With thousands of stars becoming visible above them, the world melts away under their steady swaying. The unsophisticated jug band on stage plays a slow country melody, but for them it might as well be a massive orchestra in full swing filling the air with a romantic serenade.

When the band slowly eases out of the song with the most beautiful off-key harmony, everyone leaves the dance floor - except for two embracing figures who continue moving back and forth without any music to accompany them.

Finally, Ryan gently steps back to see Lily's delicate features highlighted by the soft glow of moonlight.

"Thank you," he says, wiping a tear from her cheek.

"Well," she says, "don't feel so bad. Clearly you're not the only one who thinks they're a messed-up idiot."

Ryan's eyes remain locked on her face. "I guess we just had to learn the hard way that there's a big difference between moving on and running away. I think tonight we're both taking our first step in the right direction."

Tearfully and with a touch of fear in her eyes, Lily nods.

"And with that in mind," she says, "I should be going."

She slowly leans in to give him a soft kiss on the cheek.

As she backs away, Ryan grabs her and pulls her close. Their lips instantly connect. She embraces him as tightly as she's ever embraced anyone, and for a moment, they allow themselves to get lost in one another completely. They share the type of kiss that you only fantasize about in old-time movies, the kind that always seems to end with a happily ever after.

But they both realize that life doesn't stop when the curtain closes and the lights fade up. Tomorrow, they'll have to go back to their normal, mundane routines, back to nurturing the relationships they've damaged.

They know that as soon as they part, they're leaping off the precipice into a future that's unknown and dangerous. Instead of escaping the past, they'll finally have to come to terms with it.

But that's all merely a dream for now. This moment will last a lifetime, kept in the hip pocket to be pulled out on the darkest of days, and maybe when there's no more hope, as a tiny reminder that it's possible for something to be perfect and uncorrupted.

As their lips part, Ryan gently leans into Lily's ear and says, "No matter where life takes us, I will always be just a whisper away."

She takes a step back.

Ryan sees that her hand's still cupped closed. He lifts her fist and slowly unwraps her fingers to reveal the polished engagement ring. He takes it and gently slides it back onto her finger.

Lily places her hands on Ryan's cheeks and cradles his face. She examines his nose, brushing it with her finger.

"Looks like you've healed up real good," she says, "and handsome as ever."

With a subtle smile but yet the gnawing, bittersweet feeling of something coming to an end, she turns to leave. After a few steps, she turns back, gathers herself and looks at Ryan with a new air of calm.

"By the way," she says with a little smile, "my name's Katie, and I'm simply a little girl from Ohio." She takes a deep breath. "And I chose the librarian, too."

The volume of the crowd behind them suddenly surges and Ryan looks to see Charlie and Crystal engulfed in a messy kiss after they've smeared rich, homemade frosting all over each other's faces.

"Okay," the reverend announces to the crowd, holding up a piece of cake, "who da lucky lady who got da Skittle? As legend tell, tonight da night she find what her heart been lookin' fer."

With a big grin, Ryan looks back to Lily, only to find that she's gone.

He stands alone under the canopy of brilliant stars, white Christmas lights strung above his head, a country guitar twanging loudly and crickets chirping from the swamp. Although it's definitely Crystal and Charlie's night, deep down Ryan feels like this night belongs to him and a young woman named Katie, with whom he shares a longing for adventure, and the desire to travel as far as it takes to find and repair that little part of themselves that was broken long ago.

"You wanted to ask me a very simple question," Chloe reads from a fresh postcard, "and it's taken me months and many false starts to have the right words to answer it."

Ryan's filled the entire back of the card with his neat, masculine handwriting. Chloe absorbs each word as her office headphones block out the world around her.

"The answer is, sadly, yes, the postcards are bullshit. They're bullshit to everyone but the person who wrote them, and to me, they're everything. Sometimes when we can't say something to our best friend, or even to ourselves, we yell it at the person in the car next to us, or at the cashier who gives us the wrong change. We scream it from a mountaintop. But the fact that someone identifies with what we're screaming might just mean we're not as small and alone as we think."

A young computer programmer races down the sidewalk leading to the spanking new glass exterior of Redding Corp. Phoenix, a massive, shiny building in the middle of a well-groomed commercial park in the middle of the desert. A few strategically placed trees ensure its "green" status, even in such a brown place.

Brandon has to maneuver around the newly christened metal statue of an abstract shape. He's quickly through the glass doors and in the middle of the vast cubicle maze, where a voice emanates from one of the small workspaces.

"I really can't believe I was wrong about that. I guess you'll just have to remove me from your VIP club, and I will not be attending the Phoenix Suns' Blazing Spectacular."

Brandon peeks his head in and points to his watch.

"We're late," he mouths.

Larry reluctantly hangs up the phone, and the two hurry off to catch up with their small work group at the far end of the hallway.

"Sorry I'm late," Brandon says, a little out of breath.

Dressed sharply in long sleeves and a tie, Ryan gives him a forgiving nod. Brandon's again grateful to be working for one of the most reasonable managers at the company.

Just a stone's throw from accounting, they stop in front of a closed door. Since most of the new facility is unknown, this door could hold any number of mysteries.

Ryan reaches into his pocket and pulls out a key he obtained through much extended discussion.

"I keep trying to tell you," he says, "everything's negotiable."

It's something Larry will never believe.

When he opens the door, it's revealed to be a large room with a window that lets in sunlight. It's filled with empty cardboard boxes and discarded packing tape that has yet to be disposed of in the rush to move in.

Larry breaks out in a grin. Just what their new workplace needed - a "War Room."

"You know what we should do?" Brandon says. "We should make this into a totally awesome room that's just ours. Like a secret room."

Larry rolls his eyes at the comment from the newbie he knows has been working overtime and not even telling anyone.

"Actually," Ryan says, "I had other ideas for this space."

Larry gets a small grin on his face, eyeing his friend. "Really?"

Ryan smiles and nods.

"No more fancy office?" Larry says.

"Nope, and no more cubes for you guys. This is ours now. All of us working in here together."

The guys nod their approval as they check out the room that now holds so many possibilities.

Larry wraps his arm around Ryan's shoulder. "Can we still have the mini fridge?"

"Yes, Larry."

The answer appeases him.

"I wish Pokorski could've seen this," he says sincerely.

Ryan nods in agreement.

Brandon's confused. "What's a Pokorski?"

With that, Larry and Ryan head to the window to gaze out on their prime parking-lot view. Brandon watches on.

He's never seen anyone so thrilled over a cramped, over-looked storage closet.

Even with the happy mood, no one's in denial over the fact that the dynamics between friends have changed, and that the person who was once a buddy in the trenches is now the squad leader ... and that life moves on.

In a Southwestern-style tract home only seven miles down the road, Janet hangs a photo of her goofy husband and crazy kids splashing around in a backyard pool lined with tiki torches, beginning the lengthy process of making a new house into a home.

Ryan will still come over for Friday night dinners, and although work gripes will never be mentioned, and some familiar topics will now be taboo, certain bonds cannot be broken.

But not this Friday.

Even though it took him three months to get up the courage to make the call, Ryan will finally be seeing Chloe for the first time since New Orleans. He's already picked out a quaint little taqueria that's decorated with sombreros and paintings of Mariachis, that serves up heaping helpings of beans and rice to top off burritos stuffed to the absolute breaking point. He's set aside a few of his best jokes, and tucked away a few conversation starters, in hopes that after the bill comes and they've had their mints, Chloe's eyes will remain on him, and not the door.

In a small apartment hundreds of miles from Phoenix, Pokorski stares at a computer screen with the focus of a dedicated surgeon. Monica promotes the heck out of his fledgling data recovery business, her cherry-red fingernails wrapped around the phone.

"I'm telling you, the man's a friggin' genius," she says in the thick Long Island accent he's come to love. She looks over at Pokorski. "Kind of like our own Steve Jobs."

A little caught off guard, Pokorski smiles to himself with pride.

"We can save that drive, or have it transferred to the Cloud," she says. "And because you're a friend of the PC Doctor, chop 10% right off that bill."

Monica will insist until the day she dies that St. Joseph was the one who answered their prayers and gave them this chance at a fresh start.

She once again glances Pokorski's way, to see his admiring gaze. Not missing a beat, she playfully mouths, "Head down."

He gets right back to work.

Little does she know that in his pocket rests a small box whose contents he'll soon reveal to her, in hopes that they can make their unlikely endeavor something to last the rest of their days.

In the beautiful backwoods of Louisiana, animated as ever, Charlie leads a boatful of tourists along a waterway flanked by overgrown trees and brush.

"I got me some Wet Ones if any o' dem cranes drop a bigun," he tells them.

Now an employee of Miss Mabel's Bayou Adventures, he awes his enthralled audience with his homegrown knowledge, topped off by crawfish po' boys prepared to perfection by his loyal wife, Crystal, who couldn't be happier to toil away nurturing and growing the simple life they've worked so hard to build at the edge of the swamp. And who tucks away a few bucks here and there in a tin can covertly hidden under the sink, so that one day she can present Charlie with two round-trip tickets to whisk away to a modest little hotel along the banks of the Nile.

In a tract home in Middle America, on a street no different than most, stands a woman who, for a brief period of time, went by the name of Lily. She holds a tattered postcard with an image of a Spanish villa.

The postcard's written by a retired couple who found their way to New Orleans because of a message they received from someone with the name of "April Showers," which, for some reason, still makes them laugh. Lily smiles as she reads the bumbling adventures of two people unsuited for travel, and not exactly sophisticated about new cultural norms.

"I'd hate to think where we'd be right now if we hadn't gotten your little message," it reads.

With a smile, Lily scans the words that were obviously written by Sarah, but which Henry has signed his name to as well.

She carefully sets the postcard alongside the framed pictures on the freshly dusted fireplace mantel.

Through the window, she sees Jack outside battling a front yard that's been neglected for well over a year. His strong forearm wipes sweat from his brow and his rugged features are smudged with paint.

Lily picks up the tray that holds two glasses of iced cold lemonade, and heads outside to join the cause.

In the bright afternoon sun, they both guzzle down their drinks in record time. Jack reaches into his cup to pull out a piece of ice to cool his face, but just as quickly, he's dropping it down the front of Lily's shirt.

She tries to retaliate, but he wraps her in his arms and gives her a little kiss, which she happily returns.

Inside on the mantel, leaning against a framed photo of a young girl nestled between her adoring parents, sits a cheap 25-cent rectangular postcard. It bears the response to a message sent out by a young woman across thousands of miles to random recipients in faraway places, with no thought of implications, or even that someone would read it, and she never thought it would be seen as anything more than a handwritten fortune cookie.

But sometimes it's the simple act of telling another person, of confiding in them, that opens the door to new surprises and something unexpected.

Sometimes you find that your daily grind is everyone's daily grind, and pain and loss is not an individual experience. Although we all take different paths to get there, in the end, we're all struggling to get to the same place. And maybe, just maybe, we're not as small and alone as we think.

As night falls and the shadows grow long, an enigmatic temptress slowly comes to life as her gas lamps flicker on. She's dressed to the hilt in bright neon and the elegant architecture of a bygone era, ready to entertain her suitors who've travelled vast distances just for the chance to boast that, even for a moment, they attended one of her epic parties that live more in legend than in reality.

New Orleans knows how to hide her scars and mask her sorrow. She wears a brave face in hopes that, while her guests are with her, they can rid themselves of everything they carry around just beneath the surface.

Wild partiers and binge drinkers, coeds and international travelers, inexperienced tourists and excited families behave as if this night and this place were made just for them. Among them stands a businessman in casual dress clothes who's clearly more comfortable in a boardroom than amidst this kind of free-spirited energy.

With the crowd flowing around him, the man's a tree stump caught in a surging river, until … something within him suddenly changes, something unspoken, and his smile reveals that he has two perfect, deep-set dimples. He steps out into the crowd, comfortably flowing into the mass of humanity that works its way down Bourbon Street, becoming a part of the life and energy of a never-ending party.

The crowd flows right past the spot where a mother who's discarded her Us magazines and energy drinks now wears colorful beads around her neck.

The normally frazzled soccer mom's surrounded by her children, one of whom still proudly sports a t-shirt proclaiming, "I am the future." They've forgotten their usual temper tantrums, and hold tightly to the hands of their mother and father as they take a decisive step off the curb into the crowd.

While most have come here looking for a weekend party, an excuse to get away and indulge themselves, a select few have arrived in New Orleans in search of a place they heard about on an anonymous postcard that offered a spark of something more - whether it was a glimmer of hope, or access to some intangible truth.

The only common thread was one line inviting them to a place that's seemingly nothing more than a little dive bar, where the drinks come watered down and the food is cheap: "I finally made it to Rusty Harpoon's," "I'll see you at the best little bar in town."

A cross-section of America has ventured into the streets hoping for answers. They've risked their jobs, boarded buses and airplanes, all because of a message from a stranger that, for some unexplained reason, awoke something in them that died long ago. Or maybe that they didn't even know existed in the first place.

But they're the lucky ones who actually made it.

Many others never completed their journeys. Maybe they didn't have the money or the guts to buy an airline ticket, or maybe they stared down a scary airplane ramp only to turn and walk away. Maybe they buckled under the pressure of a demanding boss who refused their vacation request.

Some postcards got stuck in mailboxes, or arrived after their recipients moved away. Some arrived at homes that were already jaded and defeated, so they fell on deaf ears.

There are those whose life or finances confined their travel, but who now explore their own towns and communities in a new way. They're making plans they never made before, calling old friends, trying on new hairstyles. For the first time, they're finding themselves straying outside their comfort zones.

And it's possible that a happy-go-lucky swamp tour guide from the back waters of Louisiana was right, and they're discovering something new inside themselves. That indescribable feeling some call gut, some call intuition and some even refer to as "magic," that gives you a tingle down the back of your neck, brings a smile to your face and makes you feel a connection with someone thousands of miles away as if they were standing right next to you.

All because of a simple postcard … just like the one now tacked to the back wall of Rusty Harpoon's. It's been ripped down the middle and carefully repaired with a piece of Scotch tape. Next to it hangs a photo that wouldn't really stand out to most people, or be seen as anything out of the ordinary - a picture of Ryan and Charlie standing arm in arm.

The postcard's surrounded by what at first glance seems to be dozens of postcards on the wall, but upon further investigation is revealed to be hundreds, if not thousands, of cards - each with a unique photo attached.

The few regular barflies have been replaced by a bustling cross-section of travelers who've gathered there as if it's some sort of mecca - a hub for those in the know, members of a club with no leader, with no official card, but who are connected through a message that none of them can quite explain.

In the open back courtyard splashed with cherry blossoms, a boisterous crowd gets caught up in speculation and wonder about where it all began, who was the first to find a little unexpected surprise in their mailbox, and just how long something like this can possibly last.

But all of them secretly know that when they exit the old, wooden door with the harpoon handle, something small within them will have changed. They'll take something home with them, a little spark of something new, something they'll never be able to explain to anyone else.

There's no meaningful way to articulate an experience like this. Sometimes people surprise you. When they have something inside that's dying to get out, they find a way - usually one that's been right in front of them all along.

At the post office sorting center, a mail carrier watches a steady stream of miscellaneous junk mail and bills feed through the huge sorting machine in the back room, the same way it has day after day, year after year.

From time to time, he catches sight of a bright image printed on cheap card stock. The flashes of color begin to pique his curiosity. He leans forward to watch more and more flimsy novelty cards coming through the machine.

The mail carrier moves a little closer. Just then, the noisy machine suddenly lurches forward and falls silent.

"Hey, Bob!" he shouts. "You gotta come here!"

Walking around to the back, he's shocked to find that the sorter's completely jammed with rectangular pieces of mail with hand-written messages scribbled on the back. He looks up to see ... four more postal workers holding huge bins full of colorful images printed on card stock.

Across America, people write postcards to strangers.

THE END

Made in the USA
Middletown, DE
19 September 2024

61135622R00203